The Marvelous Illusion

The Marvelous Illusion

Morton Feldman's The Viola in My Life I–IV

THOMAS DELIO

OXFORD
UNIVERSITY PRESS

Oxford University Press is a department of the University of Oxford.
It furthers the University's objective of excellence in research, scholarship,
and education by publishing worldwide. Oxford is a registered trade mark of
Oxford University Press in the UK and in certain other countries.

Published in the United States of America by Oxford University Press
198 Madison Avenue, New York, NY 10016, United States of America.

Library of Congress Cataloging-in-Publication Data
Names: DeLio, Thomas, 1951- author.
Title: The marvelous illusion : Morton Feldman's the Viola in my life I-IV / Thomas DeLio.
Description: [1.] | New York : Oxford University Press, 2024. |
Includes bibliographical references and index.
Identifiers: LCCN 2024028442 (print) | LCCN 2024028443 (ebook) |
ISBN 9780197759929 (hardback) | ISBN 9780197759936 (paperback) |
ISBN 9780197759943 | ISBN 9780197759967 | ISBN 9780197759950 (epub)
Subjects: LCSH: Feldman, Morton, 1926–1987. Viola in my life, no. 1. |
Feldman, Morton, 1926-1987. Viola in my life, no. 2. | Feldman, Morton,
1926-1987. Viola in my life, no. 3. | Feldman, Morton, 1926-1987. Viola
in my life, no. 4. | Music and literature—History—20th century. | Art
and music—History—20th century. | Music—20th century—History and criticism.
Classification: LCC ML410.F2957 D45 2024 (print) | LCC ML410.F2957 (ebook) |
DDC 780.92—dc23/eng/20240701
LC record available at https://lccn.loc.gov/2024028442
LC ebook record available at https://lccn.loc.gov/2024028443

DOI: 10.1093/9780197759967.001.0001

Paperback printed by Marquis Book Printing, Canada
Hardback printed by Bridgeport National Bindery, Inc., United States of America

For my family: Kathy, Ted, Laura, and T.J.

Contents

Acknowledgments

Many thanks to Mr. Norman Hirschy, Executive Editor, Academic and Trade Publications, Oxford University Press, for his enthusiasm and support throughout the process of bringing this book to completion and publication. Also, many thanks to Ms. Laura Santo, Project Editor, Oxford University Press, for her expert guidance in bringing this project to fruition, Ms. Ganga Balaji, Project Manager, Newgen Knowledge Works Ltd. for her careful management of the production process, and Ms. Betty Passageno, for her careful copy editing. Finally, many thanks to the University of Maryland College Park for its generous support in granting a semester release from teaching through an Independent Scholarship, Research, and Creativity Award, without which the completion of this book would not have been possible.

Thanks to the following for permission to include selected materials in this book:

Universal Editions for reprint of the full score of Morton Feldman's *The Viola in My Life I*. © Copyright by Universal Edition A.G., Wien.

"The Marvelous Illusion: Morton Feldman's *The Viola in My Life I*." In *Contemporary Music Review* 32, no. 6 (2013). Taylor and Francis Group. Reprinted by permission of the Taylor Francis Group.

Robert Rauschenberg, *Erased de Kooning Drawing*, 1953. Traces of drawing media on paper with label hand-lettered in ink, and gilded frame, 25 1/4 × 21 3/4 inches (64.1 × 55.2 cm). San Francisco Museum of Modern Art. Purchased through a gift of Phyllis C. Wattis.

Robert Rauschenberg, *Studio Painting*, 1960–1961. Combine: oil, charcoal, fabric, printed paper, and printed reproduction on two canvases, with rope, metal pulley, eye bolts, clasps, woven strap, and stuffed canvas bag 72 × 72 × 2 1/4 inches: (182.9 × 182.9 × 5.7 cm:). Private Collection.

Jasper Johns, #9 from *0 – 9* (2013). © 2023 Jasper Johns and ULAE/Licensed by VAGA at Artists Rights Society (ARS), NY, Published by Universal Limited Art Editions.

Jasper Johns, *Four Panels from Untitled* (1972). © 2023 Jasper Johns and Gemini G.E.L. / Licensed by VAGA at Artists Rights Society (ARS), NY, Published by Gemini G.E.L.

Preface

As an undergraduate at the New England Conservatory of Music in the early 1970s, I became fascinated with the music of members of the so-called New York School—John Cage, Christian Wolff, Earle Brown, and, in particular, Morton Feldman. I recall that, for my very first paper for an advanced theoretical studies course in which I was enrolled at that time, I chose to attempt an analysis of one composition from a set of Feldman's early piano pieces entitled *Last Pieces* (1959). Certainly, at that time I did not really comprehend what I found so fascinating about that music, nor did I have a clear sense of either how to proceed with such an analytical project or what tools were available for such a project. Indeed, no one was focused on the analysis of such music. In the end, I stumbled forward using the only real tools available to me—my ears. This turned out to be fortuitous, for, as I continued to analyze and publish my research on the music of many contemporary masters (not just those of the New York School), I learned to rely more and more on those first tools. Over time, I studied many other analytical approaches developed since the 1970s, and along the way I started to form some core beliefs about the music to which I was devoted as well as beliefs about useful ways of talking about that music. In particular, I learned to reject proposals of a universal nature—proposals that would lead one to believe that there is only one way to look at certain types of music—and, by extension, the systematization of the analysis of music. Rather, I always try to base all my studies on one principle: that the examination of any piece of music must begin with one's perceptions. This is especially important with respect to music like Morton Feldman's, which continually forces the listener to reevaluate his or her experience as each composition unfolds. Moreover, when subsequently documenting those perceptions in an essay or book, I realized that one must take care to take into account the fluctuating nature of perception itself, for, as I note in the Introduction to this book, *how we speak of a piece of music forever colors our understanding of it and limits our ability to address it fully.* As such, I always encourage my students to vary their terminology when speaking of the sonic events of different compositions, so as to continually acknowledge their ever-changing experience of those events. Our discussions of musical works should never be static but rather, should reflect the fact that our perceptions are always evolving. This is central, not only to my approach to the study of music, but also to my work as a composer.

In this endeavor I am deeply indebted to one man, whom I consider one of the most important music theorists of the second half of the twentieth century, Robert Cogan. I met Cogan around the same time that I had embarked upon the aforementioned, ill-fated, first attempt to analyze Feldman. Cogan himself was not very familiar with Feldman's music, and together we discussed not what to say about the piece but how one might go about discovering what one might say about the piece. Throughout his career he presented a succession of brilliant insights into either music often ignored by other theorists because it could not be understood using "accepted" tools for analysis, or music often analyzed, though in the process ignoring many aspects of sound crucial to our listening experience. His studies of music from Machaut to Varèse and beyond, as well as music from around the world, are models for how we should think, talk, and write about music. Though he never wrote about, or analyzed, Feldman's work himself, this study is deeply indebted to his pathbreaking approach to the study of music. Analytical studies such as those contained in the present volume, however detailed, are in no way exhaustive, for indeed, there is always more one can learn about a great work, no matter how many times it has been studied. I hope that this book will encourage others to bring fresh ears and thoughts to the work of this remarkable twentieth-century master.

1
Introduction

> *A work of art is a form that articulates forces, making them intelligible.*[1]

Rauschenberg/de Kooning

By 1953, Willem de Kooning had become a leading figure in the American art scene, in particular as a member of the so-called Abstract Expressionist movement. One day that year, a young, as yet little known artist named Robert Rauschenberg visited de Kooning's studio and asked the master if he could have one of his drawings. He told de Kooning that his intention was to erase it. According to de Kooning's biographers Mark Stevens and Annalyn Swan:

> "There was a moment of silence. The younger man wanted de Kooning to hurry up and just give him a minor drawing so he could quickly leave. But de Kooning instead chose to take his time. . . . He told Rauschenberg: 'I know what you are doing.'
>
> De Kooning probably sensed that Rauschenberg's visit was an omen. It would not be long before art would turn away from de Kooning, for in the end it was young artists and not writers who performed the essential acts of criticism."[2]

After a very long and careful search among his drawings, de Kooning gave Rauschenberg what he had come for, though de Kooning deliberately chose a drawing that he liked and that would be very difficult to erase. Indeed, it took Rauschenberg almost a month

The Marvelous Illusion. Thomas DeLio, Oxford University Press. © Oxford University Press 2024.
DOI: 10.1093/9780197759967.003.0001

to do so, leaving behind only a sheet of paper with faint smudges here and there. The result, Rauschenberg's *Erased de Kooning Drawing* (1953, traces of ink and crayon on paper, 25¼" × 21¾"), has become one of the iconic artworks of its era (Figure 1.1).[3] For Rauschenberg this work was of great importance. He had been trying to erase some of his own drawings but felt that these works were flat and unexpressive. His decision to take a work by one of the era's greatest masters, erase it, and turn that erasure into an artwork was a conscious acknowledgment of the sources of his own art.

Guy Davenport begins his brilliant essay entitled "The Artist as Critic" with a quote from Claude Lévi-Strauss:

> When he claims to be solitary . . . the artist lulls himself in a perhaps fruitful illusion, but the privilege he grants himself is not real. When he thinks he is expressing himself spontaneously, creating an original work, he is answering other past or present, actual or potential creators. Whether one knows it or not, one never walks alone along the path of creativity.[4]

Every work of art constitutes an act of criticism. Every work is a resonance of its many predecessors—in some cases in sympathy with them, in other cases in opposition to them, in most cases a bit of both. As Gertrude Stein puts it in her "Master-pieces":

> After all there is always the same subject there are the things you see and there are human beings and animal beings and everybody you might say since the beginning of time knows practically commencing at the beginning and going to the end everything about these things. . . .it is not this knowledge that makes masterpieces. Not at all not at all at all.[5]

Stein repudiates the very idea that there are new stories to tell, and she does so in a statement in which her own subject is gradually superseded by the language of its representation. Her writing

Figure 1.1 Robert Rauschenberg: *Erased de Kooning Drawing* (1953, traces of ink and crayon on paper, 25¼" × 21¾").

inhabits a constant present in which language, in a perpetual state of formation, becomes its own subject—even as its author tells us that there are no new subjects. It is this same ongoing present in which Morton Feldman's work lives.

Throughout his career, Feldman attempted to locate sound at the moment the listener becomes conscious of its presence. His work vivifies our experience of sound *as it is in the process of being transformed into "music."* As the distinguished Belgian musicologist of twentieth-century music, Hermann Sabbe, noted:

> The immediacy, the immediate presence of each single and unique sonority or sound event . . . is absolute and unique. It cannot be repeated ("re-petitioned"). It irreversibly belongs to a present that has been. (Feldman takes the time, each time, to establish a present.) If it returns, happens to return, it is being experienced as a new present—full absolute, and unique in its own right. A chain of presents. No corrections of the past, no predetermination of the future. . . . Neither nor. . . .[6]

Feldman constantly strove to identify his compositions with this process, both as a perceptual act and as a potential conceptualization. As I have demonstrated in my previous studies of Feldman's work, order never seems to exist *a priori.* Each work appears to assemble itself for the listener as he or she experiences it. More significantly, each work appears to assemble itself *through* the listener's very engagement with the sonic evolution of the piece. Of course, this does not mean that Feldman's compositions were created by chance (he is not John Cage). Each composition is carefully crafted to center the listener in the creative process and forge the *illusion* that it is the listener who is shaping the work *for him- or herself* as he or she experiences it. Universality is cast aside in favor of an art of pure contingency.

In his celebrated essay *Cézanne's Doubt*, philosopher Maurice Merleau-Ponty tells us that Cézanne (one of Feldman's favorite painters)

> ". . . did not want to separate the stable things which we see and the shifting way in which they appear; he wanted to depict matter *as it takes on form* [my italics].
>
> Similarly, it is Cézanne's genius that, when the over-all composition of the picture is seen globally, perspectival distortions are no longer visible in their own right but rather contribute, as they

> do in natural vision, to the impression of an emerging order, of an object in the act of appearing, organizing itself before our eyes."[7]

Feldman is always careful to remove any sense that he himself is shaping sound over time, and it is in this sense that he is very close to Cage. But for Feldman sounds do coalesce and form does emerge, though it is always his purpose to articulate the process of emergence, not a resulting form. Process is always more important than goal. In each piece he tries to capture the moment when form becomes a *possibility* and to project that moment to us as vividly as possible. This is not as mysterious as it may sound at first blush. Indeed, it is a hallmark of one branch of Modernism, which sees form as immanent within its materials (a holdover from Romanticism). Feldman simply makes this immanence much more immediate than his predecessors. This is the nature of his critique of their work.

As is often noted, Feldman was intimately connected to the New York School of visual artists, including Jackson Pollock, Franz Kline, Philip Guston, and Willem de Kooning. Indeed, over the course of his life he titled and dedicated several compositions to these figures: *For Franz Kline* (1962), *Piano Piece (to Philip Guston)* (1963), *de Kooning* (1963), *Rothko Chapel* (1971), *For Philip Guston* (1984). In addition, he wrote music to two films about Pollock and de Kooning.

Such connection was shared by many members of the New York Schools of Art and Music. As art critic Dore Ashton has stated:

> As John Cage has said in his "Lecture on Something" "when starting to be abstract, artists referred to musical practices to show that what they were doing was valid." So nowadays, musicians, to explain what they are doing, say "see the painters and sculptors have been doing it for quite some time." Concerts by unorthodox composers such as Cage, Stefan Wolpe, [Ralph] Shapey, or Morton Feldman are attended by painters. Paintings

> are often dedicated to composers, and I know of at least one instance where a painter commissioned a musical composition by a contemporary New York composer.[8]

On a more personal note, in 1974, in a question-and-answer session with a class at the New York Studio School, Philip Guston himself described his connection to Feldman:

> Well, I can't explain Morty's music other than that I'm involved with it and have been for a long time. I guess it was 1950 when we met and started a very close relationship in which we each had our growing aesthetic ideas and philosophical ideas [which we] were constantly discussing. I'm devoted to his music, as I'm devoted to his mind. I'm fond of him personally. And of course, he's one of the two or three people who respond to my work, that seems. That seem related to me or how it feels to myself. And also on whom I depend a great deal.[9]

Feldman's own observations on the work of these painters, though very revealing, are clearly seen through the lens of what he and Cage were doing at the time. In his marvelously chatty reminiscence of the art scene in New York in the 1950s, "Give My Regards to Eighth Street," Feldman addresses the then current view of so-called Action Painting as reflected in the work of the aforementioned painters.[10] Action Painting is generally viewed as an approach to painting that includes the physical gestures involved in the act of applying paint to canvas. Such physical gestures include dripping, smearing, and pouring the paint, rather than applying it in the traditional manner, through careful shaping of an image with a brush. The term was introduced into the parlance of art making by the American critic Harold Rosenberg in a groundbreaking article entitled "The American Action Painters" published in the magazine *ARTnews* in December 1952.[11] However, the term has come to be associated with unfortunate images of artists randomly splashing paint on a canvas, in a spontaneous, though uncontrolled, series of actions.

Feldman was developing some of his most important ideas about his own approach to composition around the same time as Action Painting came into being. However, he sensed a different view of this development in the arts:

> Personally I have never understood the term "Action Painting" as a description of the work of the fifties. The closest I can come to its meaning is that the painter tries for a less predeterminate [sic] structure. This does not mean, however, that there was an indeterminate intention. If indeed there is an emphasis on action, it is the attempt to capture a certain spontaneity always inherent in drawing, and now applied to larger forces. [Philip] Guston's drawings, for instance, have the look of paintings while his paintings have the feel of drawings. To varying degrees, one can say the same of much of the work done in the fifties.
>
> My quarrel with the term Action Painting is that it gave rise to the erroneous idea that the painter, now being "free," could do "anything he liked." But it is not at all true that the more one is free, the more things one has to choose from. Actually, it is the academician who has the alternatives. Freedom is best understood by someone like Rothko, who was free to do only one thing—to make a Rothko—and did so over and over again.[12]

This statement is quite revealing with respect to how Feldman began to feel about his own work throughout the 1950s. The idea that the composition is the result of a random combination of sounds, lacking any sense of order, and completely free of scrutiny by a critical ear, is false with respect to his music. However, in Feldman's work, the existence of a carefully crafted order—so favored by the serial composers of this period—was kept deliberately hidden. He strove to create a music that might appear to be spontaneous but was nonetheless highly controlled whether through conscious planning or intuitive feeling. Again, as Sabbe states:

> This is not to deny that there are connections among successive elements and figures in Feldman's music. There are, on the contrary, most definitely and continually. Only they are not motivic—at least not in the original etymological sense of "motif" as a cause of motion, i.e. for immediate univocally, directed action.
>
> Let me, therefore, right away and for the sake of clearness state explicitly that, to my mind, Feldman *does not leave anything to chance.* What through his music he endeavors to impart to us is not a sense of chance, but one of causation of a circular nature.[13]

Feldman's contact with several members of the New York School of poetry were no less significant. These included John Ashbery, Kenneth Koch, Barbara Guest, and, most significantly, Frank O'Hara who wrote the liner notes for Feldman's first recording. Feldman twice set to music O'Hara's short poem entitled "Wind," which was dedicated to the composer—*The O'Hara Songs* (1962) and *Three Voices* (1982)—and wrote an extraordinary work without text entitled *For Frank O'Hara* (1973) in homage of his friend. The work of this poet clearly reflects the same artistic concerns as those of the New York Schools of composers and painters.[14]

> O'Hara advances a position that favors the exercise of "individual preference" over "system." "Expression" is an ungovernable and unpredictable field of energy that cannot—or should not—be brooked. What is praised might be described as an art of immediacy, dependent on principles of "unpredictability and possibility" and highly skeptical of theories of art and formal systems. O'Hara admiringly describes Feldman's *Structures for String Quartet* [1951] as "without sonata development, without serial

> development, in general without benefit of clergy," and writes of his identification of "a personal and profound revelation of the inner quality of sound" in Feldman's music.[15]

It seems clear that Feldman's contact with these artists and writers had a significant impact on his own work, though, throughout the 1950s, he was gradually moving closer to their aesthetic position anyway. His contact with figures such as Pollack, Rothko, and O'Hara helped clarify the thrust of his creative work from which he would never waver. As Feldman noted:

> The new painting made me desirous of a sound world more direct, more immediate, more physical than anything that had existed heretofore. [Edgard] Varèse had elements of this. But he was too "Varèse." [Anton] Webern had glimpses of it, but his work was too involved with the disciplines of the twelve-tone system. The new structure required a concentration more demanding than if the technique were that of still photography, which for me is what precise notation had come to imply.[16]

In my previous essays devoted to several of Feldman's compositions, I always took great pains to present comprehensive analyses of his music. I have shown that, in his work, a sound (perhaps an interval played by a specific instrument in a widely spaced texture) acquires meaning as the result of an accretion of contextual associations that gradually become apparent as that sound takes its place in an ongoing evolution of both similar and dissimilar sonorities. Again, Sabbe's observations are illuminating:

> Let us imagine and consider any potentially given piece of (later) Feldman music. Say it starts with the sonority C^4-B^4: not just—though also and importantly so—a major seventh, but this particular major seventh sonority, with this particular octave placement, this particular metric placement, this particular

> timbral pigmentation; and when it, eventually, changes, it may do so into a new sonority, say B^3-C^4—which would not mean just a variation of intervallic constellation (as it would even in Webern), but a modification of a global sound quality—or it may do so either into itself, in another octave placement or a different metrical placement or/and with an altered timbral pigmentation, or into itself modulated through the addition of a supplementary member of one of its pitch classes; etc. . . . and if it should later happen to return, it may do so either in one of the guises already described, or in another slightly modulated shape.
>
> In short; similar information is being presented in dissimilar/similar contexts; literal or modified repetitions occur in literally repeated or modified contexts. So, Feldman's music presents constantly differing degrees of difference and of similarity, in other words a continual differentiation of difference.[17]

These processes of accretion and transformation are intimately linked with Feldman's treatment of time, for, as I have said, in his music, order never appears to exist *a priori*, but only in the time of a composition's unfolding. Connections arise as a composition is heard. However, time is never shaped to underscore this emergence; rather, it constitutes the ground of our experience, on which sounds may or may not coalesce into some meaningful whole. This is also true of Feldman's characteristic slow and soft mode of presentation whereby sounds at first appear isolated, disconnected, unrelated, and perhaps even unrelatable. Eventually, however, relationships do emerge, though never to be acted upon, rather, only to be recognized. His compositional designs are, thus, quite precarious.

There is no universally accepted way of talking about Feldman's music, nor, I believe, should one ever expect there to be such consensus. Indeed, his music forces us to confront this very fact and, perhaps, shows us that this is actually true of *all* music. The search for universality is foolish at best, dangerous at worst. Attempts to standardize terminology and notation may be the boon of antiseptic scholarship (as exemplified in the *worst* usage of Heinrich Schenker's important theories of tonal composition, or all usage of Alan Forte's set theory), but it is the bane of artistic integrity and a barrier to true scholarly insight, *for how we speak of a piece of music forever colors our understanding of it and limits our ability to address it fully.* Thus, we may, and indeed, should often vary our terminology when speaking of the sonic events of a piece, reflecting our ever-changing perceptions of those events. Rather than search for a single codified language when speaking of Feldman's music, we should embrace the fact that the possibility of such codification is precisely what he has erased from music (à la Rauschenberg's literal erasure of de Kooning).

Now, this is not to suggest that one should become soft and unfocused in one's analytical approach—quite to the contrary. Too often, studies of Feldman's work deteriorate into superficiality as scholars substitute vague descriptions of their experience for careful attention to the unfolding of the sonic materials themselves.[18] This is usually the result of an inadequate understanding of the nature of sound as well as an inadequate understanding of the history of Modernism, which, for over a century, in myriad ways and in virtually every artistic medium, has addressed the question of how we derive meaning from experience. (Can one possibly attend to music such as Feldman's and not immerse oneself in the work of, say, the so-called Black Mountain poets or the Abstract Expressiont painters?) As a scholar, it is never a question of "I may hear this" or "I may hear that," but of identifying *the dimensions of one's hearing as discovered through a piece of music*, and synthesizing those dimensions into an understanding of one's experience of that piece of music.[19]

As I have noted in my previous analyses of the music of Morton Feldman, every sonic characteristic of each sonority is of central importance to our experience of this music. Sound must be considered within the totality of what we now consider timbre: overtone structure, register, attack noise (or lack thereof), and pitch/interval combinations. These taken together seem to determine Feldman's decisions as his compositions unfold. In this regard, Feldman has given us his own view: "My definition of composition is the right note in the right place with the right instrument."[20]

Of course, *all music is about sound.* Feldman's is not unique in this respect. It is how he composes with sound that is special; the way that he leads the listener to experience sound afresh. Unfortunately, all too infrequently music theorists consider only pitch relationships and certain rhythmic properties, ignoring (with rare exception) timbre and how timbre changes with shifts in register, amplitude, and duration. As Arnold Schoenberg wrote over one hundred years ago:

> The distinction between tone color and pitch, as it is usually expressed, I cannot accept without reservations. I think the tone becomes perceptible by virtue of tone color, of which one dimension is pitch. Tone color is, thus, the main topic, pitch a subdivision. Pitch is nothing else but tone color measured in one direction.[21]

Any experience of the great serial works of the twentieth century (Schoenberg, Webern, Boulez . . .) will exemplify this fact.

Certainly, the term *sound* itself is a vague label for many things. Rather than apply labels, the listener must begin to recognize and absorb everything that is heard into an experience of a work. For example, overtone structure and register are two equal components of the same aspect of sonority, and both are as important as simple pitch relationships. For Feldman, it seems, when he knows exactly the sound he wants, there are only a few notes in any instrument in specific registers that will suffice. From many of his statements it is clear that Feldman thought carefully about the nature of sound.

Of course, as anyone who has read Feldman's own writings and interviews know, his statements can be somewhat mysteriously contradictory. Again in Feldman's own words:

> In music it is the instruments that produce the color. As for me, that instrumental color robs the *sound* of its immediacy. The instrument has become for me a stencil, the deceptive *likeness* of a sound. For the most part it exaggerates the sound, blurs it, makes it larger than life, gives it a meaning, an emphasis it does not have to my ear.[22]

Such a statement reveals the source of his lifelong preference for very soft attackless sounds that tend to reduce instrumental colors to purer sounds, less distinguishable from one another.

In my previous analyses of Morton Feldman's work, I have avoided traditional approaches to the analysis of pitch/interval relationships. For example, in my study of his piano solo *Last Pieces* #3, I carefully separate sonorities based on the register disposition of their component frequencies as well as the density of their pitch/interval content (number of distinct pitches together with the number of distinct intervals, sounded both contiguously and separately). I also distinguish between significant moments when Feldman connects sonorities by similarity from those where he seems to deliberately isolate sonorities by creating a succession of sonorities that are different from one another, seemingly negating one another and therefore halting any sense of growth or development. In the literature, much has been made of the latter but little of the former. Indeed, these seem to always work in tandem with one another throughout his work.

In my study of *Durations* III, #3, the focus is on the emergence of a sense of order over time as it unfolds through the sonorities of a unique instrumental ensemble. (This is a constant "theme" in Feldman's work up until his late long pieces where time is frozen and perspective is thwarted, pushing the listener's experience into a constant sense of the present.)

All this is to say that many misconceptions about Feldman's music abound, the result of a lack of scrupulous and detailed analysis of *all* sonic aspects of a work (a problem with so much discussion of new music). Often I encounter one of two responses to such an analysis: there are those who cling to a false mystique that the composer wrote without thinking about his choices—as if using one's instincts, crafted over a lifetime, is not a process guided by a subconscious logic, as powerful as a conscious one. Or there are those who try to pigeonhole his work into certain methods of analysis (set theory, for instance), which seem utterly useless for the purpose of understanding this music as they negate the composer's very focus on sound. Set theory is especially misleading as it negates the emphasis on the specifics of any sonority (the register of each note, the instrumentation of a chord) in favor of an abstraction—decidedly not part of Feldman's thinking. As is always the case, analysis should unfold from the inside out, not from the outside in, from within the experience of sound rather than from outside that experience.

The Viola in My Life I, II, III, IV

The Viola in My Life is a set of four pieces written over a two-year period from 1970 to 1971.[23] The cycle was begun in Honolulu, Hawaii, and composed especially for Karen Phillips, a member of the Juilliard Ensemble. These compositions may be performed individually or in any combination. They are scored for viola solo and a variety of ensemble configurations:

The Viola in My Life I (1970, ca. 9'45"): viola (solo), flute, violin, cello, piano, percussion (timpani, vibraphone, glockenspiel, bass drum, tenor drum, temple block, wood block)

The Viola in My Life II (1970, ca. 12'): viola (solo), flute, Bb clarinet, violin, cello, celesta, percussion (timpani, vibraphone, castanets, maracas, tenor drum, side drum)
The Viola in My Life III (1971, ca. 6'10"): viola (solo), piano
The Viola in My Life IV (1971, ca. 20'): viola (solo), orchestra

Henceforth, these will be referenced as *Viola I*, *Viola II*, *Viola III*, and *Viola IV*.

This book is divided into six chapters, the central four of which consist of careful analyses of each of the four compositions in the set. The reader will note that as these chapters progress the level of detail is reduced. The analytical information is cumulative. As the book continues, analytical observations from preceding chapters naturally carry over to their successors. In each chapter I focus more on the elements that are new to the composition under consideration in that chapter. Thus, the analysis of *Viola I* is more detailed than that of *Viola II*, *Viola III*, or *Viola IV*.

The final chapter addresses the relationships among these four works. While, as we will see, there are numerous connections to be found among the four compositions—including literal quotations carried over from one piece to the next—it is important to be aware that these four pieces are still formally quite different. They were clearly not conceived as movements of a single large work, but, rather, four different works sharing materials that are treated in different ways. As such, following the foregoing discussion on labeling, I am careful never to impose the same terminology, nor the same approach to analysis, when discussing each piece in the set. For example, when discussing *Viola I*, *Viola II*, and *Viola III*, I use the term *panel* rather than *section* or *phrase*, for reasons discussed in Chapter 2. But this term seems particularly inappropriate for the discussion of the morphology of the fourth piece in the set. In *The Viola in My Life I*, I use the term *gesture* because it is more suggestive of the way materials are shaped on the molecular level, so to speak, while in *The Viola in My Life II* I refer to *sonorities* and *patterns* instead because these elements come to the fore in defining form in that work. The reasons for these and other differences in terminology will become clear as the analyses unfold. In the final chapter, I will also return to Feldman's colleagues in the art and literary worlds of New York in the 1950s and 1960s and delve further into the connections between their work and his.

The Viola in My Life set is characterized by Feldman's omnipresent use of crescendo markings on all viola tones. Again, in the composer's own words:

> The compositional format is quite simple. Unlike most of my music, the complete cycle of *The Viola in My Life I–IV* is conventionally notated as regards pitches and tempi. I needed the exact time proportions underlying the gradual and slight crescendo characteristic of all the muted sounds the viola plays. It was this aspect that determined the rhythmic sequence of events.[24]

While this is certainly one reason for the use of precise rhythmic notation, it is clearly not the only one. Whether planned or felt, a great many proportional temporal relationships are to be found among various formal units, both large and small, in each of the compositions. Again in the composer's own words:

> At the concert which the BBC recorded in March, all the pieces were precisely notated, but for different reasons than one used to notate precisely. For example, in *The Viola in My Life* underlying almost every viola sound there is a slight *crescendo*. Now in a free duration you cannot write a *crescendo, so the rhythmic proportions were brought about because of the durations of the various types of crescendo*. I've become fascinated with precise notation now, because I use it to measure other things, which ordinarily I would never have thought of. Most of my music of the past two years is precisely notated, but each piece for a different reason.[25]

One need only glance at the final pages of *Viola II* to encounter multiple events of precisely equal duration (as will be shown in the third chapter), or the remarkably precise temporal patterns that repeat verbatim in *Viola III* (as will be detailed in the fourth chapter).

One principle of compositional design will be referenced frequently in the following analyses. Central to these compositions, and indeed all of Feldman's later works, is the concept of oppositional design. More traditional compositions evolve in a linear fashion. Composers set out their materials and develop them toward a goal. This is true not only of music from the seventeenth through nineteenth centuries but also of the music of early twentieth-century composers such as Béla Bártok, Arnold Schoenberg, et al. However, a growing number of composers from the early twentieth century to the present reject the idea of form that evolves through various states of related materials toward a singular goal in favor of more nonlinear concepts of form. Such composers create designs in which elements exist in stasis, created through their constant opposition to one another.

One of the earliest and most compelling examples of such an approach is found in the music of Edgard Varèse. To take an obvious example, one might consider the design of his extraordinary electroacoustic composition, *Poème Électronique.* The first sound one hears is the very low tolling of a church bell, a sound with multiple fundamental frequencies and their respective overtones, a soft, unfocused attack, and long decay. This is followed by a sound that is completely different—the sound of a wood block or similar instrument—a high sound, nonresonating, with a very sharp attack. This too is followed by a group of sounds completely different from the first two, a succession of more pitch-based, synthesized glissandi (perhaps fashioned from sine wave generators). The composition continues in this manner. Rather than constructing a musical design from a succession of related and graduated sounds (like the tones of a scale), Varèse creates a succession of sounds that seem to completely contradict one another and exist in opposition to one another. Undoubtedly, this approach was inspired by the very nature of his sonic materials. The sounds he chose for his composition are extraordinarily varied, both created artificially (the sine tones) and drawn from the natural world (human voice, machine sounds, etc.). There would be no way to connect them in a linear fashion. As such, he devised a concept of form that places these sounds in constant opposition to one another. This oppositional dynamic continues to the larger formal levels of the piece where he opposes noise-based sounds with less complex, frequency-based sounds. The oppositional nature of this work was studied by theorist Robert Cogan, who was the first to identify its true design:

> The whole piece, and each section of it, are dominated by two opposing, alternating sonority types. In Part I it is complex spectral noise bands, percussion and machine-like sounds, that prevail. . . . Part II, on the other hand, is dominated by simpler harmonic (or quasi-harmonic) spectra, generated equally by electronic oscillators and by the vowels of human languages and voices. . . .
>
> . . . . In a similar way, the immediate local sonic interactions are also determined by the principle of sonic opposition. The *Poème* begins with the prolonged tolling of a grave bell-like spectrum. What follows the tolling bell? Not a similar sound, but rather a highly contrasting one: an acute, clipped, percussive noise-band tapping. The tapping is then followed by an oblique wash of siren-like sounds, first climbing and then falling through many octaves of audible space—a vivid contrast to the preceding tolling and tapping alike.[26]

Of course, Varèse developed this oppositional approach to composition long before he turned to electronic music. It is evident in many of his earlier instrumental works as well. Indeed, we encounter such oppositional structures in the works of many contemporary composers, but also in the works of contemporary poets and visual artists wherein the singularity of a directed evolution is replaced by a plurality of possibilities.

Feldman's music functions precisely through this same principle of oppositions. Perhaps this is his greatest debt to Varèse, a composer he greatly admired! In each of the works in *The Viola in My Life* series, the composer juxtaposes diffuse, often thick semitone clusters in the ensembles against the focused, much purer sonorities of the single tones of the muted viola (the soloist never even plays a double stop, only single tones, often isolated from one another). As will be shown, this succession of oppositions reaches its peak in *The Viola in My Life IV* where the soloist and ensemble articulate a succession of oppositions that grow in complexity and intensity.

It cannot be overstated: Feldman's music is, above all else, about sound. Inspired by the work of the great theorist Robert Cogan, throughout this book (as in much of my writing) I use spectrographs to study the actual sound of the music; to evaluate what one actually hears, not just what is notated on a printed page.[27] Though spectrographs do not constitute a comprehensive tool for this purpose (e.g., they do not tend to give useful information on attack noise, which is an important component of our experience of sound), it has nonetheless become an essential tool for meaningful analysis. Toward this end, throughout these analyses I have created spectrographs of various moments in Feldman's music using the software *Spectra Plus*, designed by Pioneer Hill Software.[28] The spectrograph provides a visual representation of the frequency spectrum of a sound. Reading such a graph, we see that the vertical axis represents frequency from low to high covering the entire range of human hearing, the horizontal axis plots sonic events through time, and the relative shading of the image represents amplitude (darker images reflect louder components of the sound, lighter images, softer; of course color graphs are more precise in this regard but were not reproduced in this volume). As will be shown, the spectrograph offers a window into dimensions of sound that clearly, deeply, affect our experience of a musical work but that we typically do not consider when analyzing music through traditional means (set theory, harmony, temporal proportions). As Cogan himself has noted:

> How can spectrographs illuminate music, all music? They do so by providing eagle-eyed views of musical forms, views at once telescopic and microscopic which allows us to engage music at two levels different from most everyday experience. Telescopically, a spectrograph affords a sweeping picture of musical *macrostructure,* of a musical work's comprehensive motion and architectural design—the forest all too often obscured by its many individual trees. At the other extreme, a spectrograph offers a penetrating and until now rarely available glimpse of musical *microstructure,* the fleeting spectral overtones that comprise music's "sub-atomic" physical reality. This microstructure is largely responsible for the rich varied palette of musical tone color.[29]

Coupled with other approaches to analysis, the spectrograph can offer a more comprehensive view of what we hear when we listen to a composition. Moreover, it is essential when we are considering music from different cultures and time periods—music not based solely or primarily on pitch relations. It allows us to consider sound and time in new terms, and so it makes us more conscious of our experience.

In preparing these spectrographs, I considered the three most readily available recordings of the work. (Several others are listed in the Discography at the end of this volume, but these three will be the easiest for the reader to locate.)[30] The first, performed by an ad hoc ensemble, was released on the CRI label but only included recordings of *The Viola in My Life I, II,* and *III.* It was supervised by the composer and, for that reason, would take precedence over the others. However, the sound quality of this recording, made in 1970 and first released on an LP disc, renders it somewhat useless for spectrographic analysis, as there is an inordinate amount of background noise that obscures much of the sonic detail of the sonorities. The second recording is by the Cikada Ensemble (in conjunction with the Norwegian Radio Orchestra), which includes all four compositions in *The Viola in My Life* series. Unfortunately, in these recordings the balance between ensemble and soloist is not ideal; often the soloist never seems to emerge from the surface of sound via the crescendo, and the tempo is too fast. The third is by the Ensemble Recherche, which is slower and closer to the indicated tempo and is generally more accurate than that of the Cikada Ensemble. Again, however, this ensemble only recorded the first and second compositions in the set. For Chapters 2 and 3 (chapters devoted to the study of *The Viola in My Life I* and *II*, respectively), I have used the recording by the Ensemble Recherche. For Chapters 4 an 5 (chapters devoted to *The Viola in My Life III* and *IV*, respectively) I have used the recordings by the Cikada Ensemble and the Norwegian Radio Orchestra.

2
The Viola in My Life I

The Viola in My Life I is scored for flute, violin, viola, cello, piano, percussion (both pitched, timpani/vibraphone/glockenspiel; and unpitched, bass drum/tenor drum, temple block/wood block). The only performance indication is tempo (quarter = 58). It is assumed that, as with all of Feldman's music, dynamics are generally very soft. The viola is identified as a soloist in the instrumentation list at the front of the score and is treated as such throughout.

Much has been made of Feldman's well-known comment that he is concerned with the "weight" of a sound: ". . . what leads me to begin a new composition is a weight, an orchestration that is new to me."[1] However, little has been made of the second part of this statement, his reference to orchestration. As even a superficial association with Feldman's music would reveal, for this composer the term *orchestration* is complex, involving a synthesis of timbre (consisting of attack and decay characteristics as well as the spectra of individual sounds), texture, register, interval, pitch, and, most important for the present study, various degrees of noise. To understand Feldman's music requires careful attention to each of these elements of sound.

Feldman's oft-noted aversion to attack noise is of importance when considering certain types of sonorities that he achieved, but it is simply not reflected in other aspects of his music. This will be particularly true of *The Viola in My Life I*, in which a broad spectrum of attack qualities—from plucked strings to rolls on a wood block—play a significant role.[2] Such aspects of musical structure as attack noise and decay are certainly as important as pitches and intervals to the music of most significant contemporary composers.

The Marvelous Illusion. Thomas DeLio, Oxford University Press.
DOI: 10.1093/9780197759967.003.0002

Music is indeed "organized sound" (to borrow Edgard Varèse's definition).

The score for *The Viola in My Life I* is fully notated with respect to instrumentation, pitches, tempo, and durations. However, Feldman has included no dynamic markings. Of course, knowledge of the entire body of Feldman's work, including other works from the early 1970s, leads to the conclusion that this composition should be played softly. The solo viola articulates every note that it plays with a crescendo (which is partly why it is experienced as separate from the rest of the ensemble). These crescendos add another dimension—perhaps best described as "depth"—to the texture. The viola always seems to be emerging from the otherwise very soft, uniform surface of the piece (somewhat analogous to the way that areas of color seem to emerge from a generally white surface in many early paintings of Philip Guston, one of Feldman's favorite abstract expressionists). The crescendo is treated as though it was a fixed characteristic of the viola's sound, in the same way that the sound of an oboe is defined by its nasal quality, or a cymbal roll by white noise.

Most importantly, the omnipresent crescendo in the viola part highlights our awareness of the juncture of sound and silence throughout the piece. As Feldman has also said: ". . . the reason my music is notated is I wanted to keep control of the SILENCE, you see."[3] Often, sounds decay into silence as they die out, robbing us of a clearly defined separation between sound and the silence that surrounds it. This is most characteristic of the numerous piano sonorities heard throughout the composition. In contrast, when each viola crescendo ends, we hear a distinct cutoff that highlights the moment when sound ends and silence begins. The crescendo, literally, defines that moment. Only in such a rarified sonic environment as Feldman has created can such subtle distinctions be rendered so vividly. Certainly, these distinctions exist in the music of other composers, but rarely is one alerted to them to such a degree as in Feldman's work, where the way a sound meets silence becomes a central part of the listener's experience.

Since orchestration is essential to the design of this piece, it will be useful to spend a few moments on this aspect of the work before moving on to a more detailed analysis. The materials of the piece span an exceptionally broad spectrum of sound, one that seems characteristic of Feldman's music of this period. Most notable is the use of un-pitched percussion. There is a great deal of emphasis on unpitched noise sounds, derived from the attack transients of the instruments. It is interesting to note that of the approximately seventy-five published works Feldman composed over the twenty-three years between 1946 and 1969 only about ten use any unpitched percussion instruments, including his only solo percussion piece, *The King of Denmark* (1964). In 1970, however, the year in which *The Viola in My Life* series was begun, the use of unpitched percussion becomes much more prominent. In fact, of the twenty-four pieces composed over the five years between 1970 and 1975, ten make extensive use of unpitched percussion. In an interview with the percussionist Jan Williams, Feldman reveals a great deal about his use of percussion in his early music:

> The first time I used percussion was in one of the first orchestral graph pieces called *Marginal Intersection*, which I wrote in 1951. But here I used percussion as categories – in a big battery of instruments—those categories were divided into metal, glass, and wooden sounds. It wasn't clear then, and it's not clear now, what really categorized the make-up of all this. I don't think I wanted conventional instruments. Now that I'm reflecting on it after all these years, I'm sure I didn't want conventional instruments. I wanted instruments for those categories that sounded like metal and sounded like glass and wood to the ear. Later on, for example, in *The King* [*of Denmark*], I would naturally bring in a solo instrument even though it would still be involved with categories. I would use "skin" sounds, but I was using conventional skin instruments in *The King*. I remember bringing in, for the first concert of *Marginal Intersection* [1951] at Cooper Union, plastic dishes and those old

> heavy aluminum pots and pans that I borrowed from my mother. My models for percussion at that time were from the Gamelan Orchestra, John Cage's early '40's pieces, and Varèse's work, where the instruments were used *en masse*, not soloistically. I used that aspect as a model in *Marginal Intersection*, except *I remember wanting the percussion to sound more like noise* [my italics].[4]

The sonic materials of *The Viola in My Life I* can be divided into several general categories ranging from the attack-filled noise of the bass drum, tenor drum, temple block, and wood block, through sustained sounds with little attack noise, to sustained sounds with crescendo. With one exception (m. 41) the percussionist always rolls on his instruments, and this somewhat tends to eradicate the distinction between attack sounds and sustained sounds, as percussion instruments that cannot truly sustain are called upon to mimic a sustaining sonority. I identify five distinct categories of sonority in this piece, ranging from pure sustained sound with little audible attack to the attack-filled noise of drum and wood block rolls (Table 2.1). In formulating these categories, all markings in

Table 2.1 *The Viola in My Life I*, Timbre Categories

noise	1. attack noise without pitch	rolls on drums and blocks
↑	2. attack noise with pitch	pizz. strings, timpani
↓	3. attack with decay	piano chords, vibes, glock.
	4. sustain with minimal attack	flute, cello
pitch	5. sustain with minimal attack and crescendo	viola

the score have been scrupulously observed (Figure 2.1). Thus, for example, chords such as those in the piano in bars 73 and 93 that contain both decaying and nondecaying piano tones are identified as such (Figure 2.21).

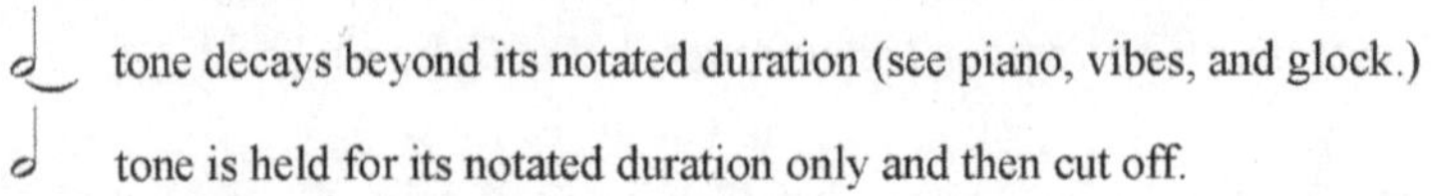

tone decays beyond its notated duration (see piano, vibes, and glock.)

tone is held for its notated duration only and then cut off.

Figure 2.1 *The Viola in My Life 1*, Notation.

In *The Viola in My Life I* Feldman engages in a play between several important sonic oppositions (Table 2.2). The piece begins with a clear delineation of these oppositions. Indeed, the very first succession of sounds forms an arc that draws all of these oppositions into a gesture of some definition. This gesture can be usefully represented three different ways: score, spectrograph, and diagram (Figure 2.2, Figure 2.3, Figure 2.4). The piece opens with a crescendo (viola) that leads up to a rapid succession of pizzicato attacks (cello), followed by a decaying sonority (piano chord), on top of which we hear a sustained pure tone (flute, softly). This is followed by its polar opposite, a quasi-sustained band of noise (bass drum roll). In this way, the piece opens with a magnification of each aspect of sound: from the attackless crescendo to the pitched attacks of the pizzicatos, to a decaying sonority from which emerges one sustained pure tone, to the final band of noise. (As we will see, in this piece Feldman typically uses rolled percussion as punctuation, separating pitched events from one another and, more importantly, erasing our aural memory of their pitch/interval configurations.) The various elements of this initial gesture reassemble themselves in different ways throughout the composition, fashioning a succession of related gestures (though not hierarchically so).

Table 2.2 *The Viola in My Life I*, Sonic Oppositions

crescendo	/	*diminuendo*
viola		piano, vibes, glock.
(always crescendo)		(typically held through decay)
attack	/	*sustain*
without subsequent sustain		with minimal attack
pizz. strings, perc.		fl., vln., cello
noise	/	*pitch*
nonpitched percussion.		fl., strings, piano,
		pitched percussion

Figure 2.2 *The Viola in My Life 1* (mm. 1–5), First Gesture, Score.

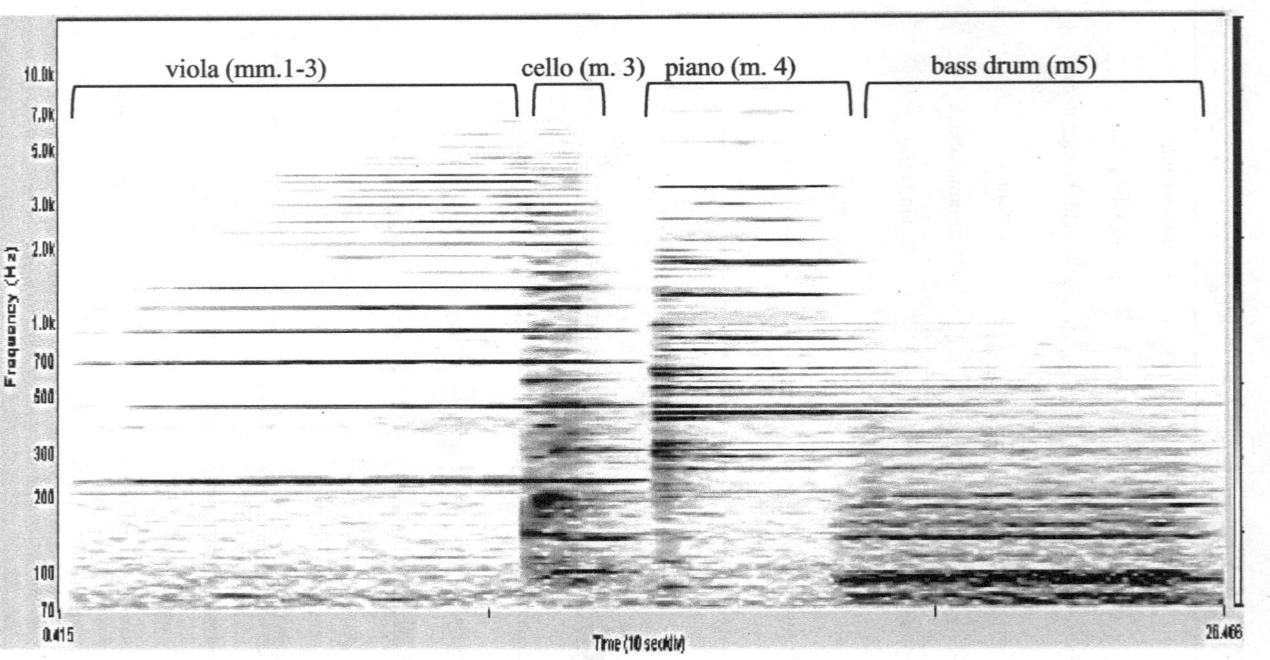

Figure 2.3 *The Viola in My Life 1*, First Gesture (mm. 1–5), Spectrograph.

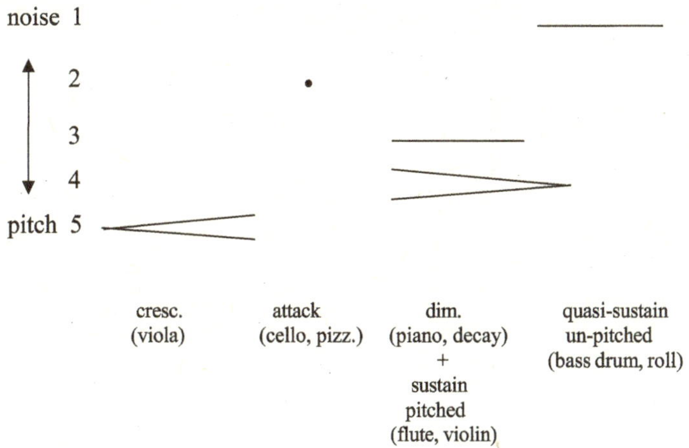

Figure 2.4 *The Viola in My Life 1* (mm. 1–5), First Gesture, Diagram.

Within the world of unpitched percussion Feldman creates gradations of sound that, as the piece progresses, move toward more articulated, attack-oriented sonorities. He gradually intensifies the articulation of attack noise as the music unfolds. The unpitched percussion is introduced in the following order: bass drum/tenor drum, temple block/wood block. The succession of attacks of a bass drum roll can certainly appear muffled and can project the illusion of a sustained band of noise, especially if the percussionist uses soft mallets. But there is no way to mask a series of attacks on a wood block, no matter what type of mallets are used. A roll on a wood block is perceived as a rapid succession of distinct, sharp attacks.

Of course, Feldman often blurs the oppositions outlined above (Table 2.2), and this is a very important goal of the piece. In one marvelous passage, he pulls us quite deliberately back and forth between the worlds of pitch and noise (Figure 2.5, Figure 2.6, Figure 2.7). At the beginning of bar 55, the piano sounds a chord primarily constructed from semitones: E F F# G# A Bb B C. Superimposed upon this is a roll on the pitch D played by the

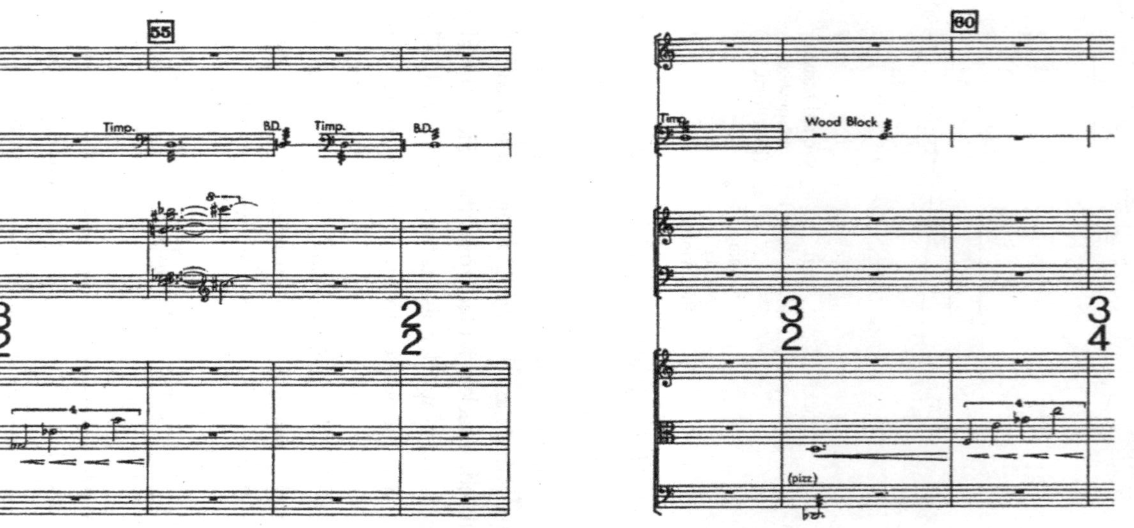

Figure 2.5 *The Viola in My Life 1* (mm. 55–59), Score.

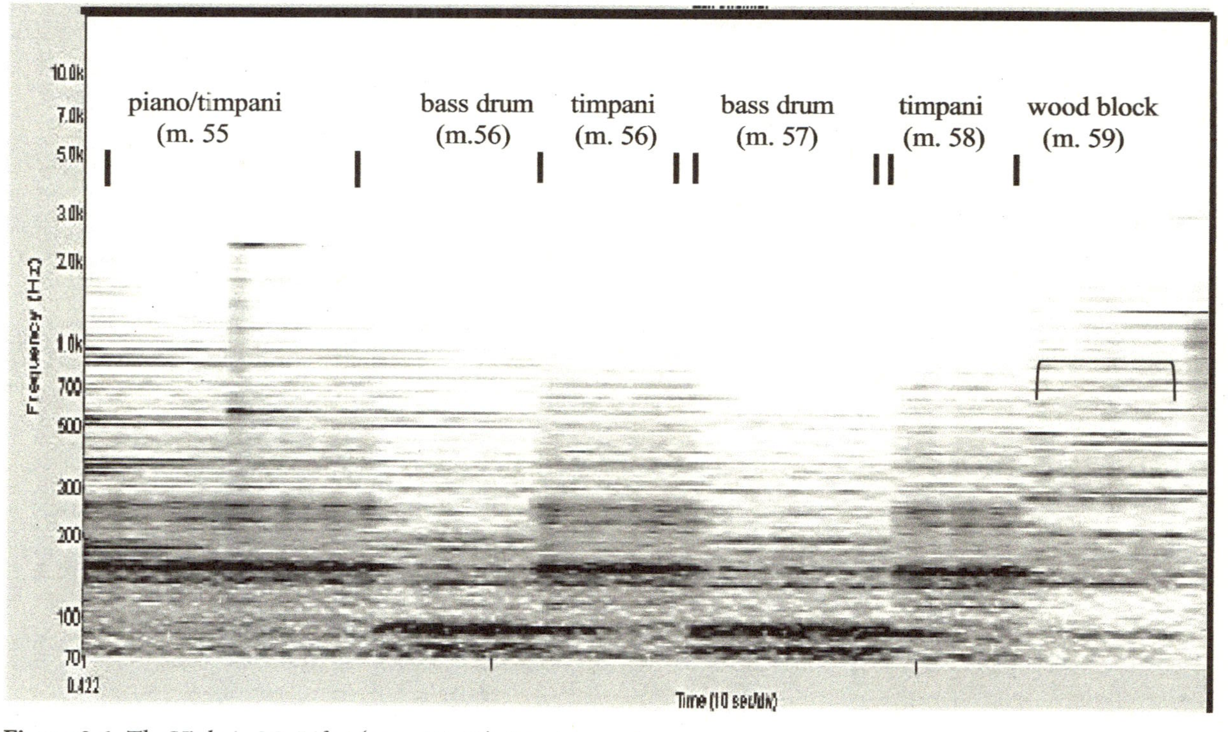

Figure 2.6 *The Viola in My Life 1* (mm. 55–59), Spectrograph.

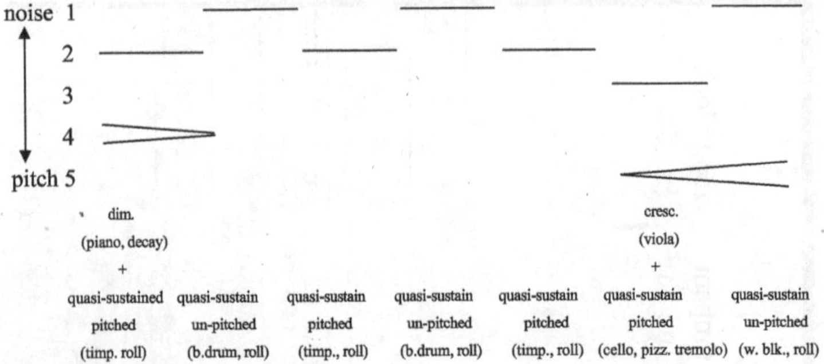

Figure 2.7 *The Viola in My Life 1* (mm. 55–59), Diagram.

Table 2.3 The Viola in My Life I (m. 55), Pitches

first piano chord	EFF# G#ABbBC	
timpani		D
second piano chord	C#	

timpani. At this point, D is the only tone in the cluster that has no link to any of the notes sounded by the piano by half-step. However, the piano then adds another pitch C#, in octaves. This, of course, provides the missing half-step connection between the tones of the initial chord and the D of the timpani (Table 2.3). Immediately following this moment, while the tones of the piano continue to ring, the percussionist plays an alternating succession of rolls between the timpani (always on D) and the unpitched bass drum. The listener is pulled back and forth—toward the pitch world of the piano and away from it. Eventually, these drum rolls are replaced by the more pitched, yet still attack-oriented, pizzicato tremolo of the cello (m. 59, one of only two such pizz/tremolos in the piece). This moment is answered by a roll on the wood block, the most attack-based, nonpitched sonority of the passage. Here noise and pitch, attack and sustain, all blend together to create a distinctive and new (though momentary) sense of unity in the piece (Figure 2.8). At

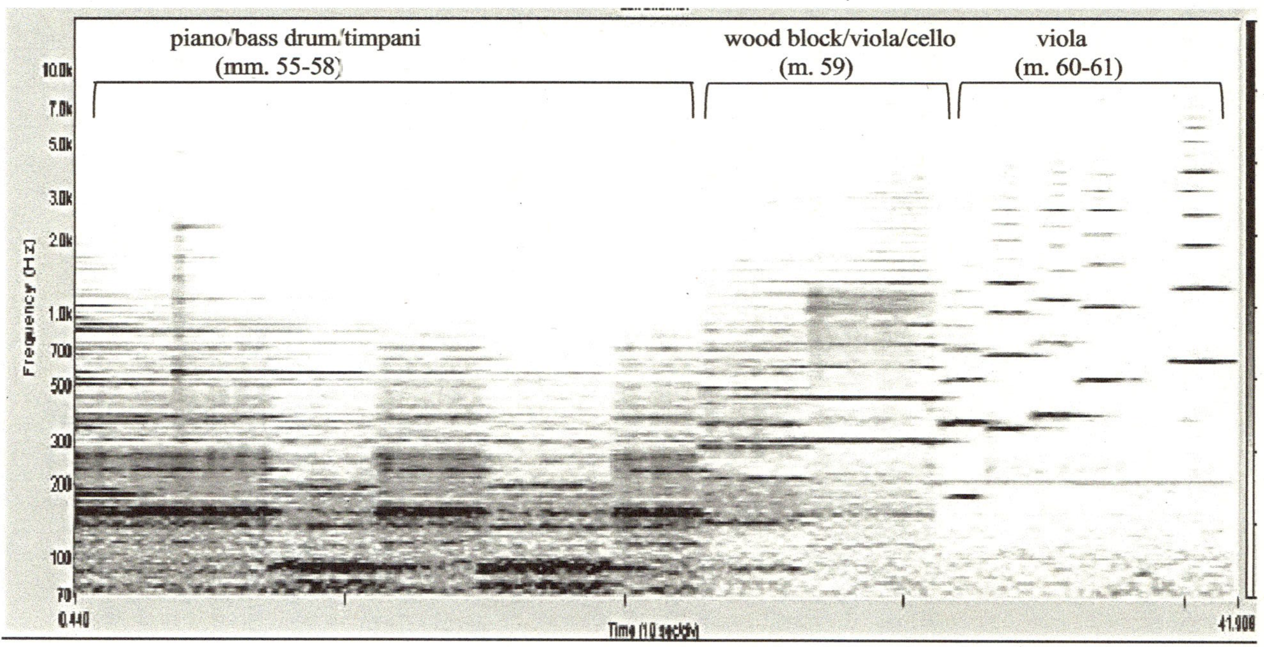

Figure 2.8 *The Viola in My Life 1* (mm. 55–61), Spectrograph.

this remarkable moment, Feldman literally obliterates the pitch/noise opposition. (We should note that this passage links two successive gestures of the piece, for, as we will see, the pizzicato cello tremolo actually introduces a new gesture.)

Form

It is always dangerous to draw parallels between music and the visual arts. That said, the general design of *The Viola in My Life I* resembles some of the works of Robert Rauschenberg and Jasper Johns, two painters with whom Feldman was quite close personally.[5]

> There was a period—*The Rothko Chapel* [1971], *The Viola in My Life* (1970–1971), a few other pieces—when I was thinking of Bob Rauschenberg's photo montages. At that time, I would use a tune just the way Bob would put a photo on a canvas.[6]

Of particular interest are those works by Rauschenberg and Johns in which they lined up multiple, equal-size panels side by side, each with differing materials and images. Rauschenberg's *Studio Painting* (1960–1961), a so-called combine of mixed media with rope, pulley, and canvas bag, consists of two adjacent, contrasting panels; while *Ace* (1962), oil, cardboard, wood, and metal on canvas, consists of five large contrasting panels (Figure 2.9).[7] Johns's *Untitled* (1972), oil, encaustic, and collage on canvas with objects, consists of four equal-sized panels placed side-by-side (Figure 2.10).[8] *Untitled* shares several remarkable, though obviously general, similarities with Feldman's *The Viola in My Life I*. Most of the panels that make up *Untitled* contain seemingly unrelated images; the two central panels are similar both with respect to

Photo: C&M Arts, New York

Figure 2.9 Robert Rauschenberg, *Studio Painting* (1960–1961), mixed media with rope, pulley, and canvas bag, consisting of two adjacent, contrasting panels.

color scheme and to the shapes employed, but these central panels are completely different from the outer two. As Steven Johnson has pointed out, the first panel (leftmost) is filled with simple repetitive lines in clearly contrasting colors that coalesce into a uniform surface, an early example of Johns's use of what are known as

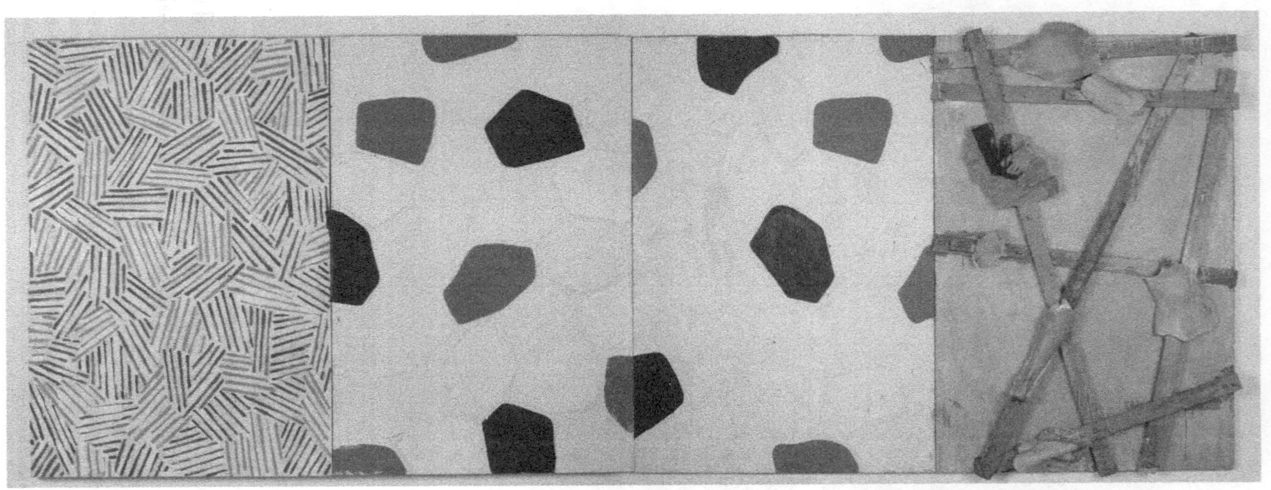

Figure 2.10 Jasper Johns, *Untitled* (1972), oil, encaustic and collage, consisting of four equal-sized panels placed side-by-side.

crosshatch marks to create a uniform visual surface.[9] In contrast, the last panel (on the right) is equally distinct: a collage of materials fashioned into a nonrepetitive, less abstract surface than the other panels, and in much more muted colors. As the eye travels from left to right, one experiences several changes in visual orientation: a change in depth perception from the flat, uninflected surface of the crosshatching on the left panel to the foreground/background layering of the right panel; a shift from the highly repetitive surface of the left panel, through the somewhat less repetitive surface of the central panels, to the singularly nonrepetitive surface of the rightmost panel; and a reorientation from the juxtaposition of contrasting colors on the left, to the muted browns and grays on the right. What is truly remarkable here is the fact that these panels share so little in common visually. It is the oppositions among the various shapes, surfaces and materials that unify them, not their similarities, which are few and far between.

In an interview with Fred Orton, Feldman once remarked that of all the painters of his generation he felt closest to Johns:

Morton Feldman: Rauschenberg and Cage. . . .There are times when their work almost coincides. . . . While Jasper [Johns] is closer to me. Jasper just keeps on going.

Fred Orton: But I get the impression that you feel closer to Johns now [1976] than when you first met him in the early 1950's.

Morton Feldman: Yes I feel very, very close to Jasper Johns. Very close to his work.[10]

Feldman's *The Viola in My Life I* projects three distinct sonic regions that resemble, perhaps in function more than anything else, the panels of Johns's *Untitled*. As such, it is suggestive to label them Panel I (mm. 1–50), Panel II (mm. 51–85), and Panel III (mm. 86–126) (Figure 2.16, Figure 2.28, Figure 2.35). The start of each panel is marked by distinct changes in gesture, rhythm, and texture. The panels themselves share similarities, but they do not evolve toward one another. Nor is there any sense of transition from one to the next. Each reflects a different facet of the basic sonic materials employed. Thus, the whole is fashioned not from any graduated evolution of sonic materials, but rather, as with Johns's *Untitled*, from the very different treatment of these materials in each part. The first panel constitutes a rather amorphous succession of gestures drawn from the sonority types outlined above and establishes the many sonic oppositions of the work (Table 2.1, Table 2.2). The second panel is quite different: The viola is used in a more linear fashion and moves to the forefront. Percussion becomes more prominent as well, while the piano is used sparingly. The third panel is, yet again, quite different. In it, fixed sonic events repeat, somewhat like ostinati. Its structure is somewhat analogous to that of a mosaic.

In terms of duration, the composition exhibits a clear proportional design: The first panel is 241 beats at MM 58 per beat (ca. 4'); the second is 180 beats (ca. 3'); and the third is 112 beats (ca. 1.85'). Thus, proportions are approximately 4:3:2. As will be shown, the third and shortest panel is also the most concentrated not only in terms of duration, but also with respect to the presentation if its materials.

Each panel is further subdivided into a series of gestures (Figure 2.11, Figure 2.21, Figure 2.28). The reason for partitioning the panels into these gestures will become clear in the ensuing discussion. Here, as in other analyses, I use the word *gesture* rather than section or phrase, both of which connote very distinct structural units with clear patterns of evolution and moments of demarcation as their start and end points. This is clearly inappropriate in discussing Feldman's music. Moreover, it flies in the face of his aesthetic position, which, as discussed earlier, asserts that there is no shaping of materials *a priori*. The term *gesture* seems to me to suggest a process of shaping materials rather than any specific end product of that process.

The gestures of *The Viola in My Life I* also exhibit a clear proportional scheme both within each panel and across the entire piece

(Table 2.4, Table 2.5). In the first panel, consisting of eleven gestures labeled a through k, gestures a through h become progressively longer, gestures i through k generally shorter again. Throughout the second panel, gestures become progressively longer, the first being its shortest, the final its longest and, indeed, the longest of the entire piece. The third panel reverses the motion of the second and, rather dramatically, drops to the shortest durations of the composition. The entire piece exhibits an arch-like shape similar to that of the first panel but expanded. Gestures become generally longer until the very end of the second panel where, as mentioned before, we encounter the longest gesture of the composition. At this point the piece rather abruptly reverses direction, and gestures become suddenly much shorter. In addition, at the very end we encounter a rare moment of regularity: four of the last five gestures are equal in length and are also the shortest of the piece, providing a somewhat cadential feeling to the ending, at least in terms of duration.

Table 2.4 *The Viola in My Life I*, Durations of Gestures within Each of the Three Panels

Panel I, Durations (in beats at MM 58):											
Gesture	a	b	c	d	e	f	g	h	i	j	k
	19	21	15	17	23	26	34	34	14	16	22
Panel II, Durations (in beats at MM 58):											
Gesture	a	b	c	d	e	f					
	14	26	26	38	30	46					
Panel III, Durations (in beats at MM 58):											
Gesture	a	b	c	a	c	a	c	x			
	38	36	10	4	4	4	4	12			

Table 2.5 *The Viola in My Life I*, Comprehensive Chart of all Durations of Gestures at MM 58

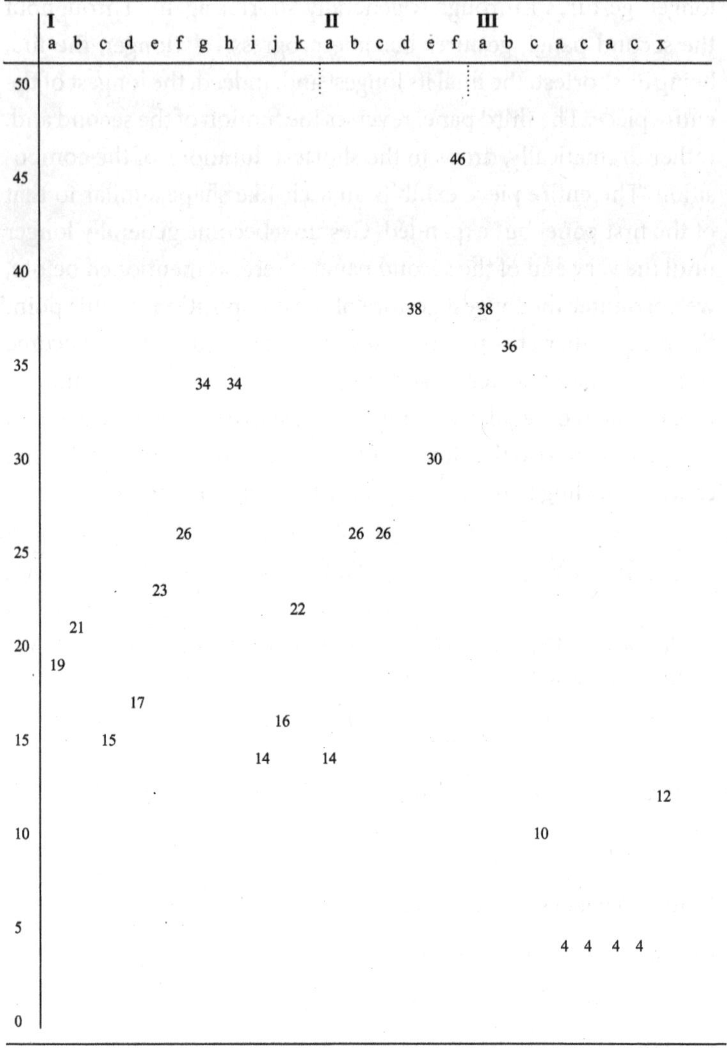

Panel I

The first panel begins and ends with rolled pizzicato chords, the only two such events in the entire composition (mm. 3 and 50). It consists of eleven gestures (Figure 2.11). As I have noted on a number of occasions, it is never a simple task to sectionalize

Figure 2.11 *The Viola in My Life 1*, Panel I, Annotated Score.

Figure 2.11 Continued

Figure 2.11 Continued

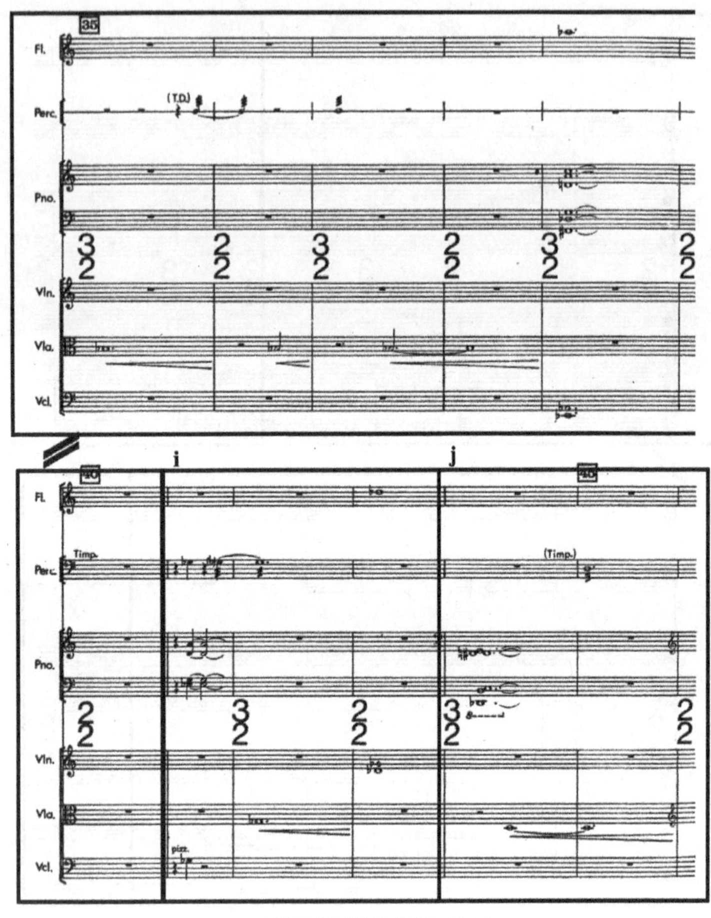

Figure 2.11 Continued

Figure 2.11 Continued

Feldman's music, and I do so primarily for the purposes of coordinating discussion of his work. The boundaries of his gestures are always subtle and, at times, deliberately ambiguous. Just when one feels that the music is taking on a distinctive shape, it disintegrates.

The gestures identified in *The Viola in My Life I* are determined by a few very obvious and basic factors. Each contains at least one piano chord and percussion roll, and these signify, respectively, the beginning and ending of most gestures. Of the eleven gestures that constitute the first panel, eight begin with a piano chord and seven end with a roll on a percussion instrument (Table 2.6).

Again, rolled percussion instruments function somewhat as punctuation, though the quality of this punctuation changes as the first panel unfolds, moving from drums to the temple block, which, of course, has very noticeable, highly articulated attack noise, even when the percussionist plays a roll on it (Table 2.7). This is the final sound of the first panel and, with respect to the

Table 2.6 *The Viola in My Life I,* Panel I, Gestures, First and Last Sonorities

Gesture	First Sonority	Last Sonority
a		perc. roll
b	piano	
c	piano	perc. roll
d		perc. roll
e		perc. roll
f	piano	perc. roll
g	piano	perc. roll
h	piano	
i	piano	
j	piano	
k	piano	perc. roll

percussion, it marks a significant shift in sonority from the low, muffled bass drum rolls to the highly articulated attacks of the rolls on the temple block. With these rolls on the temple block (and subsequent rolls on the wood block in the next two panels), attack noise is pushed to the forefront of the texture. Thus, it is the attack, the starting point of sound, rather than its decay, that finally emerges as predominant.

The gestures of the first panel are also partially determined by the evolution of tones and intervals in the viola solo (Figure 2.12). Over the course of Panel I, the viola sounds ten pitches (only G and B are missing), generally one per gesture. (Interestingly, the viola solo begins with an A, which is the only time it plays this pitch in the entire piece.)

Table 2.7 *The Viola in My Life I*, Panel I, Percussion Instruments in Each Gesture

Gesture	Percussion roll
a	bass drum
b	tenor drum
c	bass drum
d	tenor drum
e	bass drum (2x)
f	timpani
g	timpani, tenor
h	tenor drum (2x)
i	timpani
j	timpani
k	temple block (3x)

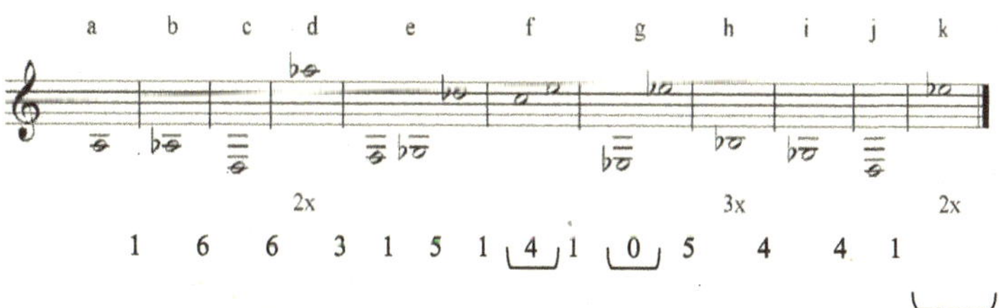

Figure 2.12 *The Viola in My Life* 1, Panel I, Pitches and Intervals of Viola Solo.

Three chords are heard throughout Panel I, and these recurrences help define certain gestures (f, g, and h in particular). Moreover, as we will see, they also help to organize them into distinctive, recognizable, and, most importantly, relatable shapes (Figure 2.13, Figure 2.14).

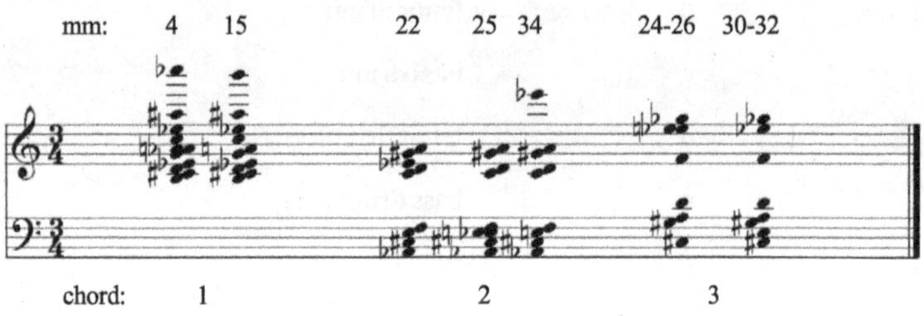

Figure 2.13 *The Viola in My Life 1*, Panel I, Primary Chords.

The first gesture of this panel was discussed earlier (Figure 2.2, Figure 2.3, Figure 2.4). The second and third gestures differ from the first and present a more typical picture. Each begins with a pizzicato attack superimposed upon a piano chord that decays. This is immediately followed by the viola, which, as a result of its crescendo, seems to emerge from that chord (Figure 2.15, Figure 2.16). The boundaries of the next two gestures (d and e) become a bit more ambiguous. At times, they seem to merge into one another and cannot always be clearly separated (Figure 2.17).

Gestures f and g are more closely related to one another than any preceding ones. They share the same two chords and close with rolls on pitched percussion (timpani). They are the two most distinctive gestures of Panel I. Each creates a context for the other and so, they become clearly recognizable as well-defined and related aural events (Figure 2.18). Gesture h begins as though it will repeat the pattern set up in f and g but then veers away from that pattern (Figure 2.19).

Gestures i and j are the most significant within this part of the composition. They draw all the elements of the previous gestures

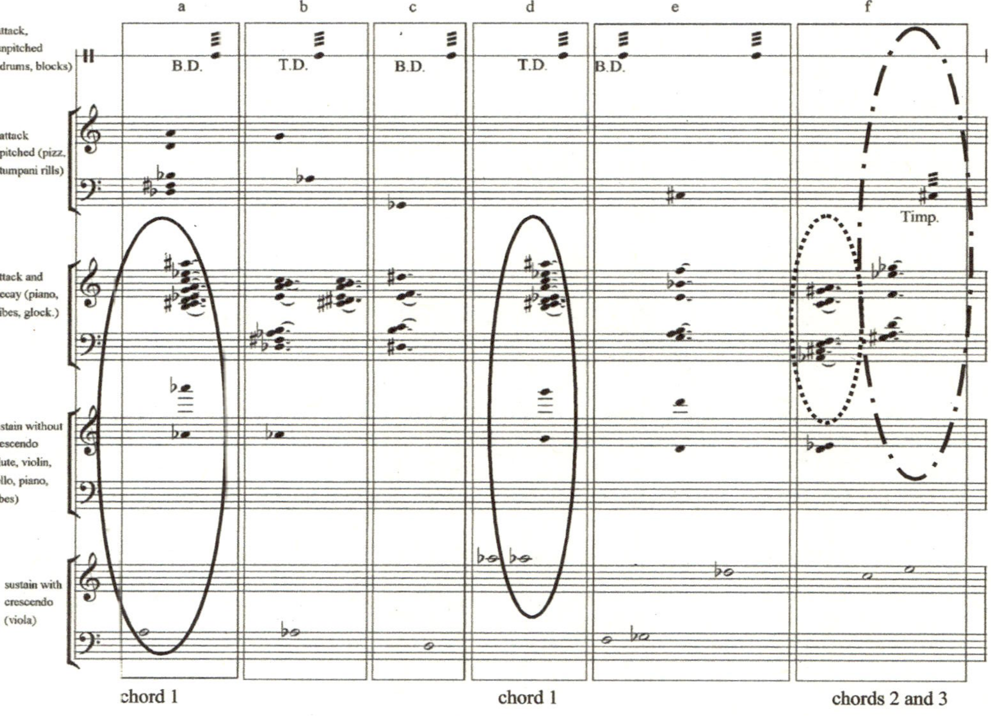

Figure 2.14 *The Viola in My Life 1*, Panel I, Summary of Pitches as Distributed among Timbres.

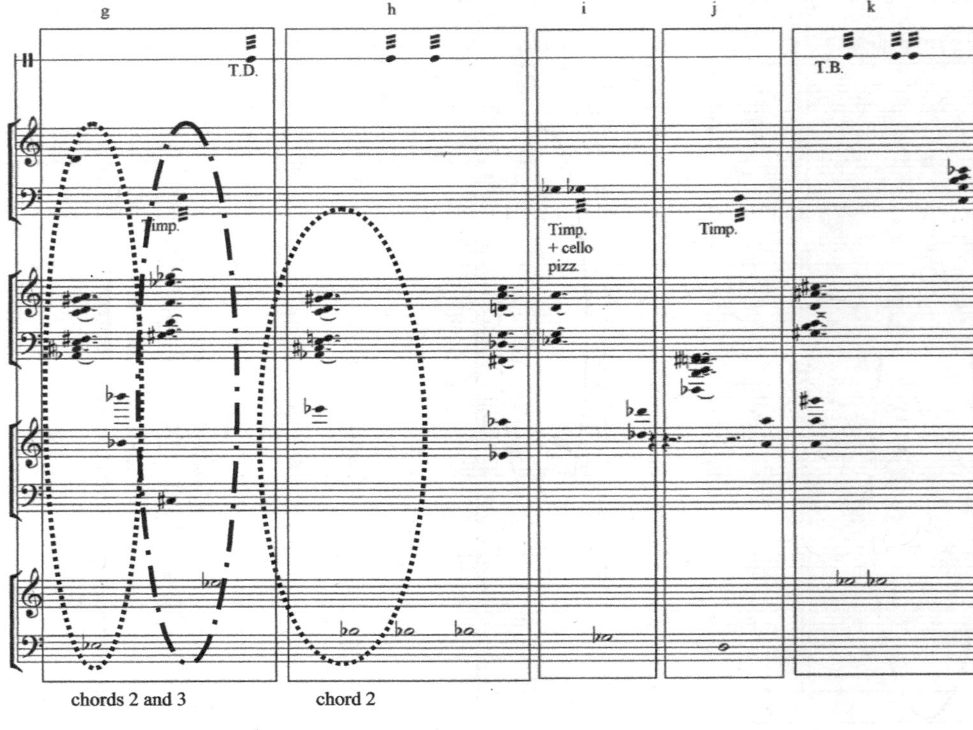

Figure 2.14 Continued

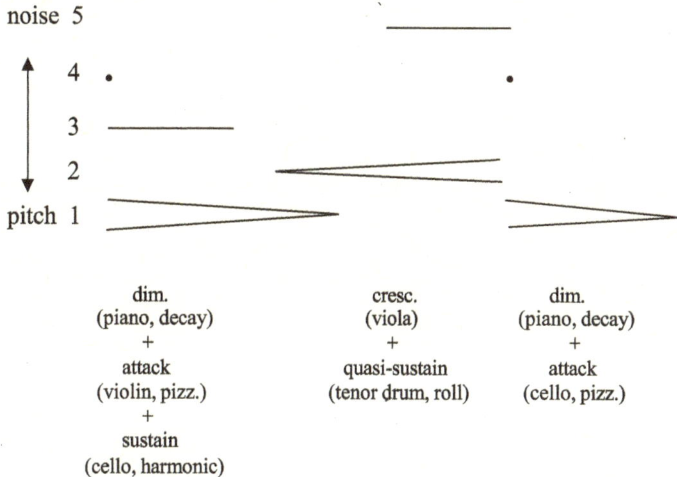

Figure 2.15 *The Viola in My Life 1* (mm. 6–9), Panel I, Gesture b.

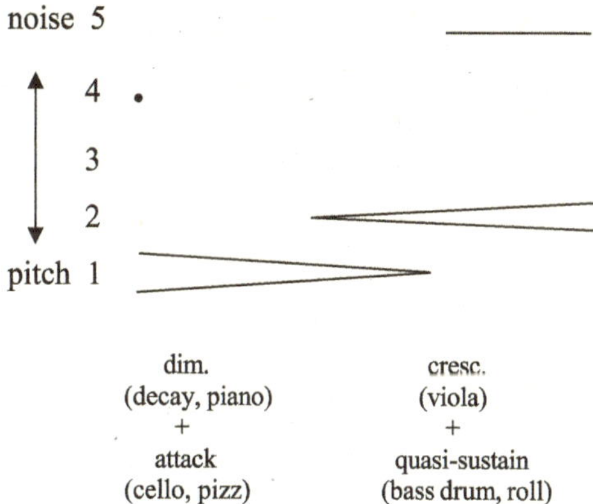

Figure 2.16 *The Viola in My Life 1* (mm. 10–13), Panel I, Gesture c.

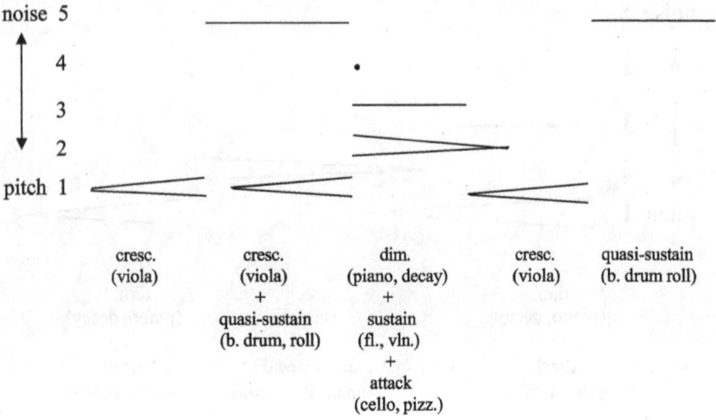

Figure 2.17 *The Viola in My Life 1* (mm. 17–21), Panel I, Gesture d and Gesture e.

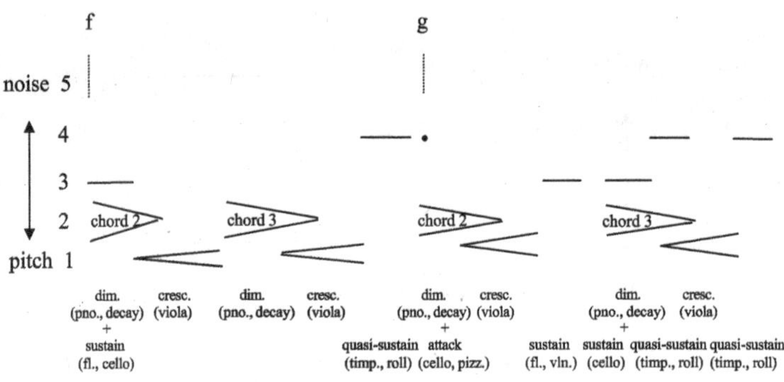

Figure 2.18 *The Viola in My Life 1*, Panel I, Gesture f (mm. 22–26) and Gesture g (mm. 27–33).

together into a pair of uniquely unified moments. One of the most striking features of the first panel is the way that the sonorities of the unpitched percussion are gradually integrated into the pitched world and thus rise to the foreground.

> Then, we have the whole problem of pitch percussion against non-pitch percussion. Making too much of a hierarchical situation out of either one or the other. That's one of the problems I have about mixing, where I don't want my percussion to become absolutely "background" if it's non-pitched, and "foreground" if it is pitched. It's one of the big problems that I have in getting my instrumental balance of percussion instruments together when I start a piece.[11]

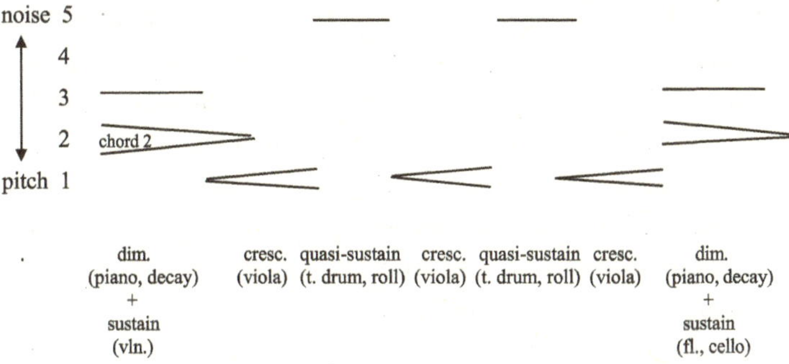

Figure 2.19 *The Viola in My Life 1* (mm. 34–40), Panel I, Gesture h.

At the beginning of Panel I, the unpitched percussion instruments function as punctuation, separating gestures. They also afford an opportunity to "cleanse" one's pitch palate, if you will, wiping away all the potential pitch/interval relationships that came to the fore as the preceding gesture evolved. Also, the individual sonorities of the initial gestures of Panel I present the various components of their respective sound worlds as separate elements—especially with respect to the unpitched percussion and the crescendo viola tones: one constitutes pure attack noise, and the other minimizes attack noise as much as possible. However, as Panel I evolves, the unpitched percussion is replaced by pitched percussion (timpani) whose tones interact with the other pitched materials. Gradually, the separation between noise and pitch disappears (Figure 2.11, Table 2.7). This process culminates in gesture i (bar 41), where the timpani sounds its only single stroke of the piece—not a roll—on the pitch Gb^3. This tone is doubled by the cello, articulating the same pitch, pizzicato. *At this moment, the identification of pitch with its attack noise is complete. As gesture i unfolds, the same pitch is rolled by the timpani into a quasi-sustained tone and, finally, is picked up by the viola, which, of course, adds a crescendo on that note. Thus, over the course of gesture i, we hear all sonic elements fuse into a single unifying tone.* Gesture i is also the shortest gesture of Panel I, and this temporal compression intensifies the synthesis of attack noise and tone.

This process continues in gesture j but in reverse. Here the viola introduces D^3, and then, a few beats later, the timpani enters on the same pitch. In gesture i noise evolved into pitch, while in j pitch regresses back into noise. All of this is prepared in gestures f and g, where the sound of the timpani is introduced. In each of these gestures the timpani and strings trade pitches: In f the viola plays E^5 and timpani follows with a roll on C#^{3}, while in g the timpani rolls on E^3 and the cello sustains C#^{3} (Figure 2.11, Figure 2.14). Timpani rolls function as quasi-sustained tones, fully integrated into the pitch world of the piece. It is interesting to note, too, that the merging of pitch and noise works both ways in this composition. This is most notable at the beginning of gesture j (m. 44), where Feldman gives us a very thick, very low chord of semitones that loses its pitch definition and takes on characteristics of a somewhat indeterminate noise band.

After gestures i and j, the texture seems to break apart once again. The final gesture, k, returns to a shape that is more common earlier in the composition; opening with a decaying piano chord and ending with unpitched percussion (Figure 2.20). In this final gesture, Feldman replaces the timpani rolls heard in i and j with a roll on the temple block, the first appearance of this instrument. At this moment the composer pulls us away from the pitch/noise merger recently enacted. More than any of the percussion instruments heard thus far, a stroke on the temple block intensifies our perception of attack noise. Unlike the soft attacks of a bass drum roll (with which percussion in Panel I began) or the timpani roll, the temple block has a hard, brittle attack that is impossible to disguise, and the repetitive attacks of a roll on this instrument only heighten our awareness of its attack noise. Indeed, the sound of a roll on a temple block presents us with a truly rich and contradictory sonority, one with an attack-filled, yet quasi-sustained quality.

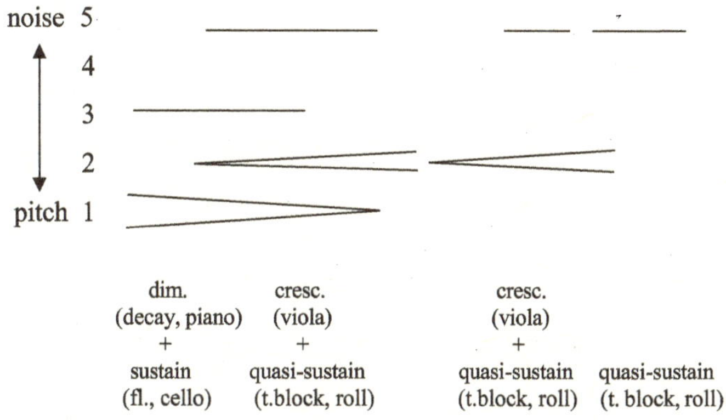

Figure 2.20 *The Viola in My Life 1* (mm. 47–50), Panel I, Gesture k.

Panel II

The first and second panels are separated by the only fermata in the piece. Moreover, the texture changes quite dramatically at the start of the second panel, which begins with the soloist initiating a crescendo with a left hand pizzicato, also the only instance of this sonority in the piece (Figure 2.21). The piano is rarely heard in this panel, sounding only four times (mm. 55, 72–73, and 78), far less than in the first panel. In contrast, the viola and percussion come to the fore. These, of course, represent opposite ends of the timbre spectrum, levels 1 and 5, respectively, on the scale outlined earlier (Table 2.1). Their juxtaposition throughout the second panel heightens the opposition of these tone color categories. The viola, in particular, stands out as each of its entrances unfolds into a brief melodic fragment (mm. 51, 54, 59–61, 64–70).

The central panel may be partitioned into six gestures (a, b, c, d, e, f), associating each of the four aforementioned fragments with one gesture (Figure 2.21). In terms of pitch content, the melodic events all seem to coalesce in gesture d; four pitch classes

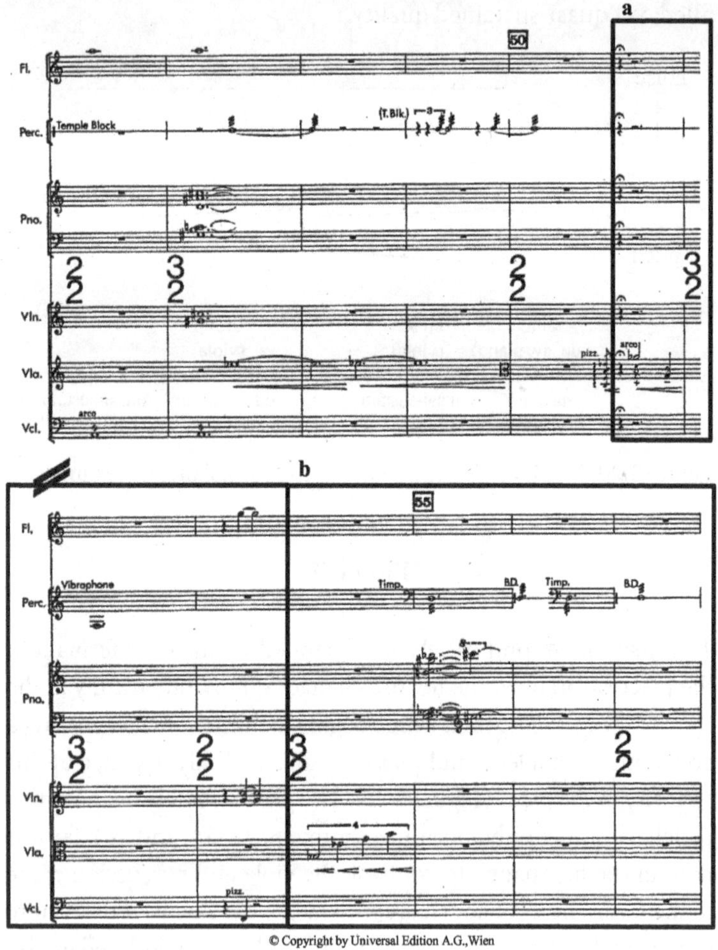

Figure 2.21 *The Viola in My Life 1*, Panel II, Annotated Score.

Figure 2.21 Continued

Figure 2.21 Continued

Figure 2.21 Continued

are carried over from gesture c to d, and one of these is carried over in the same register, the first such repetition in the viola solo in this panel (Figure 2.22). With the exception of the final three Bb^{3}s, only one pitch in the solo part is ever heard in the same register, C^5, sounded in both c and d. There is some evidence of a move toward register fixing as the composition moves from the first panel to the second, most obvious in the threefold repetition of Bb^3 (Figure 2.23). (As we will see, register fixing becomes even more prominent in Panel III.) All of this is supported by a remarkable consistency of intervallic content (Figure 2.24). Clearly, intervals 3 and 4 predominate, and this is especially true in the registrally linked passage between gestures c and d mentioned above (Figure 2.25). Despite these factors, the melodic events of the second panel never seem to cohere into a larger shape that spans and unifies all its gestures. (Such unification only emerges in the third panel where many of the nascent formal elements of the second panel crystallize.)

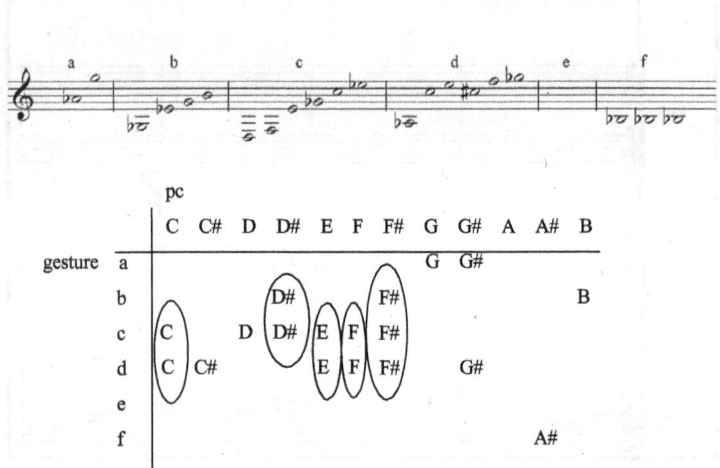

gesture \ pc	C	C#	D	D#	E	F	F#	G	G#	A	A#	B
a								G	G#			
b				D#			F#					B
c	C		D	D#	E	F	F#					
d	C	C#			E	F	F#		G#			
e												
f											A#	

Figure 2.22 *The Viola in My Life 1*, Panel II, Pitches of Viola Solo.

Figure 2.23 *The Viola in My Life 1*, Panel I and Panel II, Comparison of Register Fixing of Notes in Viola Solos.

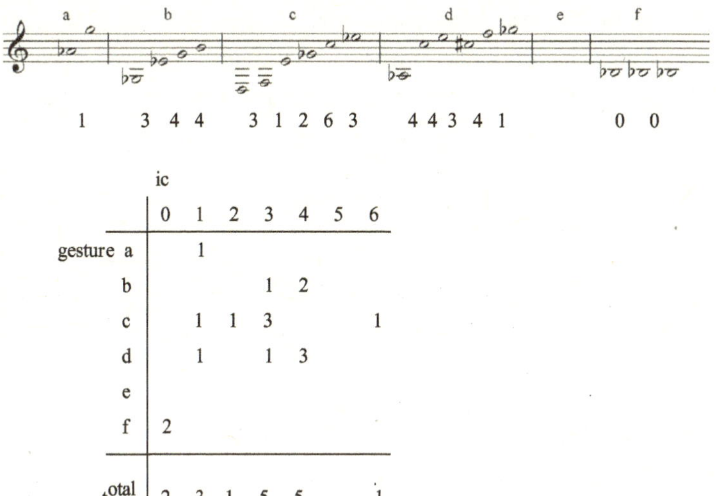

	ic 0	1	2	3	4	5	6
gesture a		1					
b				1	2		
c		1	1	3			1
d		1		1	3		
e							
f	2						
total	2	3	1	5	5		1

Figure 2.24 *The Viola in My Life 1*, Panel II, Interval Content of Viola Solo.

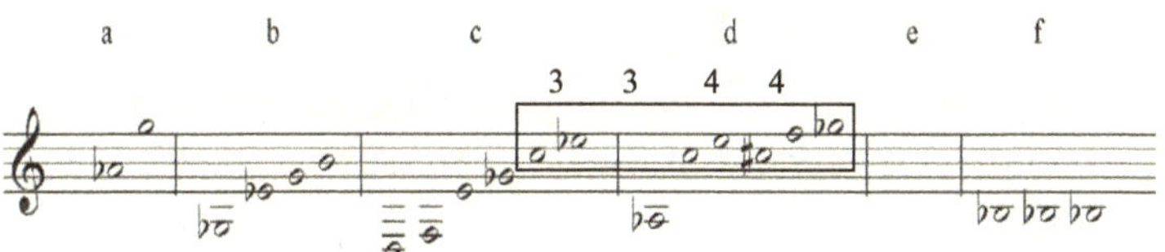

Figure 2.25 *The Viola in My Life 1*, Panel II, Interval Consistency of Notes Fixed in Register.

One of the three primary chords heard in Panel I reappears twice in Panel II. This is quite notable since there are only four chords in the entire second panel (Figure 2.26, Figure 2.27). The presence of this chord in Panel II represents an obvious link between the first two panels of the work. The memory of one sonority of the first panel lingers in the second, but it neither grows nor evolves.

As noted earlier, durations of the gestures of Panel II grow progressively longer up to gesture d, establishing the growing importance of successive melodic events (Table 2.4). Then gesture e shrinks in duration, perhaps, in part, because the soloist is silent in e. Finally, in f the viola returns and settles into the three repeated Bb^3s, fixing that note into one register and projecting a sense of stasis that concludes this part of the composition.

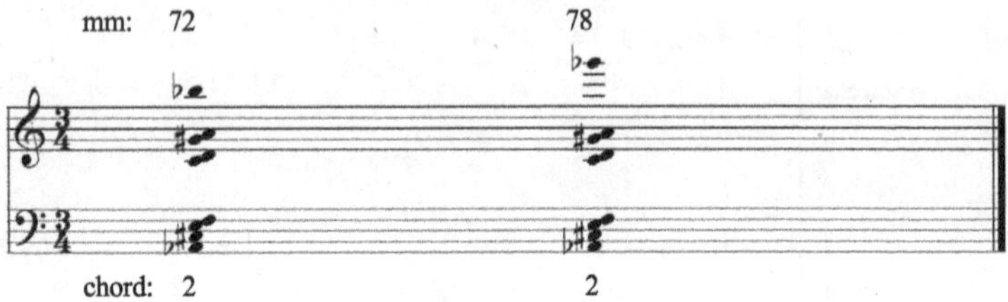

Figure 2.26 *The Viola in My Life 1*, Panel II, Primary Chords.

Percussion continues to play a central role in the evolution of the piece. The wood block is heard for the first time (mm. 59, 63–64, 76). This instrument projects an even greater focus on attack noise than the temple block (which was heard at the very end of the first panel). Moreover, we again experience the merging of pitched and unpitched sounds, here extended and intensified to a degree beyond that experienced in Panel I. This is most notable in bars 55–58, where Feldman continually rocks back and forth between pitched and unpitched instruments, alternately pulling the listener closer to pitched sonorities and then farther away from them (Figure 2.21, gesture b).

Panel III

In the third panel, the composition momentarily crystallizes into a succession of three well-defined and highly differentiated sonic events, gestures a, b, and c (Figure 2.28, Figure 2.29). Compared to the gestures of the previous two panels, the gestures of the third are remarkably concise and precisely delineated. In addition, Panel III is notable for the numerous exact and near exact repetitions

Figure 2.27 *The Viola in My Life 1*, Panel II, Summary of Pitches as Distributed among Timbres.

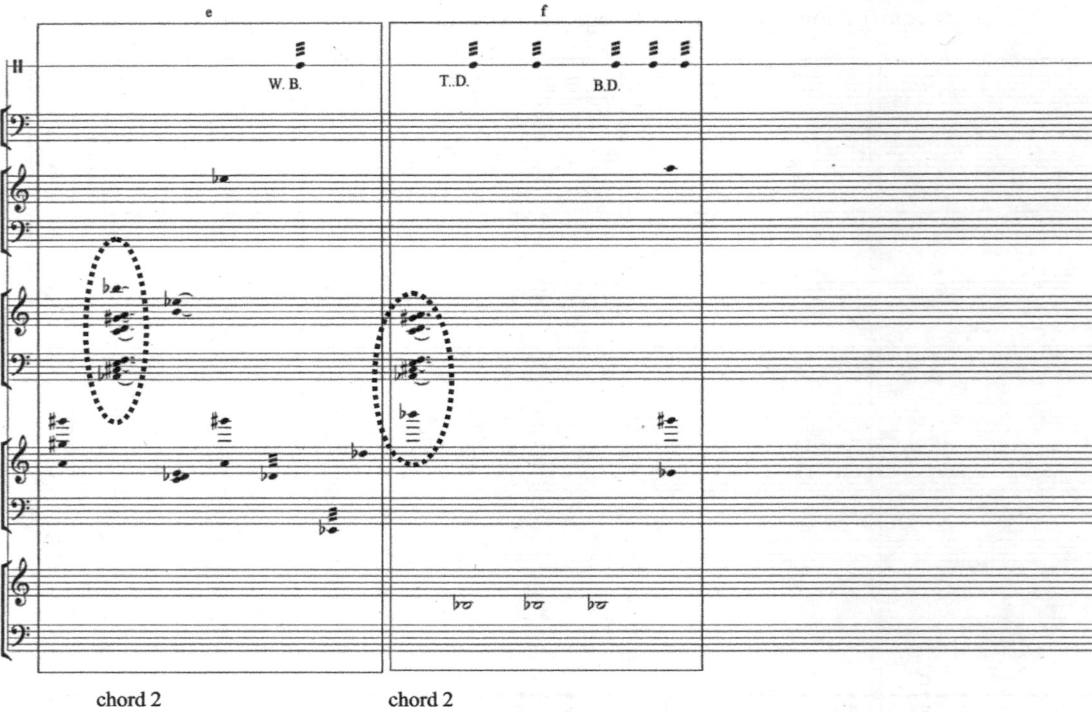

Figure 2.27 Continued

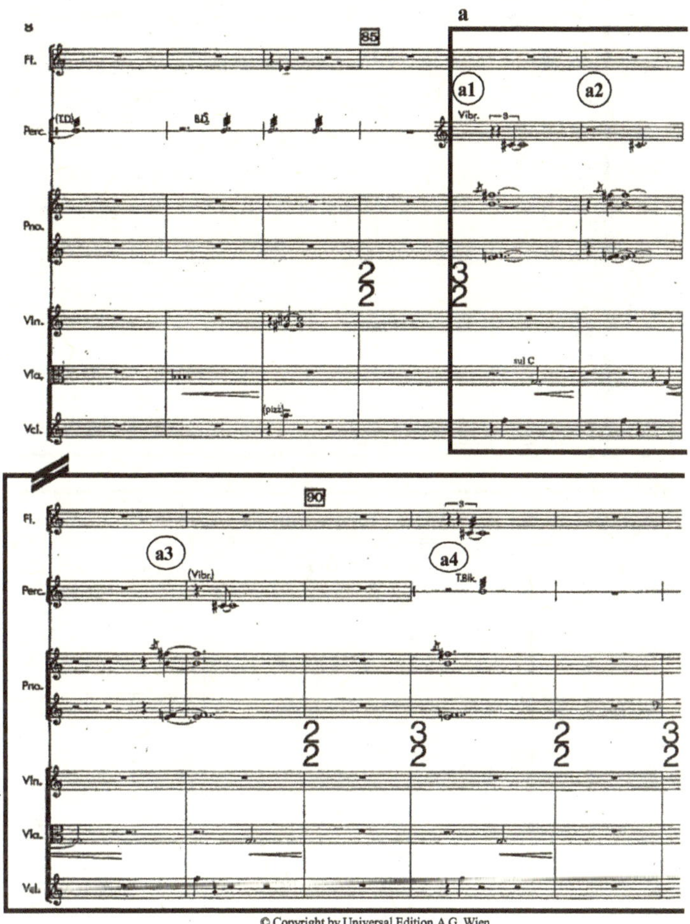

Figure 2.28 *The Viola in My Life 1*, Panel III, Annotated Score.

Figure 2.28 Continued

Figure 2.28 Continued

of its gestures, which further delineate them. Such periodicity—foreshadowing numerous later works such as *Neither* (1977), *for John Cage* (1982), and *Crippled Symmetry* (1983)—is new to this piece and, as will be shown, becomes more prominent in the next three pieces in *The Viola in My Life* set. It fixes each sonority in memory. With regard to another later work, *Triadic Memories* (1981),

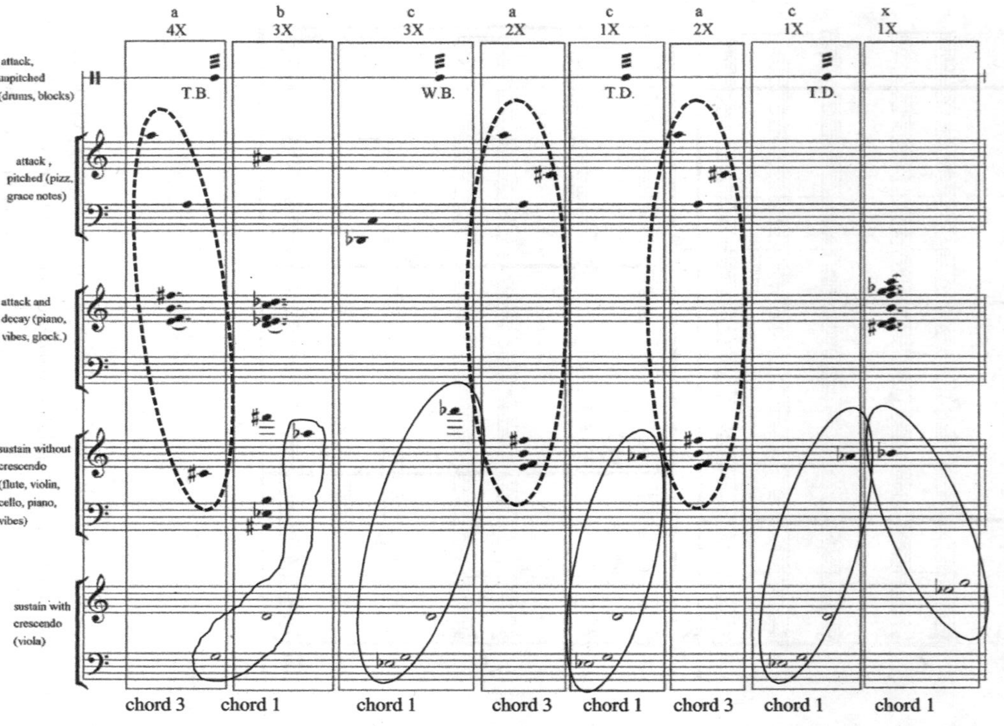

Figure 2.29 *The Viola in My Life 1*, Panel III, Summary of Pitches as Distributed among Timbres.

composed a decade after *The Viola in My Life*, Feldman noted (and it seems to me *a propos* here with respect to the third panel):

> One chord might be repeated three times, another, seven or eight—depending on how long I felt is should go on. Quite soon into a new chord I would forget the reiterated chord before it. I then reconstructed the entire section: rearranging its earlier progression and changing the number of times a particular chord was repeated. This way of working was a conscious attempt at "formalizing" a *disorientation of memory* [my italics]. Chords are heard repeated without any discernible pattern. In this regularity (though there are slight gradations of tempo) there is a suggestion that what we hear is functional and directional, but we soon realize that this is *an illusion* [my italics].[12]

It seems that Feldman attempts such a "disorientation of memory" in *The Viola in My Life I* as well. This is apparent not only in the repetitions of the gestures in Panel III, but also in the duration scheme that emerges from those repetitions (Table 2.4, Table 2.5, Table 2.8). The durations of the first two gestures of the passage (a, b) are rather long. However, the duration of gesture c is dramatically shortened. This foreshortening continues to the end of the piece, as gestures a and c alternate with one another. (In the final two bars, longer durations recur, but gestures a, b, and c are no longer present, having been replaced by a more nondistinct sonority, labeled x in the annotated score.) In addition, more silence is introduced as the panel progresses, most notably within each of the gestures (Table 2.8). These add to an overall sense of gradual dissolution. Finally, the gestures themselves seem to break apart. A comparison of the initial four statements of gesture a (mm. 86–91) with its later repetitions (mm. 109–112) reveals that elements of the initial statements have been shortened or dropped (mostly in the soloist's part) throughout those later recurrences. Later statements of gesture c are similarly truncated. The stable, well-formed identities of these

Table 2.8 *The Viola in My Life I*, Panel III, Durations of Gestures and Silences (in beats at MM 58)

◯ = silence

mm. 86				93			99				109	
a1	a2	a3	a4	b1	b2	b3	c1	c2	c3		a5	a6
7	9	11	11	12	12	12	3	3	3	(1)	4	
		7 +(4)	6 +(5)								2 + 2	
		↓	↓								1 +(1)	1 +(1)
		vla. cresc.; cut off to silence	vla. cresc.; cut off but resonance from pno. rings through silence									

113	117		121	125
c4	a7	a8	c5	x
4	4		4	12
3 +(1)	2 + 2		3 +(1)	6 + 6
	1 +(1)	1 +(1)		

figures gradually disappear as they become progressively shorter, are repeated with less insistence, and become more fragmented as the piece moves toward its conclusion. This gradual dissolution culminates in chord x (mm. 125), which is never repeated (hence, it never becomes periodic and therefore is never fixed in any way in our memory) and has little in common with the previous sonorities of Panel III (Figure 2.29). Feldman wipes away all the accumulated relationships that have formed over the course of the third panel. In a sense, chord x erases our memory of previous events. All of this is clearly evident in a spectrograph of Panel III, which vividly depicts the initial regularity of the passage and its gradual fragmentation—its "disorientation of memory" (Figure 2.30).

Again, one must note the significant role that timbre plays in this process. In the first three repetitions of gesture a (mm. 86–90), C# is sounded on the vibraphone. However, in the fourth

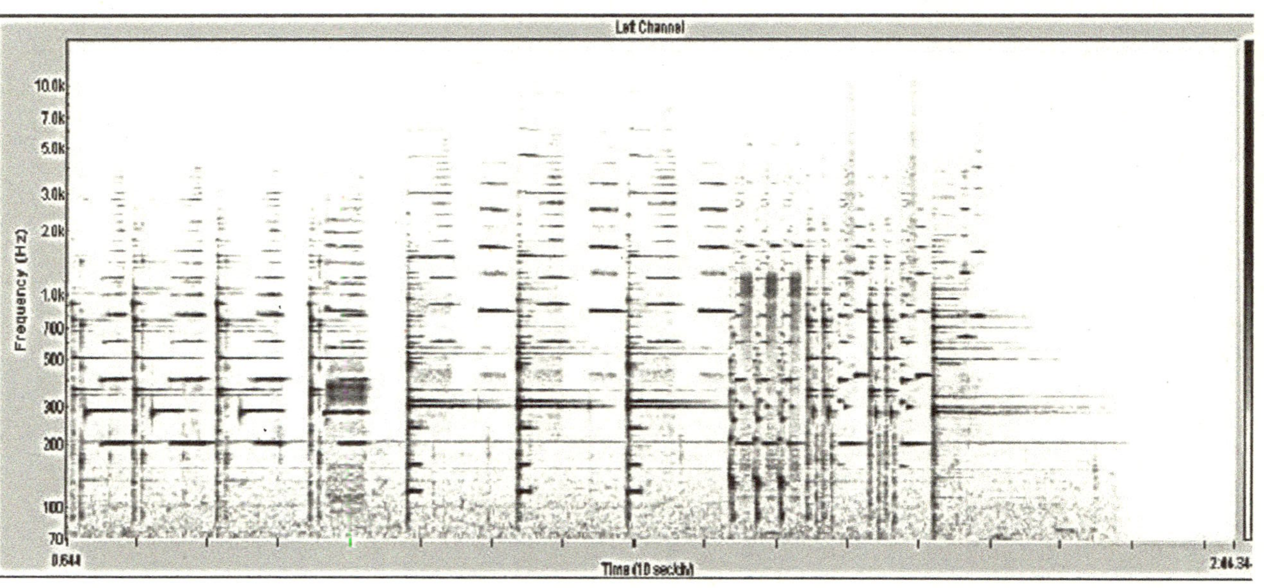

Figure 2.30 *The Viola in My Life I*, Panel III, Spectrograph.

repetition of a (m. 91), Feldman moves the C# from the vibraphone to the flute (with fluttertongue articulation). In addition, a roll on the temple-block is added at this point, overlapping with the flute. Over the course of the first four repetitions of a, we hear a transition from pitch (vibraphone) to pitched-noise (flute flutter) to an unpitched quasi-sustained roll on a wood instrument. The sonic clarity of gesture a and its numerous repetitions dissipate into a haze of noise. These changes to gesture a represent a more local instance of the dissolution experienced throughout Panel III. As will be shown, this very same sonic transformation from pitch to noise band initiates *The Viola in My Life II* and dominates its first panel!

Unpitched percussion instruments are absent from gesture b but return in gesture c and, indeed, form an integral part of that gesture. A roll on a wood block, which, once again, draws the listener to attack noise, becomes part of the repeated pattern of the gesture itself. It appears as both an extension and intensification of the attack quality of the first two notes of the gesture, the cello's pizzicato notes. It is worth noting that when gesture c returns at the end of Panel III (mm. 113–114, 121–122), the wood block roll is replaced by a roll on tenor drum, softening the attack quality of the roll. This is perhaps a reflection of the fact that, at this point, Feldman has removed the initial pizzicato sonorities from gesture c, minimizing the presence of any attack noise initiating

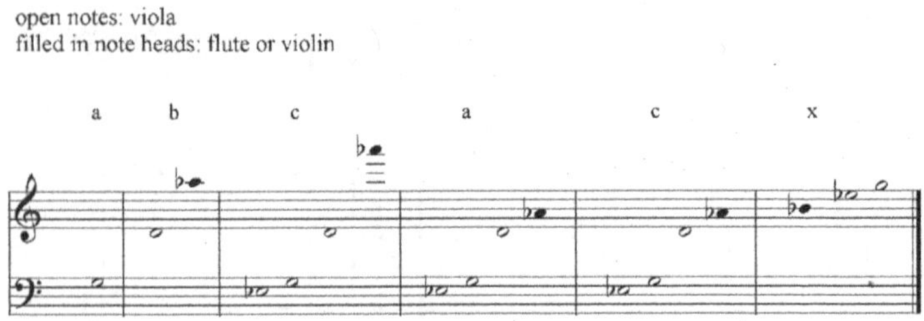

open notes: viola
filled in note heads: flute or violin

a b c a c x

Figure 2.31 *The Viola in My Life 1*, Panel III, Pitches of Melodic Fragments Including Viola Solo.

c, and further strengthening the sense of sonic separation that characterizes the end of Panel III.

As noted, in the third panel, the tones of viola solo are completely fixed in register and are now linked with those of the cello and flute, which are also, generally fixed in register (Figure 2.31). Such an exceptional degree of register fixing establishes another instance of aural memory (much like the periodic repetition of chords in gestures a and b). This too is dispelled at the end of the piece. In the final bar, the melody seems to regress and shrink back to its initial two notes, Eb and G, and these are themselves, so to speak, "disembodied," unfixed in register (transposed up two octaves from their previous position). In addition, at the end, the melodic fragment Eb-G-D (intervals 4 and 5), which has been heard throughout the third panel, is altered and reshaped into Bb-Eb-G (intervals 5 and 4). Once again, we sense the composer trying to erase our memory in these final bars; perhaps the momentary suggestion of order experienced at the beginning of Panel III was indeed an illusion.

Gestures a and b are primarily chordal. Gesture c, however, is a linear event; a melodic fragment, reminiscent of the fragments that were heard throughout Panel II, though here much more compact. Indeed, gesture c represents the most obvious example of an organized melodic event in the piece. It constitutes the point in Panel III where the gestures clearly link up with the viola's registrally fixed melodic line (Figure 2.29). Before gesture c is introduced, the viola seems to float along, disconnected from the overall texture. However, this viola line crystallizes at c, which is itself a variant of that same melodic event in diminution. This process, too, will reappear in the three succeeding compositions in the set and expand considerably in scope.

In c the linear and chordal clearly fuse. Gesture a projects its intervals into gesture c, while gesture b projects its pitches into gesture c (Figure 2.32). Thus, the linear event of c is an amalgam of a and b. Since gesture c also integrates the cello (pizzicato) and percussion into the viola's melodic event, it represents a true synthesis of all the sonorities of the composition.

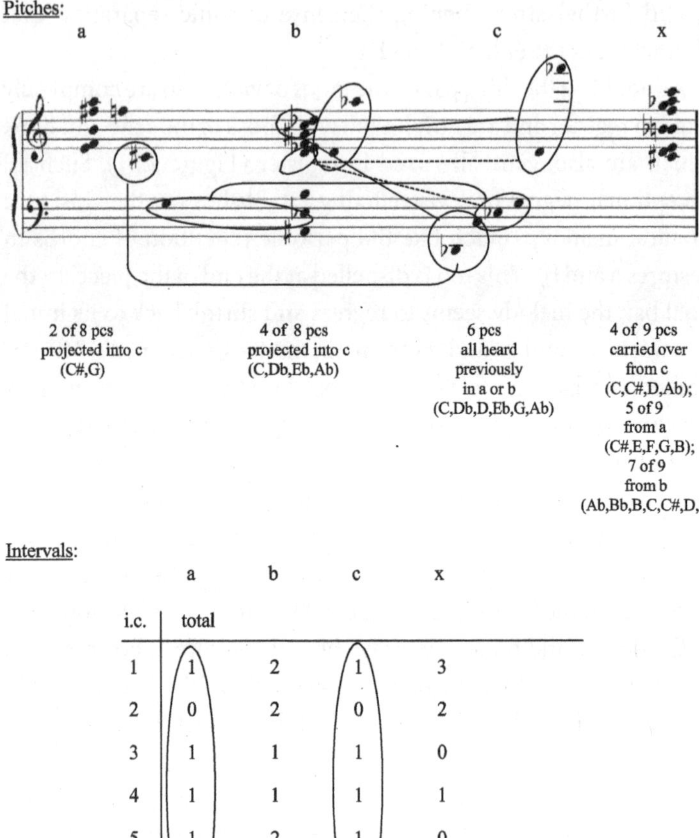

Intervals:

	a	b	c	x
i.c.	total			
1	1	2	1	3
2	0	2	0	2
3	1	1	1	0
4	1	1	1	1
5	1	2	1	0
6	2	1	1	2

Figure 2.32 *The Viola in My Life 1*, Panel III, Projection of Pitches and Intervals from Gestures a and b to c.

Synthesis

In his seminal essay "Cézanne's Doubt," Maurice Merleau-Ponty outlined the great painter's approach to the rendering of objects:

> . . . the contour of an object conceived as a line encircling the object belongs not to the visible world but to geometry. If one outlines the shape of an apple with a continuous line, one makes an object of the shape, whereas the contour is rather the ideal limit toward which the sides of the apple recede in depth. Not to indicate any shape would be to deprive the objects of their identity. To trace just a single outline sacrifices depth—that is, the dimension in which the thing is presented not as spread out before us but as an inexhaustible reality full of reserves. That is why Cézanne follows the swelling of the object in modulated colors and indicates *several* outlines in blue. Rebounding among these, one's glance captures a shape that emerges from among them all, just as it does in perception.[13]

Over the course of *The Viola in My Life I* isolated sounds coalesce into precisely delineated shapes through a similar process, which unfolds on two levels simultaneously: first, within the entire ensemble and its mixed sonic palate; second, in the solo viola part. As we have seen, these two levels fuse in the third gesture of Panel III, when the viola's evolving linear design joins with the overall sonority of the ensemble.

With respect to the ensemble as a whole, the well-defined shapes of the third panel replace the loosely formed gestures of the first. The gestures of Panel I function somewhat as frames, drawing together collections of seemingly isolated sounds. Over the course of this panel, Feldman gradually reveals that sonic connections are immanent within those sounds (gestures i and j of the first panel). In the second panel, the composer focuses more on two types of sound, viola and percussion, and in their striking opposition starts to delineate the viola's melodic potential; the viola begins to form linear connections among its tones, to form somewhat more defined gestures than those of Panel I and, in a sense, to discover the *possibility* of linearity. In the third panel, each gesture represents a fixed, highly differentiated shape that is set off from all others not only by its unique character and design but also by its deliberate repetition. The periodicity emblematic of this final panel projects a sense of order and regularity. Of course, this sense of order is an illusion, as the gestures gradually disintegrate and disappear.

With respect to the soloist, in the first panel, the viola, with its omnipresent crescendo, seems to emerge from the general texture, striving constantly to become a separate, distinguishable sonic object. In the second panel, the soloist pulls further away from the general ensemble as it starts to fashion brief linear events; having achieved enough "presence" (as a result of its crescendos), the viola becomes viable as a building block for "melody." In the third panel linearity emerges, if only briefly, fully formed both within the solo part and within the entire ensemble (Panel III, gesture c).

As noted, the opposition of pitch and noise plays a crucial role in the evolution of this piece. At the beginning, the sonorities of the unpitched percussion function as delimiters, separating materials into more or less unified sonic events, and, at the same time, wiping away all the potential pitch relationships that came to the fore as each gesture unfolded. The sonorities of the initial gestures of Panel I also project the various components of their sound world as separate elements—especially with respect to the unpitched percussion and the crescendo viola tones: one representing pure attack, the other, no attack (or as close to it as possible). But, as Panel I itself evolves, the unpitched percussion is replaced by pitched percussion (timpani) whose tones interact with other pitched materials. As the separation between noise and pitch starts to disappear, a new level of order is achieved whereby the elements of subsequent gestures coalesce into more unified shapes.

Similarly, throughout this work, Feldman slowly builds a collection of recurrences that are not quite as random as might appear at first glance. These include chord repetitions, specific pitches doubled in octaves, and, of course, identifiable melodic fragments. Such recurrences constantly suggest a push toward order. In Panel I the recurrence of chords 2 and 3 in gestures f and g, and chord 2 at the start of h, project a momentary sense that materials are coalescing into some higher unit of organization, which does, in fact, prepare us for the striking integration of pitch and noise in gestures i and j of the same panel. Chord 2 recurs in the second panel, suggesting—only suggesting—a larger resonance between the first two panels. Of course, the idea of recurrence reaches its peak in the third panel where virtually every sonic event (except the last) is repeated, frequently and with deliberation. From the general intensification of such recurrences we sense *an emergence of order* over the course of the piece. As will be shown in successive chapters, the use of such recurrences intensifies over the course of the entire set of the four *Viola in My Life* compositions and eventually becomes the central element in the fourth piece of the set.

3
The Viola in My Life II

The Viola in My Life II is scored for solo viola and a chamber ensemble consisting of flute, clarinet, violin, cello, celesta, and percussion (castanets, maracas, tenor drum, side drum, vibraphone, and timpani). The performance instructions are more specific than those of *Viola I*: extremely quiet, all attacks at a minimum, without the feeling of a beat. The tempo indication is quarter note at approximately 66 (slightly faster than the tempo in *Viola I*). The score is notated in C, the strings are always muted, and the motor on the vibraphone is off throughout until the final 14 bars of the work. The castanets are always to be played *coperto* (covered).[1] The indications for tenor drum and side drum call for deep drums typical of a marching band, one without snares (tenor drum) and the other with snares (side drum).[2]

Once again, throughout this study I often use spectrographs to analyze the sonic results of Feldman's instrumentation. As noted in Chapter 1, in general I prefer the recorded performance by the Ensemble Recherche. However, in one respect the Cikada Ensemble's performance of *The Viola in My Life II* is superior: the castanets are played truly *coperto*, and, as such, they are fully integrated into the ensemble's texture throughout the work, creating a clearer sense of transformation from pitch-based material to noise-/attack-based material, as will be discussed later in this chapter.

Formally, *The Viola in My Life II* can be viewed as constructed from two panels of sound events (continuing with the same terminology, for the same reasons given in the previous chapter, reflecting the influence of certain painters who were close to Feldman such as Robert Rauschenberg and Jasper Johns): Panel I, bars 1–99

The Marvelous Illusion. Thomas DeLio, Oxford University Press. © Oxford University Press 2024.
DOI: 10.1093/9780197759967.003.0003

and Panel II, bars 100–187 (with a slight overlap in bar 105). The initial and concluding passages of each panel are markedly different with respect to sonority, temporal organization, and linear (melodic) design. Nor is there any sense of transition from one panel to the next. Once again, the whole is fashioned not from any graduated evolution of sonic materials, but rather, from the contrasting treatment of these materials within each part.

As was the case with *The Viola in My Life I*, in *Viola II* each panel constitutes a distinct sonic region, which, on the surface, seems to be quite independent of the other. However, they do share certain characteristics. Of these, the most important is the sound of the ensemble itself, which gives unique definition to each sonic event as it unfolds. In contrast, the most notable difference between *Viola I* and *II* is the relationship between the soloist and ensemble, which is radically redefined as the piece progresses from Panel I to Panel II.

The composition opens with a rather complex sound event, the elements of which saturate the first panel. In contrast, the second panel consists of simpler, more clearly defined, static sonic events. *In this respect, the last panel of this work is remarkably similar to the last panel of Viola I.* The first panel is 299 quarter notes long. It is notated entirely in 3/4 time with only two exceptions: bar 72, which is notated in 3/2 time purely for the purpose of notating a 4:3 rhythm; and the final bar of the panel, which is a 2/4 bar of rest. The second panel is 208 quarter notes long, and throughout, meter changes quite frequently. Obviously, the ratio of 208:299 is .695, remarkably close to the Golden Mean of .618. Perhaps it was not planned, but rather felt, as was the case with some of Feldman's other works, as well as those of so many composers throughout the ages.

In Panel I the composer presents two basic sonorities that recur periodically. Throughout, one encounters a texture fashioned from the alternation and occasional interpenetration of these sonorities that at times seem to dissolve into one another. The character of Panel II is quite different. Sonic events are established and generally repeated verbatim or with slight change. In Panel II one senses a gradual crystallization of fixed sonic formations, with just enough variation to add a subtle sense of freshness. Finally, in Panel I the viola functions independently of the ensemble, while in Panel II the viola gradually merges with the ensemble and, by the end, functions as part of it.

Panel I

As noted, in the first panel, the ensemble and soloist function mostly as independent sound sources, and, initially, they will be treated as such in this discussion. Among the most notable differences between ensemble and soloist is the type of material composed for each. With respect to the ensemble, one encounters two distinct types of sonorities (combinations of pitched and/or noise-based timbres). These will be labeled *Sonority A* and *Sonority B*. In contrast, the soloist's material evolves from two basic linear ("melodic") patterns: *Pattern a* and *Pattern b*. This distinction in terminology is important because, once again, the music for the ensemble and the viola is constructed and treated quite differently. The sonorities of the ensemble and the patterns of the soloist often coincide but do not coalesce to form unified sound events (as they will quite clearly in the second panel). Here they seem to float by, gradually changing, yet functioning independently of one another.

With respect to the ensemble alone, of its two basic sonorities, Sonority A is by far the most significant and omnipresent. It first appears within the first six bars of the piece: first in bars 2 and 3, and then repeated, with variation, through the next four bars (Figure 3.1). Much of what will be heard in *The Viola in My Life II* can be found in a close examination of this sonority. As such, it is important to begin with a detailed examination of its initial statement.

Figure 3.1 *The Viola in My Life 2*, Ensemble, First statement of Sonority A and Initial Variants (mm. 2–7).

Two sonic characteristics dominate this primary sound: *pure tones*, which dissolve into *noise bands*. The pure tones are omnipresent at the outset of each statement of A. They consist of the soft, attack-free pitches in flute and clarinet, and equally soft, attack-free string harmonics. Attack noise is minimized as a result of both the soft dynamic level and placement in the register of each tone. The flute and clarinet enter softly, in low registers, with little attack noise. The result will be about as close to the quality of pure tones as one can achieve with acoustic instruments, with most energy focused on the fundamental frequencies, little on the overtones.[3] This is echoed in the violin and cello, muted, softly playing harmonics, though in a higher register.

These then dissolve into noise-filled sonorities (filled with attack noise), first via the shift to flutter tonguing by the wind instruments and then to the rolls on the castanets (*coperto*). Each of these instrument pairs adds a *slight* crescendo. When the winds reach their peaks of these crescendos, they add flutter, increasing attack noise and letting the pure tones dissolve into bands of noise. To amplify this dissolution soon after the fluttering is initiated, the percussionist enters, tapping on the castanets (*coperto*), further intensifying the loss of any sense of pitch, and the overall sonority passes into pure noise. As discussed in the previous chapter, this move from pure tone to noise was featured within the first three repetitions of gesture a of the third panel of *Viola I* (mm. 86–90), during which the sonic clarity heard at the start of that gesture similarly dissipates into a haze of percussive attacks on wood instruments.

The strings do not participate in this transition from pure tone to noise band. They serve a different purpose. The flute/clarinet pair play, respectively, D♭^{4}/C^4. At the same time, the violin/cello pair sound, as harmonics, respectively, A♭^{5}/G^4. Certainly, the A♭^{5} is heard as an overtone of the flute's D♭^{4}, while the cello's G^4 possibly alludes to an overtone of the clarinet's C^4, though an octave lower than where it would naturally sound. As the tones of the winds disappear into noise, the strings appear to brighten the sound as these higher frequencies gradually emerge (Figure 3.2). Thus, in terms of

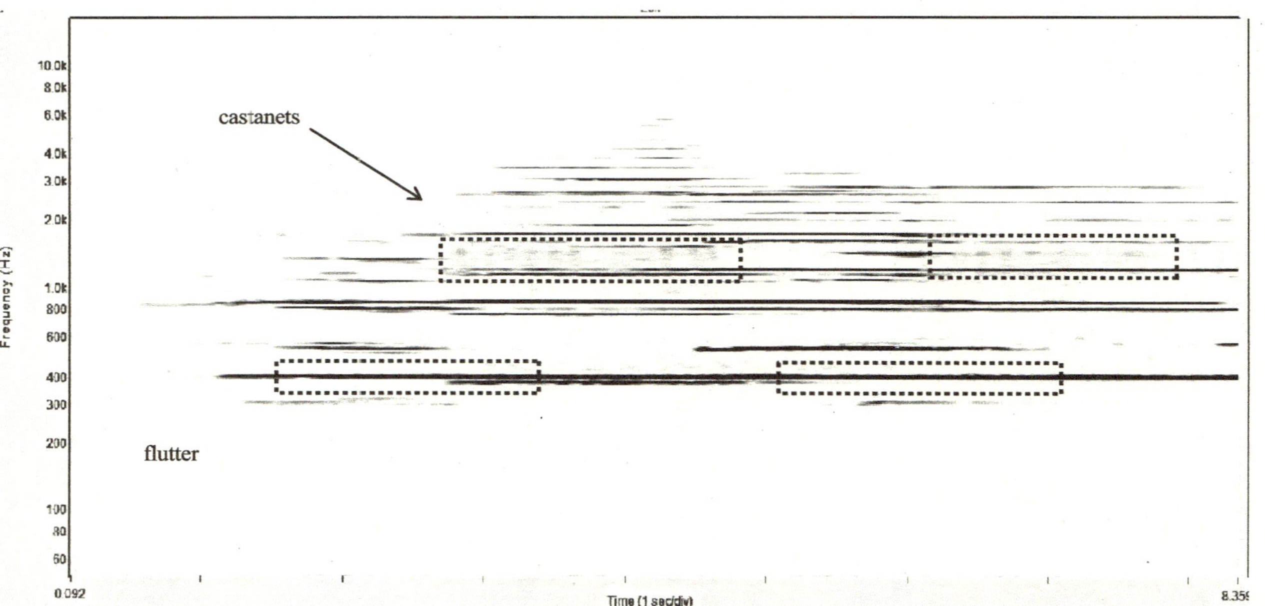

Figure 3.2 *The Viola in My Life 2*, Panel I, Sonority A, Spectrograph (Ensemble Recherche Performance, mm. 2–3); Castanets and Flutter Tonguing Outlined.

timbre, we find a very complex situation. Sonority A seems to evolve in two ways: first, transitioning from pure tone to noise—from no attack noise to extensive attack noise (woodwind pure tones to woodwind flutter to castanet rolls); second, gradually brightening the sonority as a result of the emergence of upper partials via the harmonics in the strings, which energize the upper registers of the instrumental sonorities.

This process is reinforced by the composer's choice of interval formation within the sonority itself. Sonority A is built upon a pair of half-steps. Such clustering will cause the sound to vibrate through the resultant beating (also known as the interference phenomenon). Added to this are the aforementioned crescendos, which, as they reach their peak, introduce overtones that naturally will intensify the clustering and so the beating, causing the sound to vibrate with growing intensity. As such, the process whereby pitch dissolves into noise is echoed in different ways at the opening of the piece. As will be shown, Sonority A breaks apart and dissolves into stretches of noise-filled sound in many different ways throughout Panel I.

The general characteristics of Panel I described earlier apply only to the evolution of the sonorities of the ensemble. The linear patterns of the solo part function quite differently. As such, within a discussion of each panel, I will examine the role of ensemble and soloist separately—first, the sonorities of the ensemble, and then, the patterns of the viola solo.

Panel I: The Ensemble

As discussed earlier, Sonority A is repeated, at times varied, over the course of most of the first panel (indeed, it is heard in 82 of its 99 bars). It is heard initially in bars 2 and 3, then presented wholly or in fragments throughout the remainder of that panel, and, finally, disappears from the piece entirely (Figure 3.3).[4] Though

Figure 3.3 *The Viola in My Life 2*, Panel I, Ensemble, First Three Statements of Sonority A plus Dissolution Between Each (mm. 1–15).

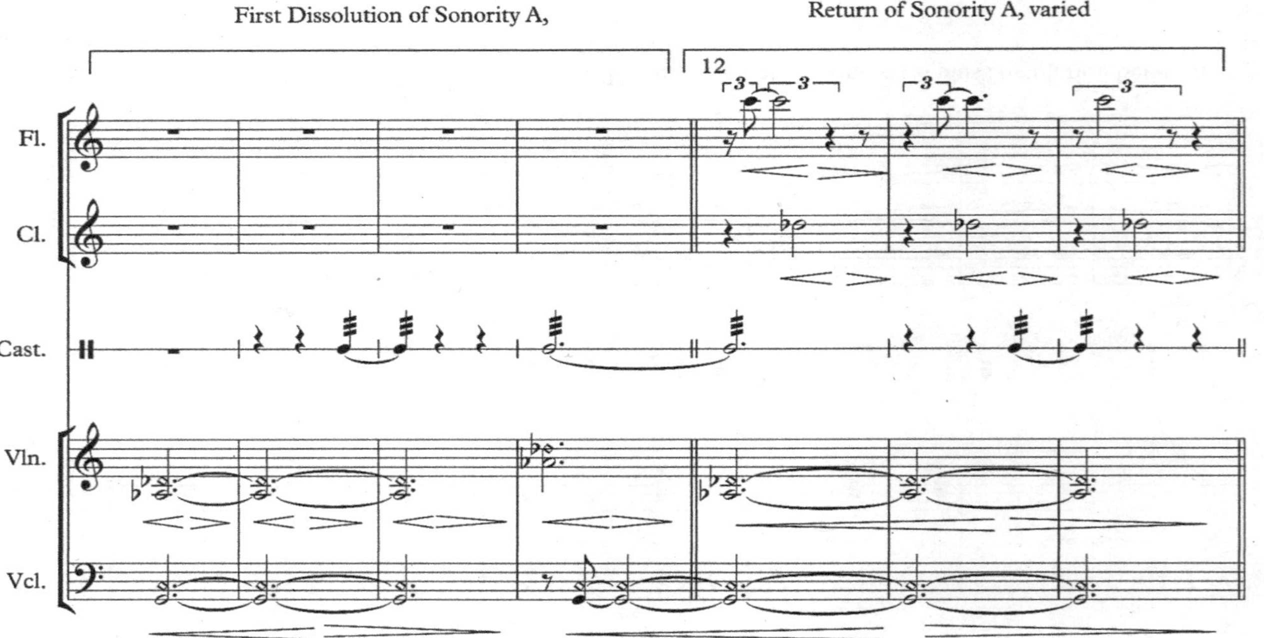

Figure 3.3 Continued

Figure 3.3 Continued

varied, Sonority A is always recognizable when it returns. For Feldman, variations project different perspectives of a sonic event rather than elements in an evolution or development of structural designs. Regarding his notion of the role of variation in his music the composer has said:

> I am interested now in a lot of music where the variation is so discrete, I would have the same thing come back again, but would just add one note. Or I would have it come back and I take out two notes. And I would vary the notes and keep the pulse, but very subtle.[5]

With respect to Sonority A, one encounters numerous examples of this concept of variation. For example, in terms of register placement, in bars 2–3 the flute sounds Db^4 and the clarinet C^4. In bar 3, the flute takes over the C and raises it one octave higher (C^5), while the clarinet sounds Db and holds it in its original register. Then, in bar 4 the flute returns to its initial tone, Db, though one octave higher (Db^5), while the clarinet returns to its initial tone, C, in its original register (C^4). This spatial configuration continues through bar 7. Then, in bar 11, both C and Db sound higher than in their first presentation in bar 2; flute with C two octaves higher (C^6), and clarinet with Db one octave higher (Db^5), bringing the entire initial sonority to a new peak in terms of register. Moreover, this is the first time the clarinet has been raised an octave from its initial position, adding an entirely new tone color to the semitone. While this transformation is taking place in the winds, the strings remain fixed in register with G^4/Ab^5 harmonics. The violin briefly shifts up one octave in bar 11, as does the cello in bars 15 and 16, after which they return to their original spatial positions for the next nine bars. It appears, then, that the strings provide a generally constant backdrop against which the various shifts of register in the winds are foregrounded. In any event, as Feldman himself suggested, such variation is not transformative, but rather serves to keep the sonority alive, less static, and fixed. In this way, Sonority A becomes more a quality of sound than a monolithic entity.

Each of these varied statements of the primary sonority, fragments of it carries through—like residue—ensuring that, on some level, its near constant presence is always felt. It creates a constant backdrop against which other material floats in and out. For example, in bars 15–20 and 24–26, the string harmonics on G/Ab continue to sound, while the winds are either silent or move away from their initial dyad C/Db. Similarly, in bar 25 the castanets—so characteristic of Sonority A—are replaced by maracas. In bars 35–41, the violin and woodwinds sustain a C in various octaves; the castanets briefly return in bars 46–50; and, finally, in bar 84, C returns as a harmonic in the cello and octaves in the winds (Figure 3.4). These are but a few examples of how Feldman keeps the elements of Sonority A in play while the complete sonority itself seems to disappear temporarily. Such moments convey a sense of the large-scale dissipation of Sonority A, which echoes, in macrocosm, the shift from pitch to noise first heard in bars 2 and 3.

With respect to the temporal domain, Sonority A remains quite fixed. In its first appearance, it sounds for six 3/4 bars (mm. 2–7), after which, every time it reappears it is heard for three 3/4 bars, starting in bars 12, 20, 43, 55, and 80. In all, Sonority A is heard in its entirety in 21 out of the 99 bars in Panel I. Whether planned or sensed, each time the primary sonority reasserts itself, it is temporally fixed (Figure 3.3). This static nature of the temporal design of Sonority A supports its constant presence and recurrence as a ground upon which everything else is heard.

The first panel of the piece also contains what will be considered a *secondary sonority*, Sonority B, which consists of a single chord sounded by the celesta. It is first presented in bar 15 and is then repeated without change in bars 24, 35, 37, 39, 41, 46, 50, and 84, after which, it too finally disappears (Figure 3.5). Occasionally, this chord too is altered in varying degrees (bars 26, 68, 70, 75, 89). However, these few variants are still played by the celesta alone,

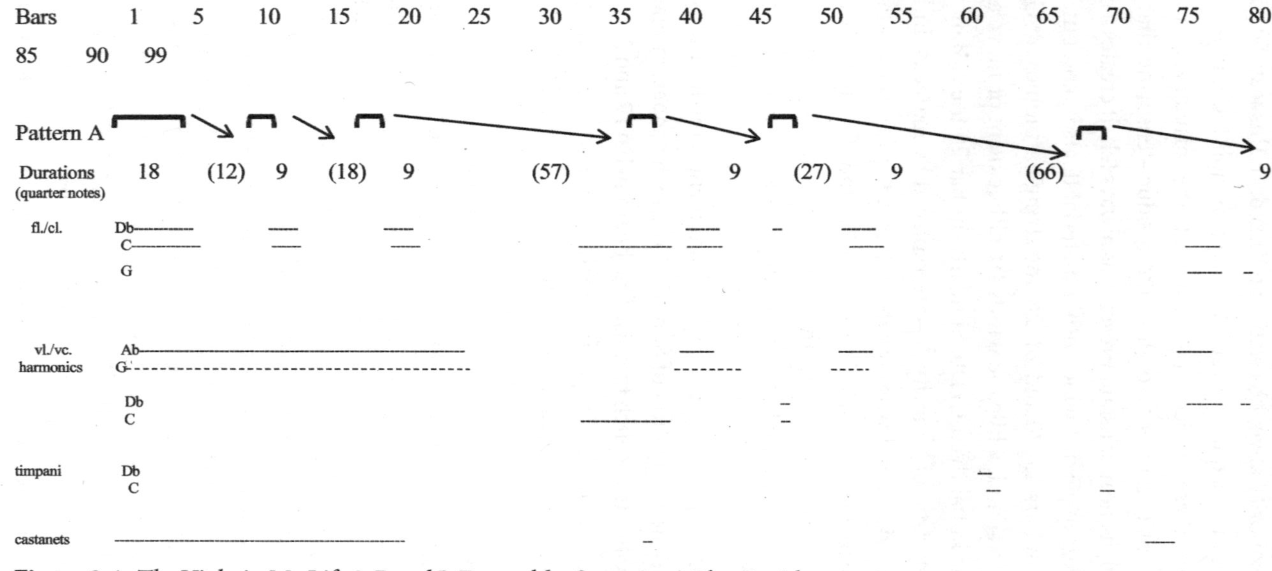

Figure 3.4 *The Viola in My Life 2*, Panel I, Ensemble, Sonority A Plus Residue.

Figure 3.5 *The Viola in My Life 2*, Panel I, Ensemble (Celesta), Sonority B.

and so they are listed as variants of Sonority B. Despite its very different sound quality from that of Sonority A, Sonority B shares a very similar interval formation with it. In fact, both very closely reflect the content of the most prominent sonority of Panel III of *Viola I* (Table 3.1). This initiates a practice of self-referencing, often

Table 3.1 Panel I Comparison of sonority from Panel III of *The Viola in My Life I* with Sonorities A and B of *The Viola in My Life II*

Vla. I Panel III m. 86	*Vla. II* Sonority A m. 1-2	*Vla. II* Sonority B m. 1
A 3 F# 1 F 6 B 6 F 1 E C# 6 G	Ab 1 G 1 6 F# 6 Db 1 C	Gb 1 F 6 B 6 F Eb Bb

resulting in direct quotation, among the four compositions of the *Viola in My Life* set—one that will become more and more prominent as the set unfolds.

It is important to recognize that both of these sonorities in the ensemble are static. Each establishes itself as aurally quite distinct from the more amorphous material surrounding it. Each recurs at various moments over the course of the piece in an overlapping manner. And each recurs in new contexts as the piece unfolds. However, there is no evolution toward a goal, and no attempt at an integration of materials is made. The result is rather more akin to a collage, a field of related recurrences. What seems to be most important is a sense not of development but of identity.

In terms of pitch/interval content, Sonority A and its variants are permutations of the same four pitches (Table 3.2). Also, all are derived from the same half-step dyads and tritone relationships that are so prominent in their initial presentation in bar 2. As noted above, Sonority B is fixed in its original form through 9 of its 14 presentations (mm. 15, 24, 35, 37, 39, 41, 46, 50, 84). Curiously, in terms of pitch/interval content, some of its variants veer closer to the formation of Sonority A (mm. 26, 68, 71, 89), as these share the same focus on half-step dyads and tritone relationships as A, an example of the occasional interpenetration of elements of the two sonorities.

Contrasting with the transformation from pitch to noise that takes place *within* Sonority A, over the course of the first panel the percussion unfolds in the opposite direction—from more attack noise to less—from rolls on unpitched percussion instruments to rolls on pitch percussion instruments, as well as the occasional related pizzicato/tremolos played by the cello (Table 3.3). Of course, what unifies all of these percussive moments is the introduction of various levels of attack noise from the rolls. Despite Feldman's indication at the top of the score ("all attacks at a minimum"), some attack noise is, at times, clearly and deliberately introduced. The castanets, which first introduced attack noise in bar 2, return

Table 3.2 *The Viola in My Life II*, Panel I, Ensemble, Sonorities A and B, Pitch/Interval Content

	Pitch	**Interval**
Sonority A {1,4,5,6} plus castanets (tremolo)		
m. 2	C Db G Ab	1 6 1
mm. 3, 21–23	Db G C Ab	6 5 4
mm. 4–7, 55–58	C G Db Ab	5 6 5
mm. 12–14	G Db C Ab	6 1 4
mm. 43–45	C G Ab Db	5 1 5
mm. 80–82	Db C G Ab	1 5 1

All permutations of the same four pitches plus castanets (tremolo).

	pitch	interval	
Sonority B {1,2,5,6}			
mm. 15, 24, 35, 37, 39 41, 46, 50. 84	A# Eb F B G	5 2 6 5	moving away from B
m. 26	Gb B C E F B	5 1 4 1 6	
mm. 68, 71	G# A D Eb	1 5 1	
m. 75	Eb F C Gb	2 5 6	
m. 89	C E F B E F	4 1 6 5 1	

All chords with same timbre (celesta).

three times (Table 3.3). These seem to be the most articulated attack-filled sounds in the composition and initiate three large-scale motions toward more pitched percussion rolls with less distinct attack noise. Each of these three such motions starts with a succession of rolls on castanets and moves toward rolled pitched

Table 3.3 *The Viola in My Life II*, Order of Percussion Instruments plus Cello (pizzicato/tremolo). Castanets, maracas, violoncello, tenor drum, side drum, vibraphone, timpani.

Bar (first appearance of each instrument type)

2	25	27	28	29	30	31	32	35	36	39	41	50	53	53	54	59	78	80	82	89	93
Cast	Mar	Vcl	TD	Vcl	TD	Vcl	SD	Vcl	Vib	Vcl	Cast	SD	Vib	Vcl	SD	Timp	Cast	Mar	Vcl	Vib	Timp
→			→		→		→				→				→		→				
40 bars											18 bars						15 bars				

Overall movement from unpitched to pitched tremolos, on two structural levels. Each of the three such movements on the larger level starts with rolls on Castanets. The first ends with rolls on Vibraphone and Cello; the second and third with rolls on Timpani. Final rolls on Timpani (mm. 93-97) pick up the C/Db semitone prominent in Sonority A throughout the first Panel, completing a transfer of significant pitch material of A from pure tones of Fl/Cl to percussive, attack filled rolls in pitched percussion. Significant moment in this transition takes place in bars 80- 82 where the Db, for the first time in a statement of A, appears in the Cello. In bars 80 and 81 it is bowed, but in 82 it is sounded as a pizzicato tremolo.

sounds. The first such evolution ends with rolls on vibraphone and tremolos on cello; the second and third, with rolls on timpani.

Of great significance are the final rolls of Panel I, played on the timpani (mm. 93–97). These pick up the C/Db semitone prominent in *every statement of Sonority A throughout the first panel*, completing a transfer of significant pitch material from the woodwind component of that sonority to the attack-filled rolls of the pitched percussion. This transfer is prepared in several earlier moments in the work such as bars 80–82 where Db, for the first time in a statement of Sonority A, is presented by the cello: in bars 80 and 81 the Db is bowed, but in 82 it is sounded as a pizzicato/tremolo, setting in motion the transition of the C/Db semitone from the winds to the pitched percussion (timpani). *Thus, what began as a transfer of frequency (pitch) to noise is transformed into a merger of noise and frequency*. Also, significantly, once this transfer is complete, the unpitched percussion instruments disappear from the composition, as well as any kind of attack-filled roll or tremolo; the only reminders are the occasional rolled pizzicato chords in the cello, but these are individual attacks rather than tremolos.

This is all in distinct contrast with what happens in *Viola I* in which the piece progresses toward more articulated, attack-oriented sonorities. As noted in Chapter 2, over the course of *Viola I*, the unpitched percussion instruments were introduced in the following order: bass drum/tenor drum, temple block/wood block. Feldman gradually intensified the articulation of attack noise as the music unfolded. The succession of attacks of a soft bass drum roll can certainly appear muffled and project an illusion of a *sustained* band of noise, especially if the percussionist uses soft mallets. But there is no way to mask a series of attacks on a wood block, no matter what mallets are used. A roll on a wood block is perceived as a rapid succession of distinct, sharp attacks. In contrast, in *The Viola in My Life II* each evolution moves from rolls of such distinct, sharp attacks toward more sustained, and in this case, pitched bands of sound (Figure 3.6).

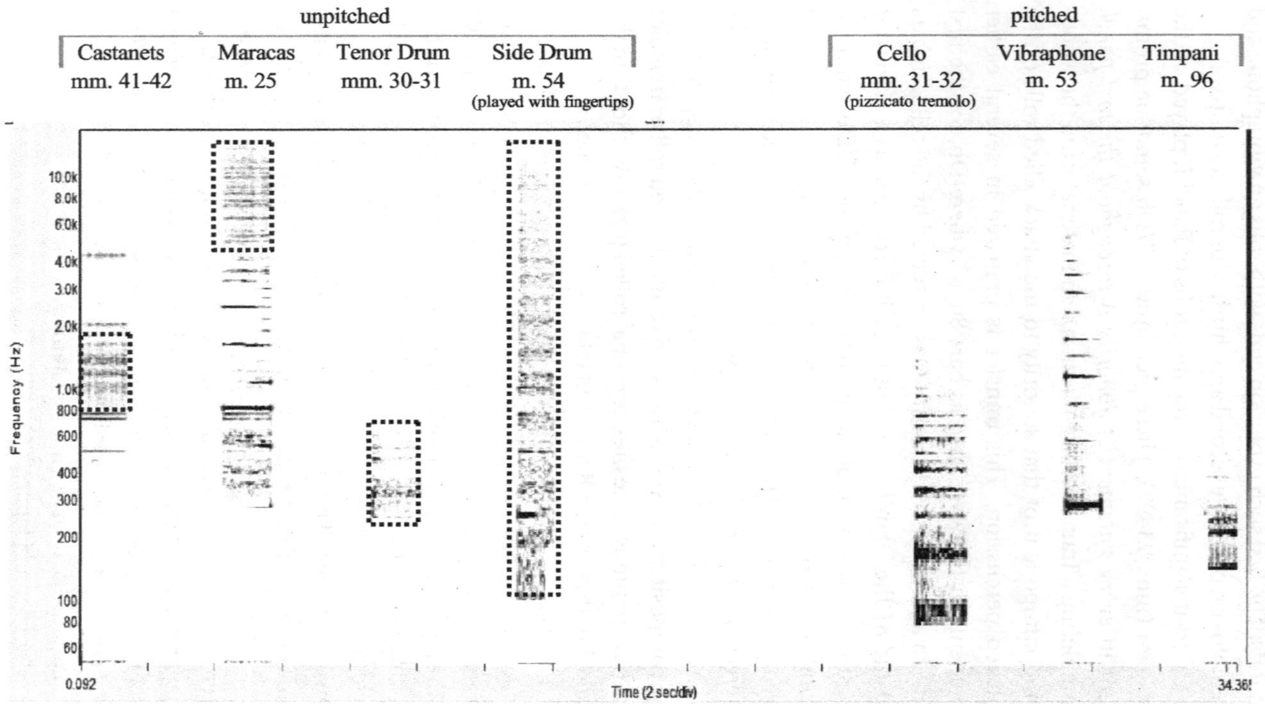

Figure 3.6 *The Viola in My Life 2*, Panel I, Spectrographs of All Percussion Instruments and Cello (pizzicato/tremolo).

Panel I: The Viola Solo

The viola functions quite differently from the ensemble in Panel I. In general, there are very few moments of such exact, or near exact, repetition, and those appear toward the end of the panel (spilling over into the beginning of Panel II, where such repetition is much more common). As with *Viola I*, the constant presence of the crescendo conveys a sense that the viola is emerging from nothing and floats above the texture of the ensemble, an effect enhanced, once again, by muting. Also, as in *Viola I*, the omnipresent crescendo in the viola part highlights, for the listener, his or her awareness of the juncture of sound and silence throughout the piece, especially in those moments when the viola counters the decay of the celesta, here, of course functioning as the sole decaying instrument, as did the piano in *Viola I*.

In contrast to the ensemble, the soloist constantly forms and reforms various pitch sequences (Figure 3.7). Pattern a and its variants consist of very short pitch/interval statements, while Pattern b evolves into longer melodic statements, concluding with a series of exact or near exact repetitions.

Panel I: Soloist and Ensemble

When one considers the combination of the solo part with the ensemble, one can sense a nascent relationship between the two slowly emerging. In general, the sonorities and patterns of ensemble and soloist, respectively, stagger, overlap, and interconnect in what appears to be a very nonlinear mosaic of events (Table 3.5). However, it becomes clear that, over the course of Panel I, while Sonority A gradually breaks apart and eventually disappears, Pattern b slowly crystallizes into a fixed melodic shape. Thus, what unfolds is a clear oppositional structure between soloist and

Figure 3.7 *The Viola in My Life 2*, Panel I, Viola, Evolution of Pattterns a and b.

ensemble (a type of structure that will form the basis for *Viola IV*). Not only are the sonorities and patterns following opposite lines of evolution (sonorities dissolving, patterns forming), but they represent very different sonic characteristics (Figure 3.8). That of Sonority A is very static, fixed in a register; while that of the viola

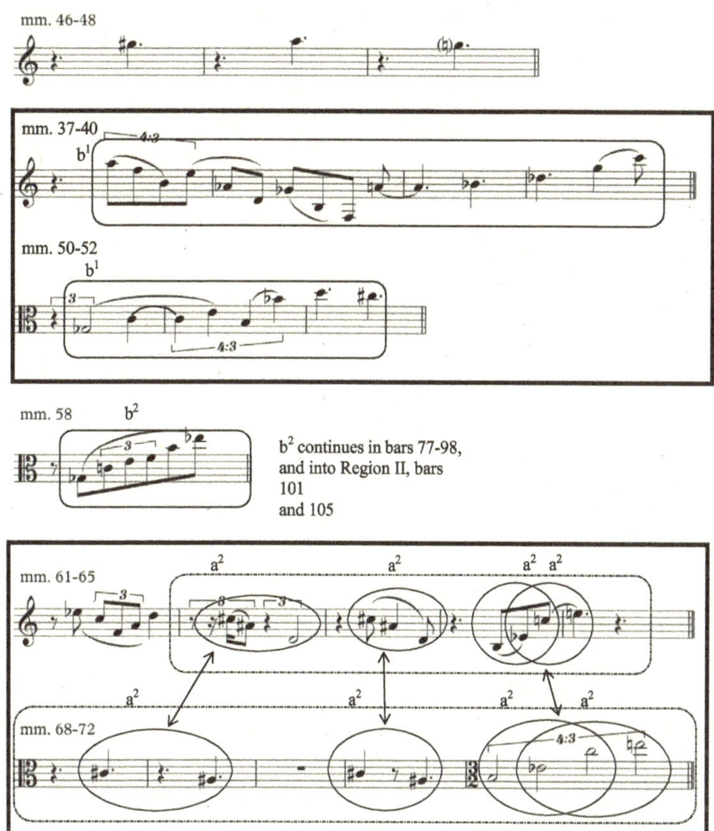

Figure 3.7 Continued

(through its melodic contour as well as changes in its spectrum as a result of the crescendos) is more dynamic.

Foreshadowing, the final interconnection between soloist and ensemble is the subtle intervallic link established in the first few bars of the work and then abandoned until the second panel. As noted above, in bars 2–4 the viola presents the first statement of Pattern a consisting of F# G# B (intervals 2 and 3). These are surrounded by the ensemble sounding G/Ab and C/

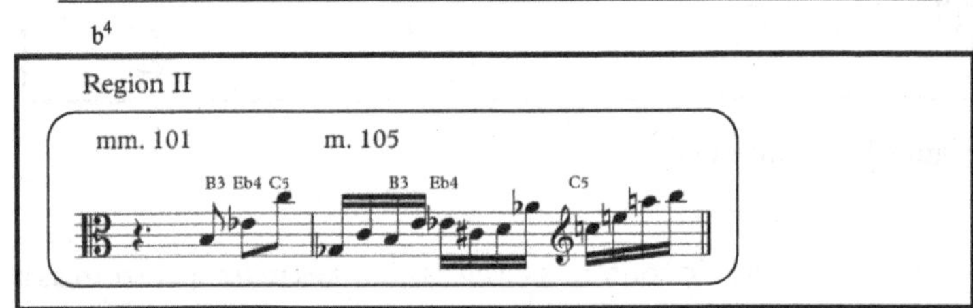

Figure 3.7 Continued

Table 3.4 *The Viola in My Life II*, Panel I, Viola Patterns, Pitch/Interval Content

Pattern	Pitch	Interval
a[1] {2,3}		
mm. 2–4	F G# B	2, 3
mm. 8–11	F D C	3, 2
mm. 24–30	D C Eb	2, 3
a[2] {3,4}		
mm. 6–7	D Bb Db	4, 3
mm. 17–20	A C E	3, 4
mm. 35–36	Ab C Eb	4, 3
mm. 61–65	C# A# D	3, 4
b[1] {1,4,5,6} (These are most abundant intervals; 2 and 3 are rare.)		
m. 37	A F B E Ab D Gb B F A Bb Db G C	4, 6, 5, 4, 6, 4, 5, 6, 1, 4, 6, 5
m. 50	Gb C E B Bb D C#	6, 4, (3), 1, 4, 1
b[2] {1,4,6}		
m. 58, 98	Gb C E F B Eb	6, 4, 1, 6, 4
b[3] {1, 2, 4, 5, 6}		
mm. 77–95	Gb A E F G B C Eb	6, 5, 1, 6, 4, 1, (3)
b[4] {1, 3, 4, 5, 6}		
m. 83	Gb C B E Eb C# D Ab C E A B	6, 1, 5, 1, (2), 1, 6, 4, 4, 5, (2)

Table 3.5 *The Viola in My Life II*, Panel I, Chart of Ensemble Sonorities and Viola Patterns

bar	1	10	20	30	40	(50)
Viola	aaa aaaaaaa	aaaa aaaaaa	aabbbb			
Ensemble	AAAAAA	AAAB	AAABB	B B B B	AAAB	

bar	50	60	70	80	90	99
Viola	bbb b	bbbb bbbbb	b	b	b b	
Ensemble	B AAA	B B B	AAA	B B		

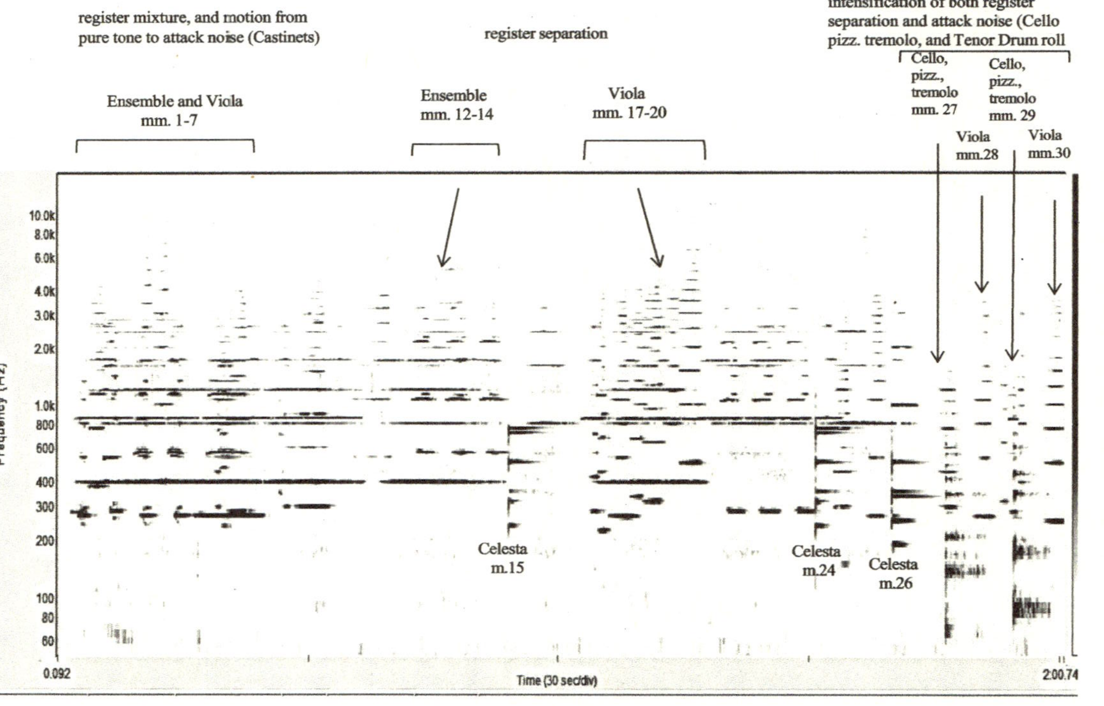

Figure 3.8 *The Viola in My Life 2*, Panel I Spectral Oppositions between Ensemble Sonorities and Viola Patterns (mm. 1–30).

Db, two pairs of half-steps. The F# of the viola links up with the ensemble's G by half-step, and the viola's G#, to the ensemble's Ab in unison and G by half-step. Finally, the soloist's B is also tied to the ensemble via half-step with the sounding of the ensemble's C. Such intervallic connections between soloist and ensemble soon disappear in Panel I, until they are reasserted in Panel II. (As will be shown, these links via half-step are omnipresent at the start of *The Viola in My Life IV* which amplifies these same connections.)

Panel II

The aforementioned regularity of Panel II is revealed most vividly in the new relationship of the soloist with the ensemble as they gradually become much more integrated as the second panel unfolds. Toward this end, unpitched percussion disappears almost entirely in the second panel, while pitched percussion is used sparingly—only the occasional single stroke on the vibraphone and the occasional pizzicato notes on cello and viola remain. There are three sonorities established by the ensemble (C, D, E) and three patterns by the soloist (c, d, e) (Figure 3.9, Figure 3.10). In terms of pitch/interval content, rhythm, and texture, the ensemble's three sonorities are remarkably consistent, always recurring as exact or near exact repetitions (Table 3.6, Table 3.7). The soloist's three patterns are also quite static in terms of pitch/interval content as well as melodic contour, as the patterns are always exact or near exact repetitions. In addition, it is clear that, as Panel II unfolds, the two instrumental groups—soloist and ensemble—work in tandem more and more.

Figure 3.9 *The Viola in My Life 2*, Panel II, Ensemble, Patterns C, D, E.

Figure 3.10 *The Viola in My Life 2*, Panel II, Viola, Patterns c, d, e.

Table 3.6 *The Viola in My Life II*, Panel II, Ensemble, Patterns C, D, and E; Pitch/Interval Content.

	Pitch	Interval	
Sonority C {1,3}			
mm. 100, 103, 106	F# A Bb G# B	3 1 2 1	
m. 108	F# Bb A Bb G# B	4 1 1 2 3	
mm. 114–115	Bb F# A Eb G# B	4 3 1 5 3	(extension: Eb F# G# A Bb B)
mm. 134–135	Bb F# A Eb G# B	4 3 1 5 3	(extension: Eb F# G# A Bb B)
m. 130	Bb F# A G# B Eb	4 3 1 3 6	(extension: Eb F# G# A Bb B)
m. 132	A F# Bb Eb G# B	3 4 5 5 3	(extension: Eb F# G# A Bb B)
m. 137	Eb F# A G# B Bb	3 3 1 3 1	(extension: Eb F# G# A Bb B)
G# B (3) constant and fixed in register.			
Sonority D {5,2}			
mm. 110, 118–120	Bb F G	5 2	
mm. 121–129	Bb F G	5 2	
mm. 139–147	Bb F G	5 2	
Sonority E {4,3,4}			
mm. 149–161	D Bb C# F	4 3 4	ensemble alone
mm. 174–186	D Bb C# F	4 3 4	ensemble with viola

Table 3.7 *The Viola in My Life II*, Panel II, Viola, Patterns c, d, and e; Pitch/Interval Content

	Pitch	Interval	
Pattern c {3,5}			
mm. 109, 113, 117	D B E C#	3 5 3	
Pattern d {2,3,4,5}			
mm. 121–129, 139–147, 163–172	Bb C E D A C E	2 4 2 5 3 4	Viola
	D B A	2 3 2	Ensemble
	F G	2	
Pattern e {3,4}			
mm. 149–161	D Bb C# F	4 3 4	Ensemble alone
mm. 174–186	D Bb C# F	4 3 4	Viola with ensemble

Throughout Panel II we hear clear and distinct patterns gradually forming, with soloist and ensemble coalescing into a series of elongated sonic events (Table 3.8). This gradual transformation—the gradual merging of soloist with ensemble—is revealed clearly through a close examination of the beginning and ending passages of the second panel. Panel II begins with a clear opposition between ensemble and soloist, not only in terms of pitch/interval content but, more importantly, of sound itself (Figure 3.11). Here one experiences a clear alternation of soloist and ensemble with no overlap. However, at the end, one finds quite the opposite as the two interpenetrate, unifying sonority and pattern (Figure 3.12). Specifically, at the end of Panel II, Sonority E is heard twice, first with clarinet and cello (mm. 149–161) and later with vibraphone and viola, which concludes the composition (Figure 3.13, Figure 3.14). Of course, by replacing the cello with the viola on exactly the same pizzicato figure, Feldman seals the merger of soloist with ensemble. In both cases, they play the very same chord in the same register and are virtually indistinguishable. For the first time the viola functions as a member of the ensemble and does so by literally replacing a member of the ensemble in a verbatim repeat of an earlier passage.

The shift from clarinet to vibraphone in Sonority E is also significant, with respect to both the local and large-scale evolution of the work. In the first statement of Sonority E, the clarinet holds B♭[3] for six beats. A spectrograph of this moment shows that the clarinet tone is steady, with, as expected, a clear sounding of the first, third, and fifth partials, a well-known characteristic of the spectrum of the clarinet (Figure 3.13). However, the second statement of Sonority E is quite different as the same B♭ is sounded by the vibraphone. Here the sound dies out over the life of the note, until the pedal is lifted and the tone is stopped. In addition, *for the first time in the piece*, Feldman indicates that the vibraphone's motor should be turned on, creating a vibrato-like effect, often associated with the instrument's tone color (Figure 3.14). The change from steady clarinet tone to a decaying/vibrating vibraphone sound is striking.

Table 3.8 *The Viola in My Life II*, Panel II, Chart of Sonorities and Patterns

bar	100	110	120	130	140	(150)
Viola	bb b	c c c	ddddddddd		ddddddddd	e
Ensemble	C CC C C D	CC DDD	DDDDDDDDD	C C CC C	DDDDDDDDD	E

bar	150	160	170	180	190
Viola	eeeeeeeeeeee	dddddddddd	eeeeeeeeeeeee		
Ensemble	EEEEEEEEEEEE	DDDDDDDDDD	EEEEEEEEEEEEE		

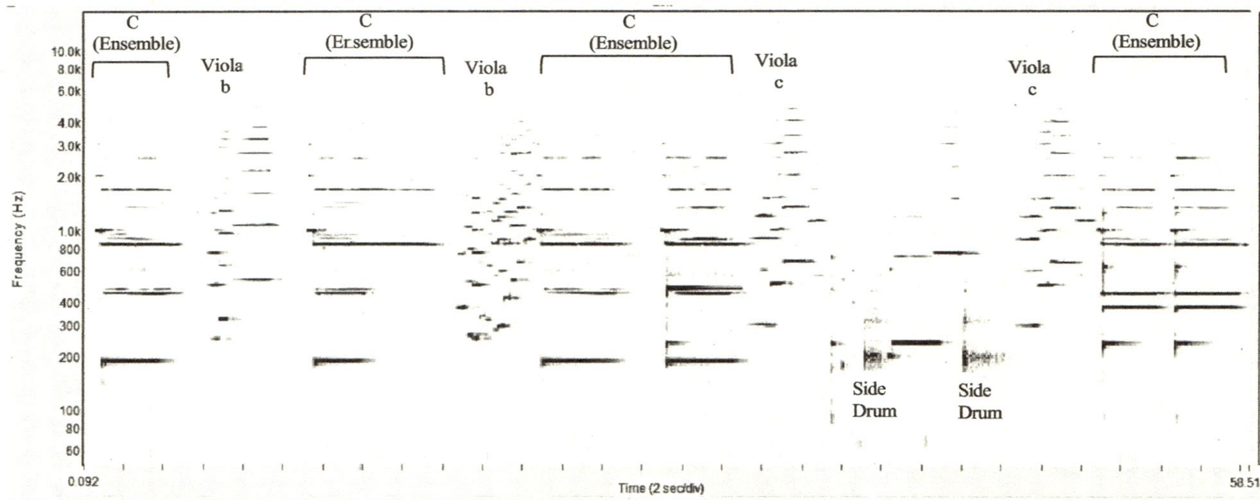

Figure 3.11 *The Viola in My Life 2*, Panel II, Spectrograph of Sonic Oppositions Established at the Beginning of Panel II (mm. 100–115).

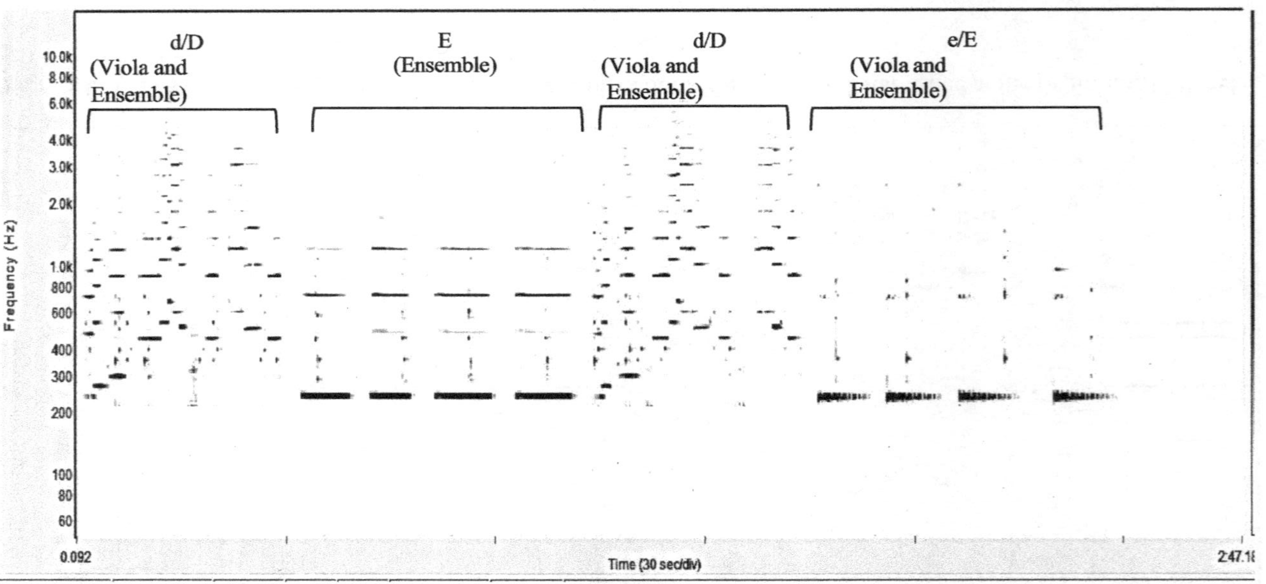

Figure 3.12 *The Viola in My Life 2*, Panel II, Spectrograph of Interpenetration of Patterns d, e, and Sonorities D, E at Ending of Panel II (mm. 139–187).

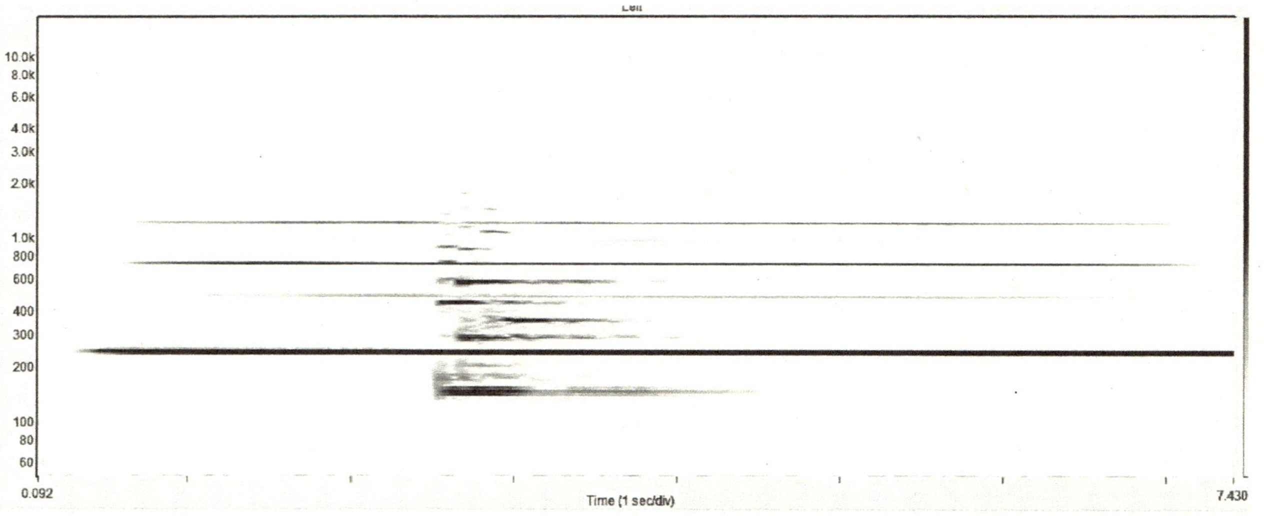

Figure 3.13 *The Viola in My Life 2*, Panel II, Ensemble, Sonority D, Spectrograph, Clarinet and Cello (Ensemble Recherche performance; (mm. 149–150).

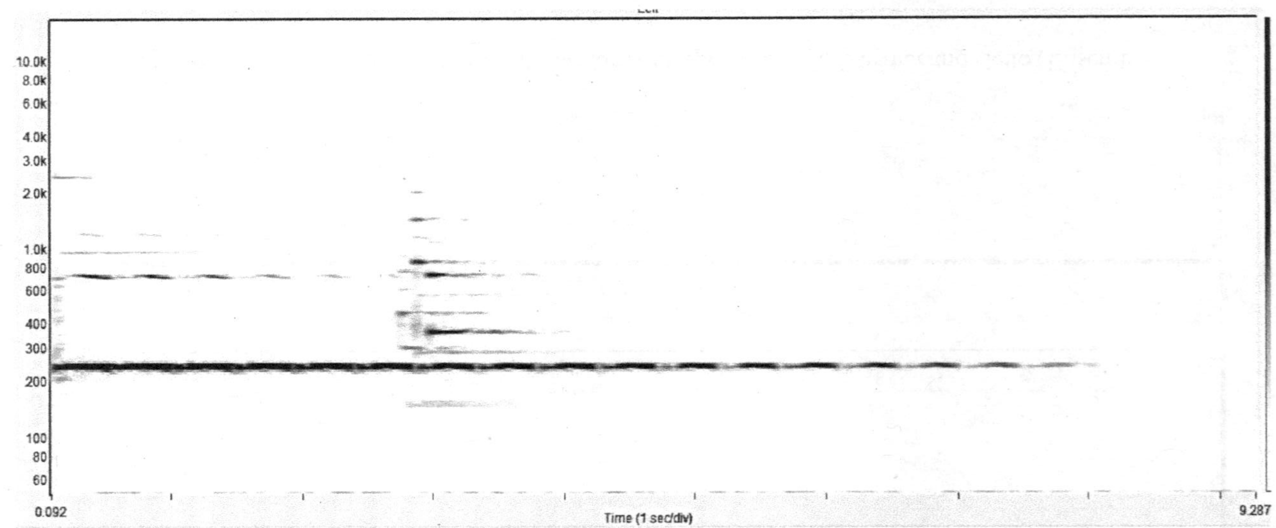

Figure 3.14 *The Viola in My Life 2*, Panel II, Viola and Ensemble, Sonority E/Pattern e, Spectrograph, Vibraphone and Viola (Ensemble Recherche performance, mm. 149–150).

The latter reflects, in a subtle, elongated manner, the shift from sustained sound to vibrating sound first encountered in the first few bars of the work, where the sustained woodwinds dissolve first into flutter tonguing and then into the rolls on the castanets (and the succeeding rolls and tremolos that are heard throughout the piece on various instruments). At the end, the vibraphone provides a wonderful, graceful echo of the opening sonority and of its characteristic sonic transformation of sound enacted in different ways throughout the piece.

The Entire Composition

A comparison of the opening bars of each panel reveals the trajectory of the composition as a whole (Figure 3.15, Figure 3.16). The first few bars of each panel differ markedly. Panel I opens with a statement of its basic sonority, which, as discussed, is filled with noise in various ways. In contrast, at the start of Panel II the ensemble is free of noise; the instruments are less often clustered into semitones; and there is no shift to flutter and no percussion rolls.

In addition, at the beginning of Panel I, the viola is superimposed onto the ensemble's statements of Sonority A and, as noted, seems to emerge from the mass of sound of that sonority. In contrast, at the start of Panel II the ensemble's Sonority C and viola patterns are not superimposed but are stated successively, not simultaneously. Moreover, Sonority C presents a static, nonchanging spectrum, while the viola line is constantly changing. One clearly differentiates the static spectrum of the ensemble from the rising sonority of the viola line. This opposition is enhanced by the opposition of the various instrumental timbres. As noted earlier, the strings and winds of the ensemble produce near-pure tones—playing in lower register, softly, strings with harmonics. As such, the winds and strings lose considerable strength in the upper partials (which is no doubt the reason Feldman chose these two wind instruments rather than

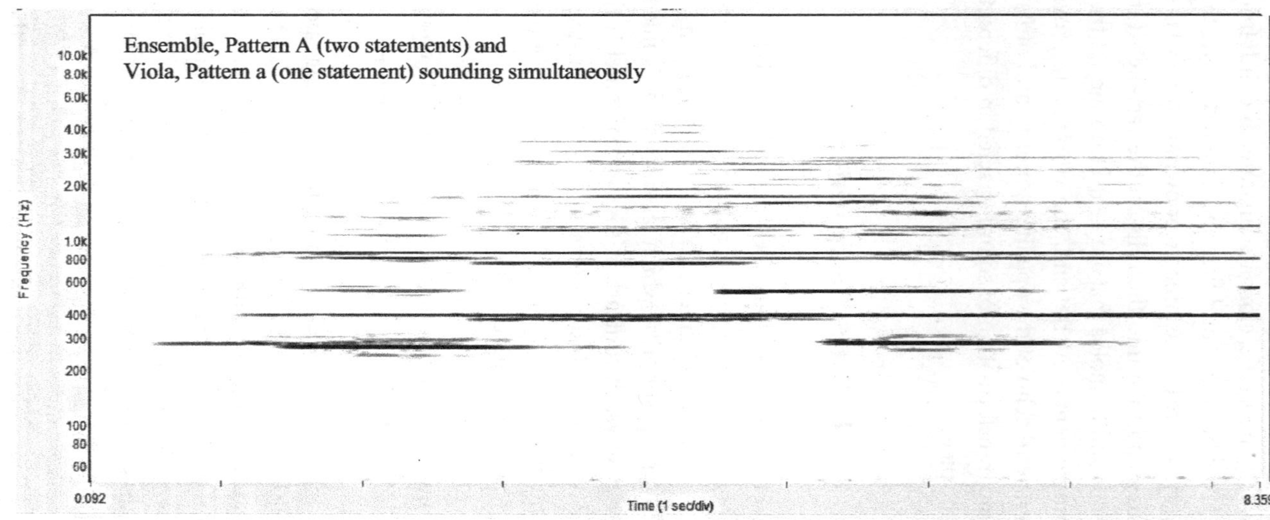

Figure 3.15 *The Viola in My Life 2*, Panel I, Ensemble and Viola, Spectrograph, Initial Sounds (mm. 1–3).

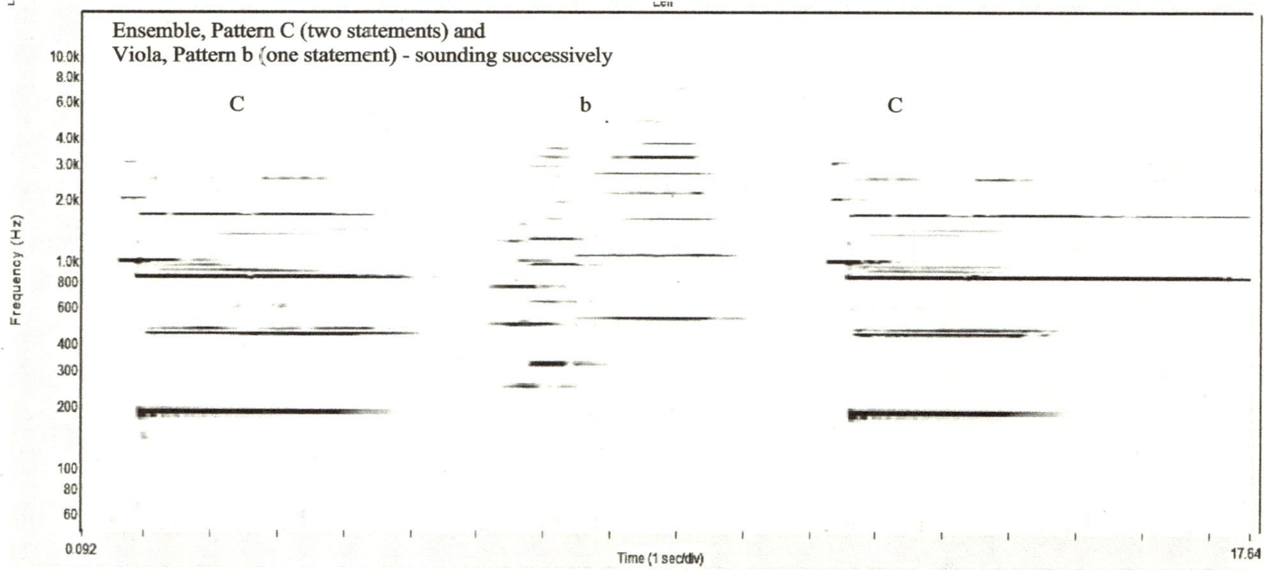

Figure 3.16 *The Viola in My Life 2*, Panel II, Ensemble and Viola, Spectrograph, Initial Sounds (mm. 100–104).

an oboe, for instance, which would not come close to approaching the quality of a pure tone no matter what the register or volume). In contrast, despite being muted and soft, the viola is still rich in upper partials.

These differences between the opening passages of the two panels establish the sonic character of each. In Panel I the primary sonority of the ensemble, Sonority A, is slowly teased out over the course of the panel and gradually dissipates, while the viola solo does the opposite and eventually emerges with a set of clearly defined patterns (indeed, to such an extent that its final pattern, b^4, lingers on into the second panel). In contrast, Panel II is characterized by much greater formal clarity with respect to both viola and ensemble. Sonorities become longer and repeat to a much greater degree, as do the viola's patterns. Finally, the soloist merges with the ensemble.

One final note: there is a significant sonority in *The Viola in My Life II*, which is borrowed almost verbatim from *The Viola in My Life I*. Gesture a, from Panel III of *Viola I*, re-appears as Sonority C in Panel II of *Viola II*. Each version of this sonority is composed of the same basic contour of a grace note falling down a minor third to a chord. Each exhibits the same basic intervallic structure as well as emphasizing the half-step and tritone. The two sonorities are only distinguished from one another through their differences of tone color: gesture a is sounded by the piano alone, while Sonority C is stated by winds, strings, and percussion (in fact, there is no piano in the second piece of the set). Thus, as gesture a is transferred from *Viola I* into *Viola II*, the piano sonority is "colored" by the wind and string timbres. One other figure first heard in *Viola I* in bar 99 (and then repeated several times) is carried over into *Viola II*. This is the brief, eighth-note dyad played pizzicato by the cello that reappears in *Viola II*, first in bar 121 and repeated many times thereafter, though with different intervals. As we will see, such borrowing becomes progressively more common and more obvious in *The Viola in My Life III* and *IV*.

4

The Viola in My Life III

The Viola in My Life III is scored for piano and violin. The tempo is the same as that of *Viola II* (quarter = 66). The only other performance indication is "extremely quiet." Following the earlier labeling practice used in discussions of *Viola I* and *Viola II*, and for the same reasons, *The Viola in My Life III* will be divided into four panels of sound material with one transition between the first two: Panel I, mm. 1–18 (consisting of two repeating parts, mm. 1–9 and 10–18, to be labeled Panels Ia and Ib) and mm. 19–20 (which constitute a transition to the next panel); Panel II, mm. 21–31; Panel III, mm. 32–40; and Panel IV, mm. 41–56 (a quasi-return to I; at the end of Panel IV, bars 51–56 constitute an extended ending, here labeled Extension). The most obvious elements providing contrast among these panels are the presence or absence of crescendo and diminuendo markings in the viola part and the presence of either nonsustaining piano chords (marked *tenuto*) or sustaining chords (Table 4.1). In addition, there are both clear instances of coordination between the two instrumental parts and well-defined moments where they share the same duration scheme. Throughout this discussion, coordination is characterized by the presence of a simultaneous attack point between the two instruments, where the piano provides a quasi-attack for each individual note sounded by the viola (Figure 4.1). This is the primary gesture heard in the piece (a single sustained note from the viola initiated by a single chord from the piano).

These panels differ from those of the two previous compositions, however, in that they are constructed from *very similar* materials. Those materials still do not evolve in any way,

The Marvelous Illusion. Thomas DeLio, Oxford University Press. © Oxford University Press 2024.
DOI: 10.1093/9780197759967.003.0004

Table 4.1 *The Viola in My Life III*, Panels I–IV, Formal Divisions

Viola: cd – crescendos and diminuendos ncd – no crescendos and diminuendos
Piano: s – sustaining ns – non-sustaining (tenuto)

Coordination: sa – simultaneous attacks nsa – no simultaneous attacks
Duration Patterns: rp – repeating patterns nrp – no repeating patterns

	Viola	Piano	Coordination	Duration Patterns
Panel I, first 9 bars	ncd	ns	sa	rp
second 9 bars	cd	s	sa	rp
transition, 2 bars				
Panel II, 11 bars	ncd	ns	sa	mostly rp
Panel III, 9 bars	cd	s	**nsa**	mostly rp
Panel IV, 10 bars	cd/ncd	s/ns	sa	rp
Panel IV, Extension, 6 bars	cd	s	sa	rp

In Panel IV two chords are sustained, one via sympathetic vibrations.

Figure 4.1 *The Viola in My Life 3*, Primary Gesture of Composition.

but, as in the first two pieces in the set, they rather coexist in the same sonic space). Occasionally, the viola may break into a brief succession of single tones (mm. 15, 19, 46–48), but, generally, the basic gesture of one note from the viola and one chord from the piano, struck simultaneously, is maintained. The most significant variation with respect to the presentation of this gesture has to do with the temporal relationship between these two elements. Changes to this temporal relationship are a central form defining elements in the work. Quite simply, at the start, the piano provides an attack for each of the soft, attack-free tones sounded by the viola. Gradually, they disengage from one another and play more independent roles, as will be shown. At the end, the coordinated attack points between the two players return and bring the work back to its origins.

Perhaps it is fanciful, but the relatively narrow range of sound material presented here may remind one of the monochromatic, monotype prints of one of Feldman's favorite painters, Jasper Johns. Johns's work *0–9* (2013) is a series of ten lithographs, each of which presents a number from the series one to ten, stripped of its content as a value and reinterpreted as a visual image (Figure 4.2).[1] In this set of ten prints, the subject matter is deliberately simple (numbers in sequence), but their representation is complex visually. Perhaps most significant with respect to Feldman's *Viola III* is the fact that color is removed (they are all black and gray with different degrees of shading). Monotype refers to a typeface in which individual characters (letters and numbers) are set individually and may be different, unlike linotype, which sets type an entire line at a time. In Johns's number pieces, each number in a series is represented in a different way with respect to color, shape, and typeface. This may parallel Feldman's use of one simple gesture represented each time it appears with slight, subtly shaded variation provided by the changes in dynamics (crescendo) and texture (*tenuto* or sustain), as well as pitch/interval content and register. These all provide a rather monochromatic quality of variation

Figure 4.2 Jasper Johns; *0–9* (2013); one from a series of ten lithographs.

similar to the look of Johns's monotype prints. Such subtlety of distinction is characteristic of *Viola III* and sets it apart from the other three pieces in the set.

The Viola in My Life III contains many echoes of *The Viola in My Life I* and *II*:

- The soloist's very prominent Pattern b from *Viola II* is quoted verbatim three times in *Viola III* in bars 8, 17, and 55. Indeed, *Viola III* ends with a quote of this pattern!
- The passage from bars 17–18 and 35–36 in the *Viola II* is heard in bar 19 in *Viola III.*
- The material of bar 29 in *Viola II* is heard in bar 19 in *Viola III.*
- There are distinct similarities between bars 67–70 in *Viola I* and bars 46–48 in *Viola III,*

With respect to the aforementioned quote of Pattern b, introduced in *Viola II,* each time it reappears in *Viola III* the tempo accelerates, from quarter note at 66 (.9" per quarter) to quarter note at 80 (.825" per quarter). This may simply be an attempt to bring the eighth-note statement of b in *Viola III* closer to the speed of the sixteenth-note statement of that pattern in *Viola II,* though it also just may be due to a preference for a slightly faster speed for this figure in the third composition. All such borrowing is yet another reflection of Feldman's penchant for revisiting old ideas in new contexts, again much in the manner of his painter friends Jasper Johns and Robert Rauschenberg. As we will see, such borrowing of previously used material becomes even more pronounced as the set continues through *Viola IV,* which is filled with quoted material. However, the presence of such material from other works, providing a new framework for material already heard in the first two pieces in the set—original though this practice may be—is not the most unusual characteristic of *Viola III. The Viola in My Life III* is primarily about time: the marking of time.

On the macrostructural level, proportions among the four panels, in half notes, are quite regular: Panel I is 50 half notes long (Panels Ia and Ib, each being 25 half notes). The transition between Panels I and II is 5 half notes in duration. Panel II is 29 half notes long, close to the duration of each part of Panel I; Panel III, 25 half notes, the same duration as each part of Panel I; and Panel IV, 42 half notes, close to the duration of the entirety of Panel I. Panel IV may be subdivided into two sub-panels, the first 27 half notes and the second 15. The former is the main section of the panel and the same duration as Panels Ia, Ib, and III; the latter is the aforementioned Extension. Each of these panels, and the transition, are further subdivided into bars of 3 or 2 half notes. No other meters are used (Figure 4.3, Figure 4.4). (At this point, it should be noted that, in these compositions meter never refers to pulsation, but rather is used to measure units of time.) In each of Panels Ia and Ib the meters are presented in a specific sequence (where 2/2 bars are always silent) and repeated without change:

Panel Ia: 3/2 3/2 3/2 3/2 3/2 3/2 2/2 3/2 2/2
Panel Ib: 3/2 3/2 3/2 3/2 3/2 3/2 2/2 3/2 2/2

In Panel II, a new pattern is formed with internal repetition:

Panel II: 3/2 3/2 2/2 3/2 2/2 3/2 3/2 2/2 3/2 3/2

Panel III returns to the same pattern as Ia and Ib:

Panel III: 3/2 3/2 3/2 3/2 3/2 3/2 2/2 3/2 2/2

Panel IV, before the extension, presents a succession of patterns shrinking in size, while the extension repeats the sequence 3/2 2/2 three times, articulating the most compact repetitive pattern to conclude the work:

Panel IV: 3/2 3/2 3/2 3/2 2/2 3/2 3/2 2/2 3/2 2/2
Extension: 3/2 2/2 3/2 2/2 3/2 2/2

Within Panels Ia and Ib, attack points between instruments are precisely synchronized, which is quite a change from the previous two pieces in the set! The differences between the two repeated statements within the first panel have to do with the articulation of

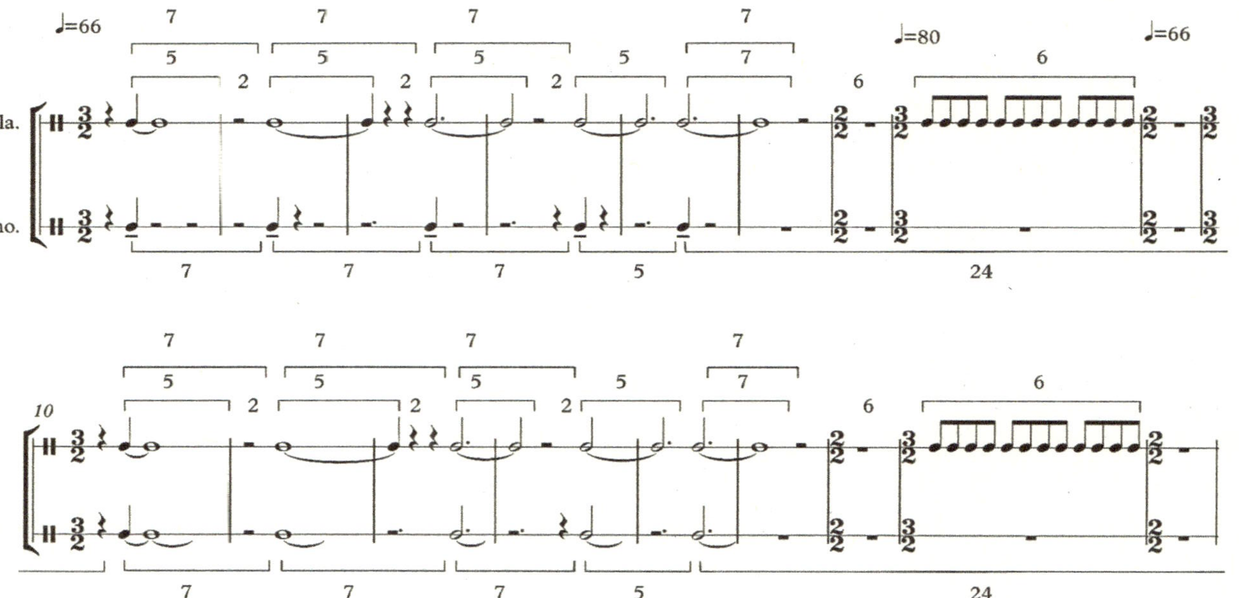

Figure 4.3 *The Viola in My Life 3*, Panel I, Chart of Durations.

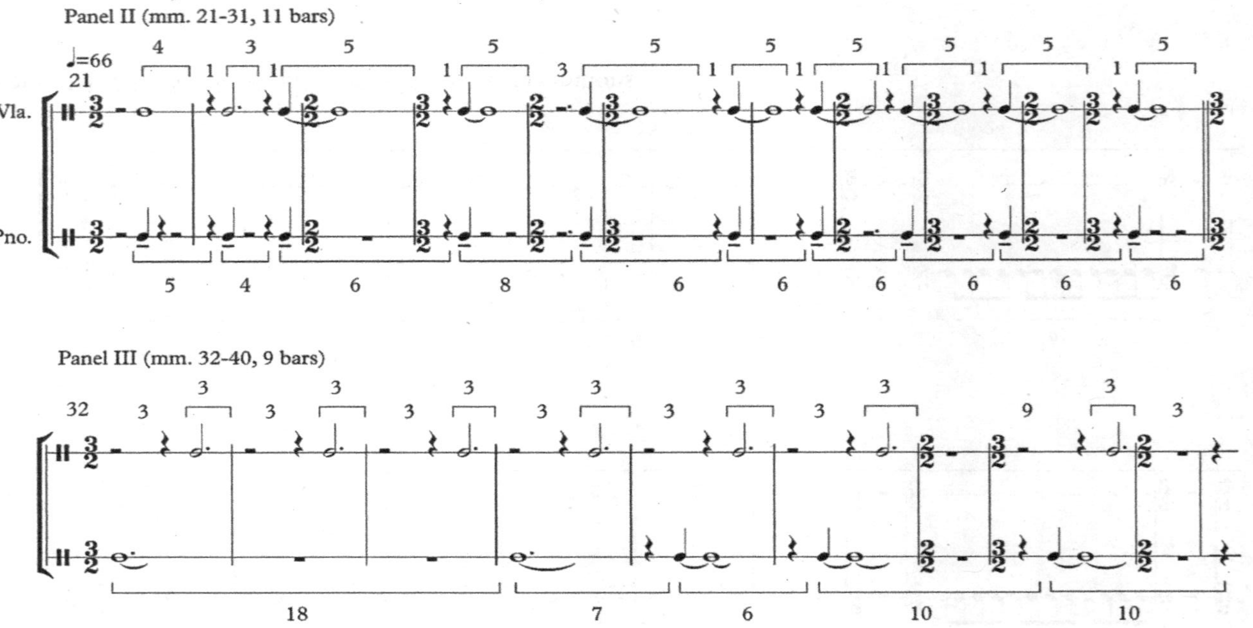

Figure 4.4 *The Viola in My Life 3*, Panels II, III, IV, Chart of Durations.

Figure 4.4 Continued

the piano chords. In the first statement, the chords in the piano are played *tenuto* and, as such, are not sustained beyond their notated duration. This leaves distinct, equally long silences after each piano chord. In the second statement, each chord is allowed to decay through its notated duration, until the next chord is sounded. In this way, the aforementioned silences are obscured (Figure 4.3). In terms of the viola part, for most of the passage, each tone is sounded for a fixed, repeating duration and then followed by an equally fixed duration of silence. With respect to such patterning of durations, one would do well to consider once again Feldman's own words with regard to his move to more fixed notation in his music:

> I've become fascinated with precise notation now, because I use it to measure other things, which ordinarily I would never have thought of. Most of my music of the past two years is precisely notated, but each piece for a different reason.[2]

With respect to *The Viola in My Life III*, the reason seems to have been a desire to create large patterns of temporal coordination and repetition. Perhaps too, it was a desire to create a different concept of quotation; one involving temporal reflections rather than recurrences of either chordal sonorities or linear pitch patterns, as has been the case up to this point in the *Viola* series. The local and large-scale repetition of temporal patterns heard in this work conveys a sense of quotation of temporal shapes rather than melodic shapes. Initially, this may seem fanciful, since all music, certainly prior to the twentieth century, contains repetition of many kinds—melodic, harmonic, and temporal. But, upon further consideration, we note that, in the context of the other three compositions in *The Viola in My Life* series, such strict temporal repetition is an anomaly and, as such, stands out quite noticeably. The only other elements in to which the listener may relate these moments of exact or near exact repetition are the melodic quotations heard in this work as well as the previous works in the set.

As mentioned, throughout Panel I, the viola and piano are perfectly synchronized with one another and fixed within rigidly repeating patterns of duration (though still unfolding within the slow, soft texture and general floating temporal aesthetic so common to all of Feldman's music) (Figure 4.3). A close examination of the first nine bars of Panel I reveals the remarkable degree of temporal rigidity that provides the framework for this music both on the macro- and micro-compositional levels. The viola enters every seven quarter notes. These durations are then subdivided into five quarter notes of sustained tone followed by two quarter notes of silence. This pattern is repeated three times. Feldman then changes to five quarter notes of sustained tone followed by six quarter notes of silence rather than two as previously occurred. This change allows him to transition to Pattern b, which sounds for six quarter notes, though in a new tempo. Simultaneously, the piano echoes the viola similarly sounding a chord every seven quarter notes three times, followed by a chord struck every five quarter notes. This is all repeated verbatim over the next nine bars.

Panel II moves away from the rhythmic regularity so prevalent in Panel I. It eschews the seven quarter duration featured in the first panel but carries over the five quarter note duration that was of secondary importance in that panel (Figure 4.4). From the middle of Panel II onward (mm. 25–31) in the viola, each tone begins every six quarter notes; each sounds for five quarters and is followed by a silence of one quarter. The piano follows suit, from the same point initiating every chord at six quarter note intervals. This second panel opens with a distinct lack of rhythmic regularity and coordination between the instruments, but it gradually settles into a regular six quarter repetition, reestablishing a degree of rhythmic coordination between the two instruments.

In Panel III the composer completely disengages the two instruments from one another (Figure 4.4). They never enter at the same time. Moreover, while the viola articulates a rigidly repeating pattern of three quarter notes of sound followed by three of silence, the piano articulates an irregular series of durations.

Panel IV, once again, must be considered in two parts: the first ten bars followed by the six-bar extension (Figure 4.4). In the first part, Feldman initially reverses the trend of Panel III. At the start, it returns to the seven quarter duration scheme first encountered in the first panel, but it gradually breaks away from it into a more irregular scheme. However, the attack points of the instruments are once again consistently coordinated, a distinct contrast with the previous panel. The extension to Panel IV reinstates a condition of absolute temporal regularity. Both instruments coordinate their attacks at all times. A larger pattern of ten quarter notes repeated three times is established within which the viola twice sounds two tones for six quarters followed by four quarters of rest. The final ten quarter duration is simply divided as six quarters followed by four of rest. Such temporal rigidity is not something we associate with Feldman's music at this point in his career, though it does reappear a great deal in his long, late works.[3]

With respect to its macrostructure, in *Viola III* one experiences the reverse of the trajectories that characterized the first and second pieces in the set, both of which started with rather amorphous, scattered fragments of sound that slowly coalesced into larger shapes, which were repeated several times and then were gradually shaped into recognizable identities. In contrast, to those earlier two pieces *Viola III* opens with a nine-bar passage characterized by the absolute coordination and synchronization of the two instruments. That passage is then repeated verbatim—an echo in time. Starting in Panel II, however, the two instruments gradually become less synchronized as each, independently, initiates a pattern of repetition that fails to continue (Figure 4.4). This lack of synchronization culminates in Panel III, where the instruments *never coincide rhythmically*. Finally, synchronization returns near the end of the work, in Panel IV, where coordination between the two players gradually reappears until it is firmly reestablished in the final bars of the piece in the aforementioned Extension (mm. 41). In addition, echoes of the duration, linear pitch patterns, and chords of the opening of the composition also return at the end of the work. This process culminates with the return of exact repetition and synchronization in the final six bars of the piece, the Extension, both with respect to duration and pitch.

The play between the presence or absence of crescendo markings in the solo part is a significant characteristic of *Viola III* as well and one that also sets it apart from its predecessors. Unlike the other pieces in the set, *Viola III* opens with no crescendo indications in the viola part in the first statement of the initial pattern (Figure 4.3, mm. 1–9). The lack of such markings presents a rather flat surface texture, putting viola and piano equally within the same acoustic plane. Upon its repeat (mm. 10–18), the viola adds a crescendo on each note. These crescendos, coupled with the new indication for the pianist to sustain his or her chords, leaves the listener with the sense that each tone of the viola is emerging from the decay of the piano sonority. At this point, a multilayered sonority evolves—the piano fades out as the viola fades in. Throughout the second panel, Feldman, once again, removes the indication for crescendos (mm. 21–31) marking a return to the flat surface encountered in Panel Ia, and he again puts the viola on a par with the piano within the same sonic space. The crescendo markings return in the third and fourth panels, allowing, once again, the viola to sound as if it is emerging from the decay of the piano sonority. Whenever Feldman adds the crescendos to the solo part, he creates a nascent sense of emerging melodic figuration—the beginnings of a linear ordering of tones, which is not present at the outset of the work. I believe that this is the key to understanding this composition. The opposition of the viola and piano is striking. The viola alternately seems to join with the piano texture or strives to emerge from the decay of that texture.

With vivid clarity, spectrographs reveal this relationship between the viola and piano as the former adds crescendos while the latter sustains and decays through the entire notated duration of each chord (Figure 4.5, Figure 4.6). In the spectrograph of the first nine bars, one can clearly see each viola tone functioning as an extension of each shortened piano chord, as if it is a fixed part of that chord. But the spectrograph of bars 10–18 vividly shows each viola tone slowly emerge from the decay of each sustained piano chord, an effect amplified by the addition of the crescendo markings in these measures. Clearly, Feldman wanted to alter the relationship between the viola and piano. In the first nine bars, we encounter a flat surface devoid of contrast. But in the second we find a more dynamic relationship. The two instruments separate sonically. As each note of the piano decays, its partials gradually disappear, while as each note of the viola increases in volume, its partials grow in intensity. One sonority literally replaces the other.

In terms of pitch choice, throughout Panel I Feldman presents one fixed sequence of chords in the piano part and a different sequence of tones in the viola part (Figure 4.7). The order of the piano chords varies slightly from the first nine bars to the repeat in the next nine bars. The chords themselves are generally unrelated to one another except with respect to register. This seems to reflect Feldman's oft-noted concept of presenting chords in succession that seem to cancel each other, denying any sense of harmonic evolution. In contrast, the pitches of the viola's sequence remain unchanged from the first presentation to the second.

As noted earlier, the degree of both synchronization between the instruments and the repetition of duration patterns varies throughout Panels II, III, and IV (Figure 4.4). Most notable are the temporal separation and lack of coordination in Panel III. A spectrograph reveals the degree of interpenetration that occurs between the sounds of each instrument as a result of this separation of their attack points (Figure 4.8). First, the viola seems to attempt to draw its sequence of pitches together to form an embryonic melodic statement (mm. 32–36); the ascending contour of its pitches seems to reinforce this. The piano supports this motion. The lowest tones of its chords also rise in tandem with the viola, from A^1 (m.

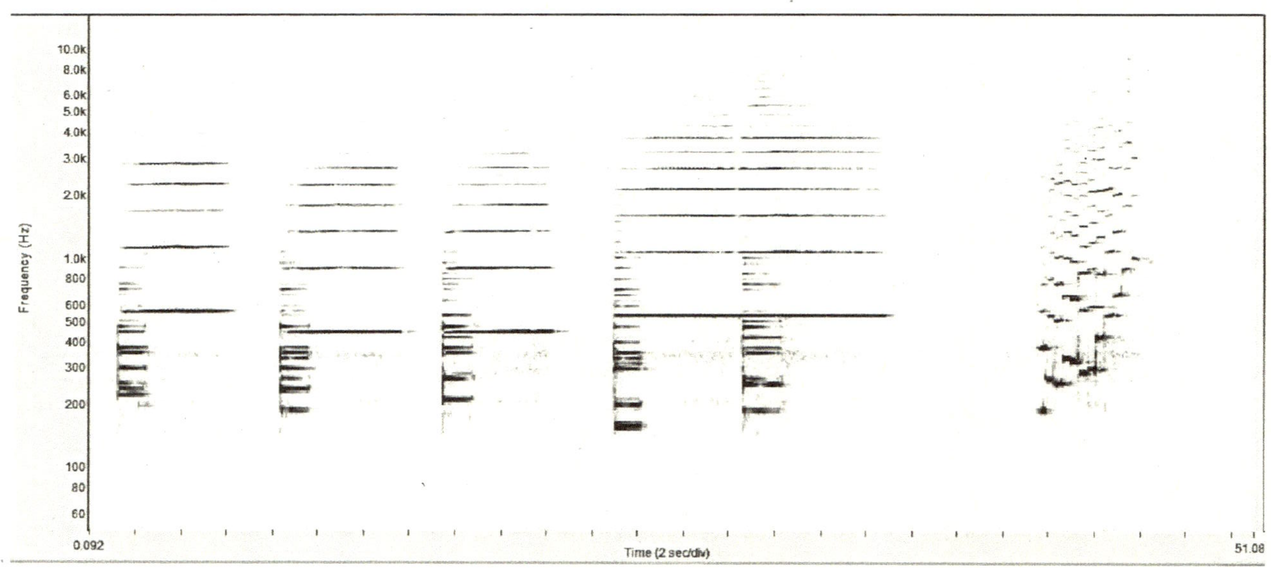

Figure 4.5 *The Viola in My Life 3*, Panel I, Spectrograph (mm. 1–9).

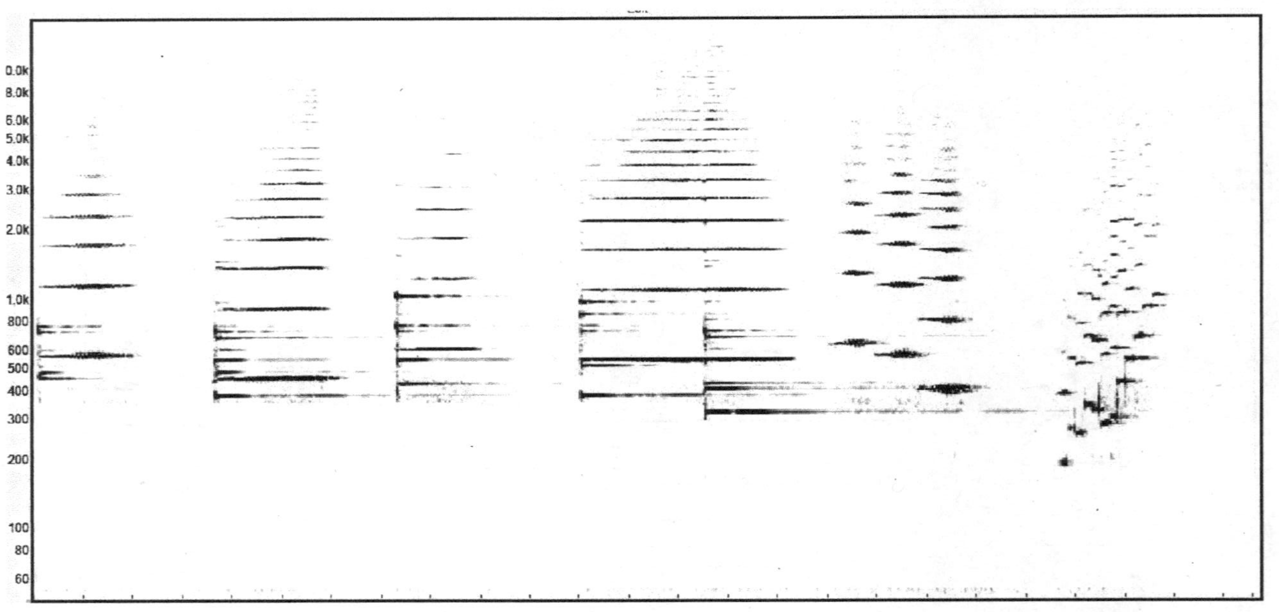

Figure 4.6 *The Viola in My Life 3*, Panel I, Spectrograph (mm. 10–18).

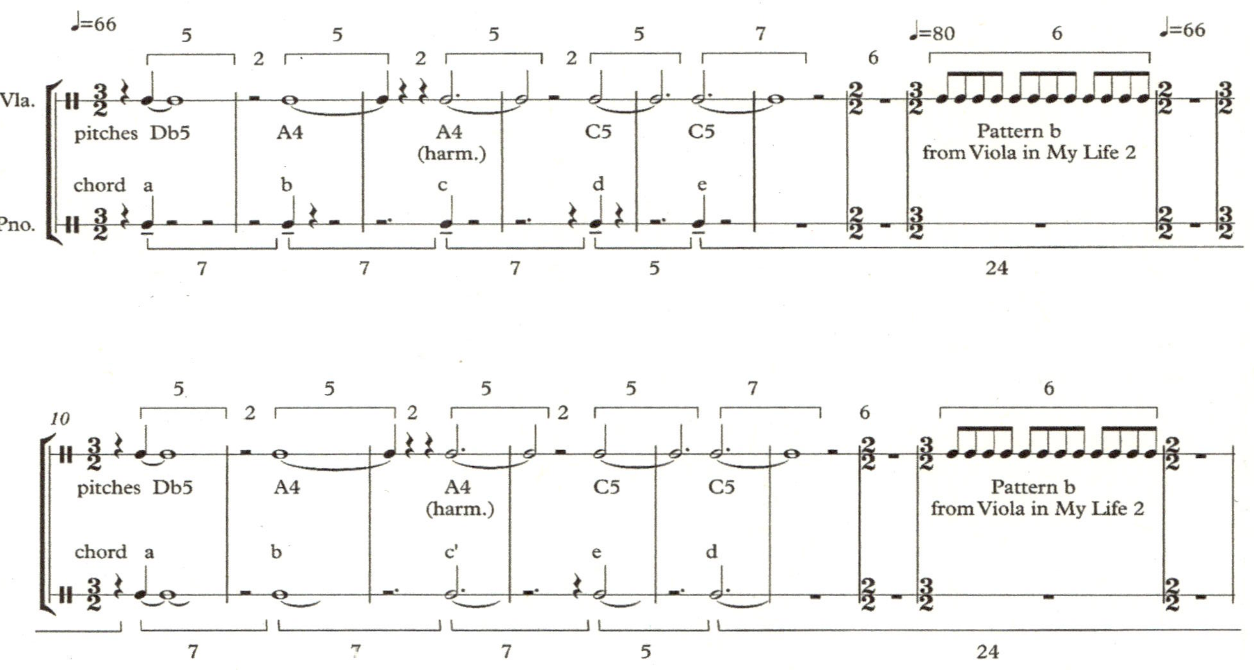

Figure 4.7 *The Viola in My Life 3*, Panel I, Pitch/Duration Coordination.

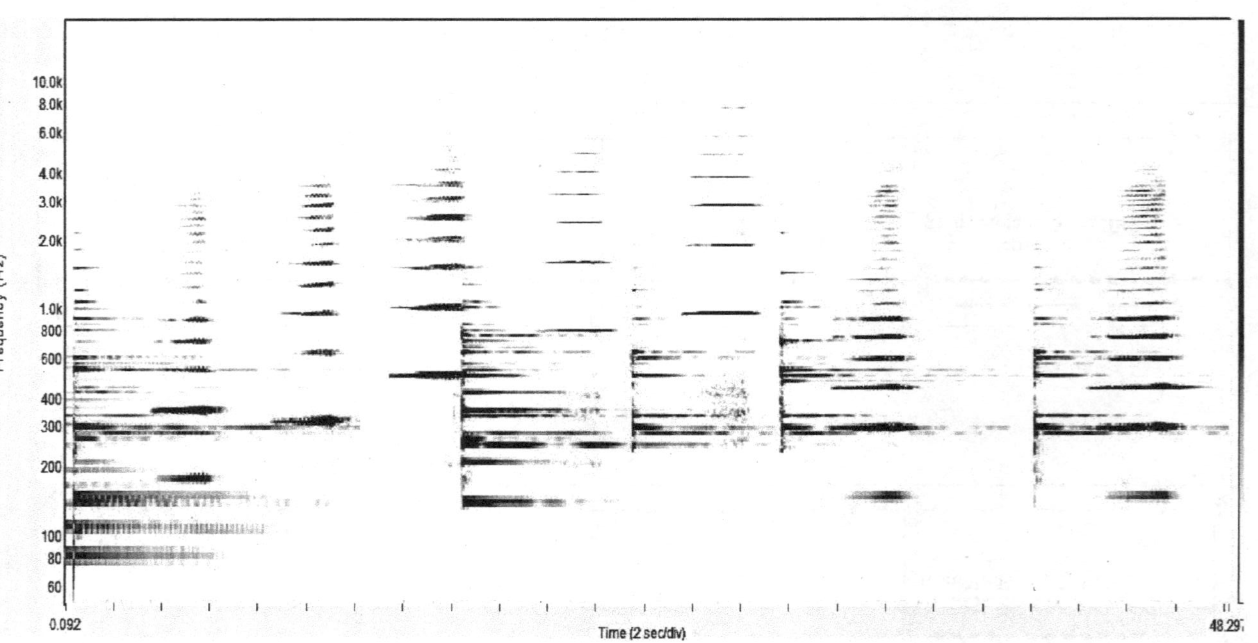

Figure 4.8 *The Viola in My Life 3*, Panel III, Spectrograph (mm. 32–40).

32) through Db^3 (m. 35) to C^4 (mm. 36–38). The viola spectrum not only seems to emerge from the decay of the piano chords, but also to complete them. They intertwine to form, for the first time in this piece, a more extended, continuous sonic event. They work together, but in a way that is new to the piece, to create a moment of real melodic/harmonic continuity. Surrounded by many, more isolated events, this moment in the composition stands out and feels like the birth of a future, more extended, linear music. This feeling of potentiality is immediately halted when Panel IV begins and essentially returns to a varied repetition of Panel Ia (Figure 4.5, Figure 4.9).

The pitch sequence presented in the viola part of Panel I returns in Panel IV, as does the aforementioned primary gesture of simultaneous attack points, as well as the overall sense of durational coordination between the instruments (Figure 4.3, Figure 4.7). As with duration, in terms of pitch, a general feeling of stasis develops as the presence of exact repetition gradually returns at the conclusion of the work. Near the end of Panel IV (mm. 44–49), the top three tones of the chord remain constant, while the lower three first slide down a half step from D# E F (m. 44) to C Db D (m. 46), and then they return to D# E F (m. 49), though in a different register, one octave lower than in m. 44—perhaps to make the return less obvious. Reinforcing this sense of return, the viola repeats the same tone, though again in a different register: first D^3 (m. 44–45) and then D^4 (m. 49), one octave higher and with a different timbre (harmonic vs. *normale*). The viola's D returns in the same two bars where the piano's sonority D#EF returns (mm. 49). (Coincidentally, this is the only measure in the piece in which Feldman calls for a tone to be depressed silently in order to produce sympathetic vibrations, adding to the underlying chord and perhaps marking this as a unique moment.)

A sense of accreting stasis continues through the Extension of Panel IV (mm. 51–56). In bars 51 and 53, the piano plays the same chord in the same register, the only time this happens in the

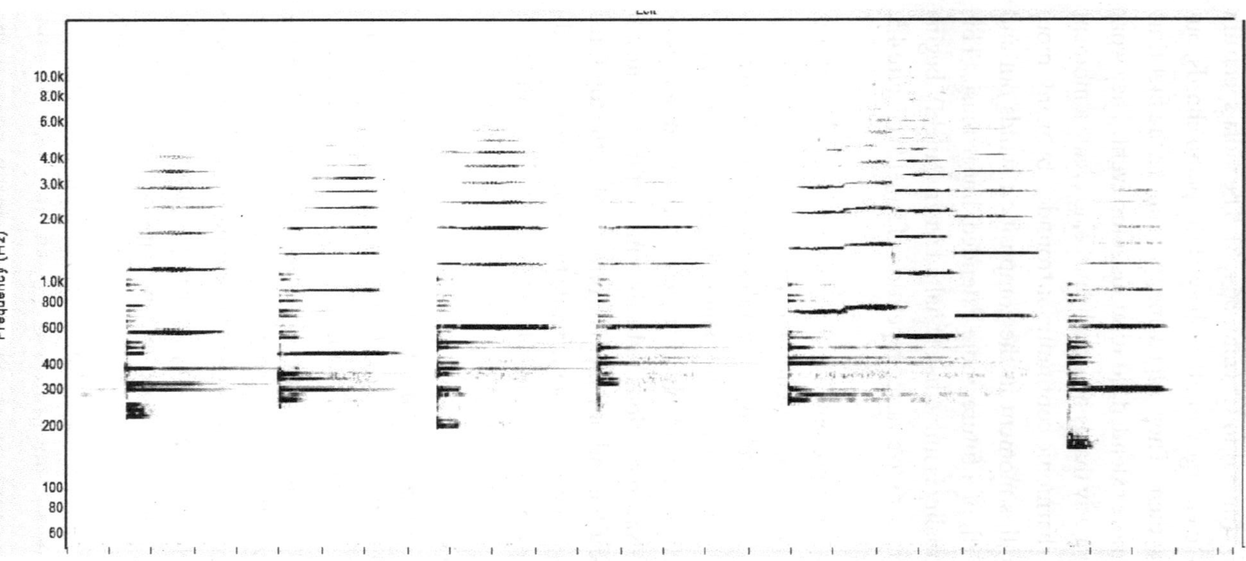

Figure 4.9 *The Viola in My Life III*, Panel IV, Spectrograph (mm. 41–49, parallels mm. 1–9).

work. Simultaneously, the viola plays the same tone but in a different octave and with a different timbre (*normale* vs. harmonic) (Figure 4.10). The slowly developing sense of equilibrium that gradually settles into Panel IV is surely meant to bring to the composition some feeling of conclusion. In this respect, the ending of *The Viola in My Life III* is similar to that of *Viola I* and *Viola II* (and, as will be shown, that of *Viola IV*). All three end with obvious passages of repetition. The first two, however, gradually progress toward such moments, while the third begins at that state (Panel I), moves away from it (Panels II and III), and returns to it at the conclusion (Panel IV).

Figure 4.10 *The Viola in My Life 3*, Panel IV, Extension, Repetition in Final Bars.

Feldman chose to end *Viola III* with a repetition of Pattern b from *Viola II*, providing a sense of repetition on a larger scale—from one composition to the next! As noted above, Pattern b appears three times in *Viola III*: at the end of Panels Ia and Ib, and then at the end if Panel IV. Thus, it marks the end of each of the most clearly fixed passages in the work with respect to repetition of temporal and harmonic material. As such, one of its functions is to draw our attention to these parallel moments in the piece. The reference back to *Viola II* will be obvious to anyone familiar with that earlier work. However, even if one is not familiar with *Viola II*, Pattern b is so different from any of the other music of *Viola III* that it certainly will stand out from the remainder of the piece. Its relatively rapid rhythmic articulation (intensified by the increase in tempo from half note = 66 to half = 80 each time it appears), as well as the fact that it is repeated verbatim each time it appears, marks it as a special event in this work. Moreover, it is a special "melodic" event, fully formed from its inception. In all other instances in *The Viola in My Life* works, melodic events unfold gradually, in fits and starts, surrounded by fragments and variants. They never otherwise appear out of nowhere fully formed. All of these factors ascribe to the presence of Pattern b in *Viola III* a sense that it is borrowed from somewhere else, whether one knows from where or not. As will be seen in the next chapter, this also signals that the use of quotation will play an even larger part in the next composition in the series, *The Viola in My Life IV*.

All in all, one can see that there is logic and order in the structure of this piece. It appears to be intentionally designed, countering the general feeling that Feldman's music was subconsciously formed rather than consciously planned. This might seem at odds with the overall quality of the sound world he has created: very slow, soft successions of either individual sounds or short sound events, with little apparent connective tissue and little surface inflection from dynamics or local rhythmic shaping. Perhaps it is precisely this contradiction that he is after in *The Viola in My Life III*. He creates a real sense that, while the sounds of the piece seem to float by the listener in apparent isolation, beneath that surface there exists a design that is governed by often rigid consistency, with only the slightest sense of variation.

5

The Viola in My Life IV

The Viola in My Life IV was commissioned by the *Venice Biennale* in 1971 where it was premiered in that year. It is scored for viola soloist and full orchestra. As was the case with the earlier pieces in the set, the score for *The Viola in My Life IV* is in C. In addition to the viola solo, the instrumentation includes two flutes, two oboes, English horn, two clarinets, bass clarinet, two bassoons, two horns, two trumpets, two trombones, tuba, harp, celesta, piano, strings, and percussion (timpani, side drum, tenor drum, bass drum, maracas, temple blocks, wood blocks, tubular bells, crotales, glockenspiel, vibraphone). The performance instructions are the same as those of *The Viola in My Life II*: very quiet (though there are actually three instances of notated dynamic inflection in the score), all attacks at a minimum, with no feeling of a beat. The tempo of quarter note at approximately 63 is a bit faster than that of *Viola I* (quarter = 58), and slower than that of *Viola II* and *Viola III* (quarter = 66).

Throughout *The Viola in My Life IV*, brass and orchestral strings remain muted. In contrast, unlike the case in the three previous works in *The Viola in My Life* set, in *Viola IV* the soloist occasionally removes the mute. Specifically, the soloist is:

- muted in mm. 1–37
- unmuted in mm. 38–86
- muted in mm. 87–168
- unmuted in mm. 169–208
- muted in mm. 210–285.

The Marvelous Illusion. Thomas DeLio, Oxford University Press. © Oxford University Press 2024.
DOI: 10.1093/9780197759967.003.0005

Overall, it is muted more often than not, but it is significant that, in this work, Feldman chooses to release the unmuted sound of the solo viola for the first time in the set. This is not only the case because the viola must compete with an ensemble much larger than that of any of the other three works. Indeed, the viola rarely sounds with the full ensemble; rather, it is typically heard either unaccompanied or accompanied by various small subgroups of the orchestra, as, for example, in bars 150–158 (Figure 5.1 and Figure 5.2). More importantly, Feldman chooses to have the mute removed at certain moments to alter the timbre of the instrument, allowing it to project the full spectrum of its overtones. This brightens the sound considerably and enables the violist to project a feeling that, at such moments, his or her sonority is emerging from the overall texture more forcefully than before. This is apparent upon examination of the score but is represented vividly through a spectrograph of such passages, as will be shown.

As was the case with the discussion of *The Viola in My Life II*, I will revert to labeling contrasting elements as sonorities and patterns. The orchestra generally presents isolated chords that will be labeled sonorities, while the viola presents more melodic figuration, to be labeled patterns. However, unlike the earlier works in the set, in this piece there are no identifiable, large formal divisions. The work does not separate into clearly defined structural units such as the panels of *Viola I*, *Viola II*, and *Viola III*. In those three compositions in the set, there are either obvious, large areas of related material (*Viola I* and *Viola II*), or areas filled with clear, large-scale repetition of distinctive events that become fixed in time (*Viola I*, *Viola II*, and *Viola III*). Nor do fixed, complex temporal patterns emerge either locally or on a large scale as seen in the design of *Viola III*. The structure of *The Viola in My Life IV* is quite different from that of any of the previous compositions. It constitutes a design more akin to a collage, much like those of one of Feldman's favorite painters Robert Rauschenberg. The work comprises individual moments, some as short as one chord from the orchestra or one tone from the viola soloist, or as long as a complete melodic event from either orchestra or soloist several measures in duration. In *Viola IV*, Feldman projects an image of individual events floating freely in time, never fixed in any temporal grid. Nonetheless, a fascinating structure emerges based on the constant juxtaposition of contrasting sonic events. These events are drawn together through a succession of oppositional pairings between ensemble and soloist.

In terms of the evolution of each composition in the set, *Viola IV* is also quite different from its predecessors. *Viola I* contained

Figure 5.1 *The Viola in My Life 4*, Example of Separation of Muted Viola from Orchestra (mm. 150–158).

Figure 5.1 Continued

distinct gestures that led to the emergence of repeating patterns in its final moments, though, in that work, such patterns remained quite short. In *Viola II* longer patterns emerged that culminated in long-range repetition and, ultimately, a merging of ensemble with soloist. *Viola III* exhibited a rigidly fixed set of patterns from its inception, as it was built from a set of well-defined duration schemes, articulated through the repetition of one basic, unifying gesture. These patterns gradually broke apart but returned by the end of the piece. In contrast, as noted, *Viola IV* appears, on the surface, to contain a succession of inchoate sonic events. Certainly, as in *Viola I*, *II*, and *III*, in *Viola IV*, repeating patterns abound (again with slight variation each time,

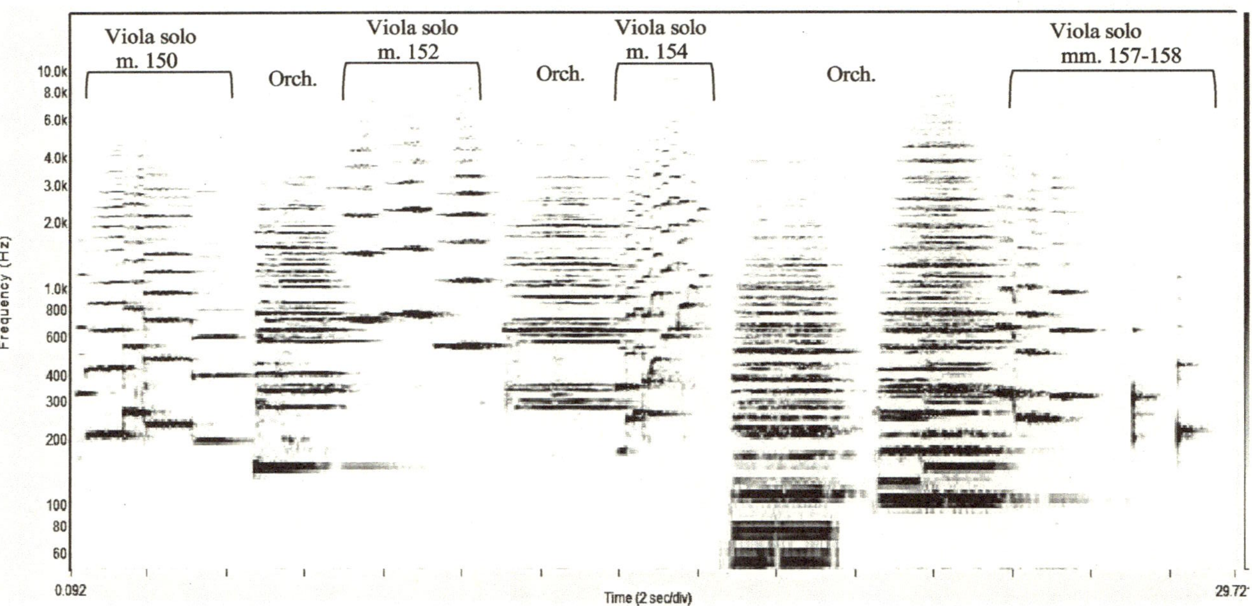

Figure 5.2 *The Viola in My Life 4*, Example of Separation of Muted Viola from Orchestra, Spectrograph (mm. 150–158).

here especially in terms of timbre given the varied instrumentation available from the orchestra), as do numerous quotations drawn from the previous three works in the set (similarly varied). However, these patterns and quotations also never synthesize into large-scale formal units. Rather, they too are joined throughout as pairs of contrasting sonic events that are then scattered about in the collage-like surface noted earlier.

Quotations

As noted, in *The Viola in My Life IV* we encounter numerous quotes from previous pieces in the set. One of the most obvious is the semitone sonority that forms a constant backdrop for all that occurs in *Viola IV*, as it often did in earlier compositions (Figure 5.3). The static nature of this chord structure fashions a ground against which variations of timbre come to the fore. These cluster-like sonorities are enriched by different orchestrations, creating a soft, shimmering texture of changing colors throughout the piece. This is evident from the outset. Considering just the first few chords sounded by the orchestra, it is obvious that each chord, again while similar with respect to interval content, is quite different sonically, occupying different registers and exhibiting differences of density (especially among their overtone spectra), attack noise, and tone color (Figure 5.4, Figure 5.5). A spectrograph of the initial five bars of the composition reminds one of Schoenberg's *Farben* movement from his *Five Pieces for Orchestra*: dark colors filled with noise-based clustering, alternating with light, open sonorities (Figure 5.5).[1]

On a more microstructural level, quite noticeable from the outset is the close relationship between the initial sonority of *Viola IV* and important sonorities of *Viola I* and *Viola II* (Table 5.1). They share the very same interval content and construction,

Figure 5.3 *The Viola in My Life 4*, Semitone Sonorities (mm. 1–21).

predominantly of half-steps and tritones, in formations of nearly identical spatial disposition. Those half-step/tritone sonorities found in *Viola II* and *Viola IV* each open their respective compositions, awarding them a place of prominence, while that of *Viola I* initiates its third and final panel. In addition, these sonorities repeat verbatim throughout their respective compositions, further emphasizing their importance in those contexts. Moreover, the sonority that initiates *Viola IV* expands the configuration of the half-step/tritone sonority encountered in those earlier works and saturates much of that work. (Sonorities

Figure 5.3 Continued

throughout *The Viola in My Life III* are not clearly related and, as such, have not been included in Table 5.1.)

In addition to the aforementioned sonorities, a number of other quotes or near quotes from earlier works are found in *Viola IV*, as well as several very prominent repeating patterns that are new (Figure 5.6, Figure 5.7, Table 5.2). Immediately, one notes the presence of the Primary Gesture of *Viola III* in the very first bar of *Viola IV* (tenuto quarter notes, in the orchestra, initiating sustained tones from the viola). This is a clear reference to the previous work,

Figure 5.3 Continued

affording a sense that *Viola IV* is picking that Primary Gesture as its starting point.

In terms of orchestral sonorities, as in the previous compositions in the set—though here greatly intensified—the preponderance of the aforementioned half-step clusters in *Viola IV* creates a thick sonority, filled with beating (also known as interference phenomena). Such beating is further intensified among the tightly packed, microtonally clustered, upper partials of the fundamental tones of these sounds (Figure 5.3). These densely packed sounds of the orchestra form a constant texture that saturates much of the composition, which provides a distinct contrast with the more open sonorities of the viola solo. Against the thick textures typically projected by the orchestra, Feldman highlights the purer tone quality of the viola (for example, mm. 77–80, 103–105, 150–154). When one adds the occasional percussion strokes and rolls that intensify the constant background of noise-based sounds from the orchestra, the viola's purer sonority stands out even further (as, for example, mm. 69–75). This all echoes the character of Sonority A from *Viola II*, where pure tones were gradually transformed into noise bands, a constant motion featured throughout the first panel of that work. This transformation is intensified throughout *Viola IV* as the pure sonorities of the viola are constantly juxtaposed against the dense, noise-filled sonorities of the orchestra in myriad ways.

Figure 5.4 *The Viola in My Life 4*, Initial Sonorities (mm. 1–5).

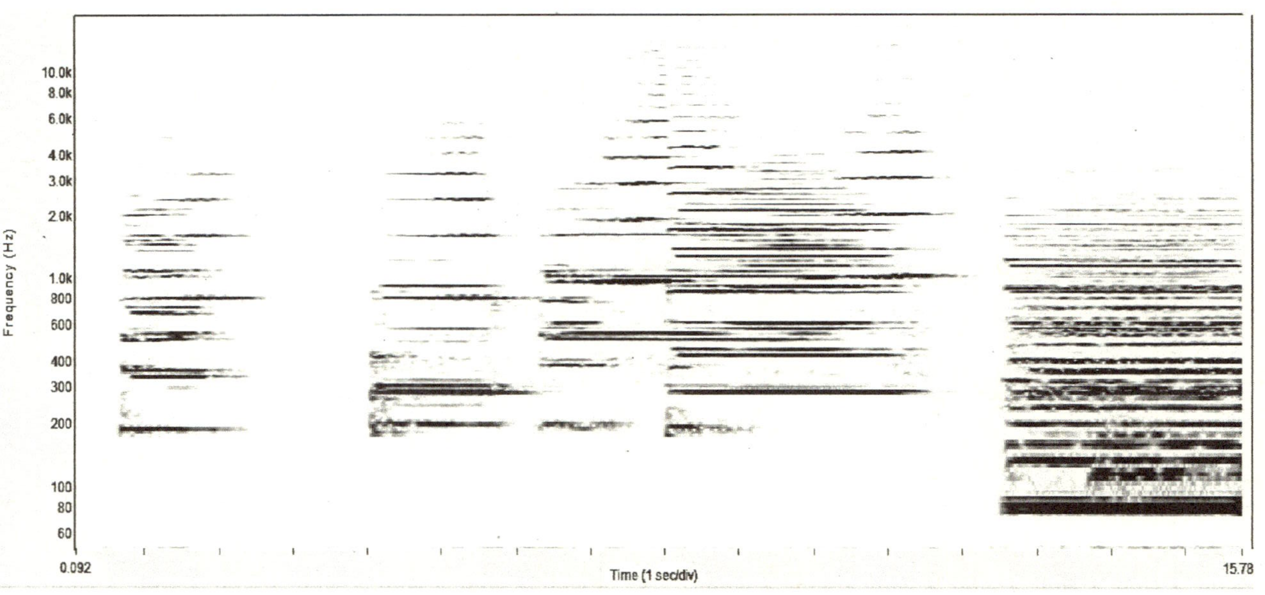

Figure 5.5 *The Viola in My Life 4*, Initial Sonorities, Spectrograph (mm. 1–5).

Table 5.1 *The Viola in My Life IV*, Shared Sonorities among *The Viola in My Life I, II*, and *IV*

Vla. I Panel III m. 86	*Vla. II* Sonority A m. 1-2	*Vla. IV* m. 1
A 3 F# 1 F B 6 F 6 1 E 3 C# 6 G	Ab 1 G 1 6 F# Db 1 C	G C 1 B 1 6 Gb F 1 1 E

Certain melodic events in the viola part are also quite closely aligned with those of earlier works (Figure 5.8 and Table 5.3). Patterns in the viola solo can be related to moments in the previous three works through pitch content, interval content, rhythm, contour, or any combination of these (Figure 5.8). In various ways, and to varying degrees, they echo earlier events and create a floating haze of reflections and memories. Other moments in the solo part, however, are new. Indeed, in *Viola IV* some such moments are impossible to connect in any way to earlier works in the set as they either consist only of single notes (bars 19, 35, 126, 128, 130) or fragments of two or three notes. While, in the composer's mind, these might reflect back to previous events, here they seem too tenuous to be clearly designated as related to specific linear configurations in any of

Figure 5.6 *The Viola in My Life 4*, Orchestra, Quotes from Previous Works in the Set.

the earlier compositions in the set—which may, of course, be the point.

The most obvious and often repeated quote in *Viola IV* was first heard in *Viola II* (mm. 118–129, 139–147, 163–172), labeled in the analysis of *Viola II* Sonority/Pattern D/d (Figure 3.12). This material returns *six times* in *Viola IV* (mm. 53–64, 84–96, 188–198, 210–220, 252–259, and 274–282). Each time it is slightly varied,

Figure 5.7 *The Viola in My Life 4*, Orchestra, Prominent Repeating Patterns.

occasionally truncated, and, once, between bars 188 and 220, two statements of this quotation are concatenated to make a much longer event. This quote is one of the most striking in the composition. Not only because it is quite long compared with all other events in *Viola IV* but also because its material is so different from anything else heard in the piece: its melody is diatonic (almost folk like . . . another memory) and, so, it contrasts sharply with all the half-step sonorities heard elsewhere. In this way, it functions as an important referential event as the piece unfolds, a stable, self-contained moment to which the composition returns periodically.

Table 5.2 *The Viola in My Life IV*, Orchestra, Sonorities, Pitch/ Interval Content

Pattern	Pitch	Interval
from *Viola I*, mm. 86, 87, etc.		
from *Viola II*, Sonority A, mm. 2–7, etc.		
in *Viola IV*, mm. 1, etc.	E F B C Gb G	1, 6, 1, 6 1
from *Viola II*, Sonority D, mm. 118–125, 139–147,		
in *Viola IV*, mm. 53–64, etc.	Bb F G	5, 2
The following sonorities from *Viola IV* contain frequently repeated patterns. However, they do not refer back to earlier compositions. They may be related by pitch content, interval content, contour, and/or rhythm, in various combinations. In the examples below, pitch/interval content is only given for the first statement of the pattern in *Viola IV*.		
X Similar interval content and repeating two-chord pattern.		
mm. 106, 112, 114, 116, 117, 133, 143, 151, 153	Bb C B Ab D C# (chord: highest note to lowest)	2, 1, 3, 6, 1
Y Same two-bar melodic pattern and very similar pitch/interval content.		
mm. 176–177, 178–179, 180–181, 182–183, 184	E D G F	2, 5, 2
Z Same one-bar melodic pattern (neighboring pattern).		
mm. 235, 237, 240 242, 245, 250	D# Bb D# F E F C B C Gb Db G (chords: highest note to lowest)	5, 5, 1, 1 1, 1 5, 5

Quoted Patterns, Verbatim and Varied

The Viola in My Life 4 (mm. 1-7); from *The Viola in My Life 2*, a1 (mm.2-4, 8-11, 24-30); same interval set.

The Viola in My Life 4 (mm. 17-18, 77-78); from *The Viola in My Life 2*, b1 (mm.37-38); m. 17 minus the initial A, m. 77 with th A.

The Viola in My Life 4 (mm. 23-24, 26, 45, 48-49, 66, 71, 119); from *The Viola in My Life 2*, b2 (mm.58, 98).

The Viola in My Life 4 (mm. 113, 144, 154, 225, 227, 229, 231); from *The Viola in My Life 2*, b3 (mm. 77, 95).

The Viola in My Life 4 (mm. 105); from *The Viola in My Life 2* and *3*, b4 (*Viola 2*, mm. 83, 105); *Viola 3*, mm. 8, 17, 55)

Figure 5.8 *The Viola in My Life 4*, Viola Solo, Quoted Patterns and Original Patterns.

The Viola in My Life 4 (mm. 56-64, 84-96, 188-198); from *The Viola in My Life 2*, d (mm. 118-129, 139-147, 163-172).

The Viola in My Life 4 (mm. 80, 150); from *The Viola in My Life 2*, c varied (mm. 113, 117, 125, 143, 167).

Original Patterns in *The Viola in My Life 4*

x (mm. 13-14, 27-28).

y (mm. 38-40, 50-51).

Figure 5.8 Continued

Table 5.3a *The Viola in My Life IV*, Viola Patterns, Pitch/Interval Content

Quotes or Variants of Material from *The Viola in My Life II* and *III* used in *Viola IV*.		
In the examples below, pitch/interval content is given for only the first statement of the pattern in *Viola IV*.		
Pattern	Pitch	Interval
from *Viola II* a1, mm. 2–4, 8–11, 24–30		
Variants of original in *Viola IV*: same interval content, varied rhythm and contour.		
in *Viola IV*, mm. 1–7, 15–16	G Bb Ab B (G Bb)	3, 2, 3 (3)

(*continued*)

Table 5.3a Continued

from *Viola II* b1, mm. 37–38		
in *Viola IV*, mm. 17–18 QUOTE minus initial A	F B E Ab D Gb B F	6, 5, 6, 4, 5, 6
in *Viola IV*, mm. 77–78 QUOTE with initial A	A F B E Ab D Gb B F	4, 6, 5, 6, 4, 5, 6
from *Viola II,* b2, mm. 58, 98		
Variants of original in *Viola IV*: same six-note ascending pattern, generally related by size, contour, and rhythm. Though perhaps more tenuous than the other groupings listed here, they nonetheless seem associative.		
in *Viola IV*, mm. 23–26, 45–48 66, 119, 269–272	C# E F B Eb G	3, 1, 6, 4, 4
from *Viola II,* b3, mm. 77, 95		
Variants of the original: same ascending contour, in sixteenth notes and all starting with a tritone.		
in *Viola IV*, mm. 113, 225, 227, 229, 231	E A# C# F A C#D Gb Bb C (decuplets)	6, 3, 4, 4, 4, 1, 4, 4, 2
in *Viola IV*, m. 154	F B C F# Bb D Eb G B C# (decuplet)	6, 1, 6, 4, 4, 1, 4, 4, 2
in *Viola IV*, m. 144	F B D# E F Ab C D	6, 4, 1, 1, 3, 4, 2

Table 5.3b *The Viola in My Life IV*, Viola Patterns, Pitch/Interval Content

from *Viola II,* b4, mm. 83, 105; from *Viola III*, mm. 8, 17, 55		
in *Viola IV*, m.105	Gb C B E Eb C# D Ab C E A B	6, 1, 5, 1, 2,, 1, 6, 4, 4, 5, 5, 2
from *Viola II,* d, mm. 118–129, 139–147, 163–172		
in *Viola IV*, mm. 56–64, 84–96, 188–198	Bb C E D A C E D B A E D B A	2, 4, 2, 5, 3, 4, 2, 3, 2, 5, 2, 3, 2

Table 5.3b Continued

in *Viola IV*, mm. 210–220, 252–259, 274–282	Bb C E D A C E D B A	2, 4, 2, 5, 3, 4, 2, 3, 2

from *Viola II*, c, mm. 113, 117, 125, 143, 167

Variants of the original: same contour and rhythm.

in *Viola IV*, m. 80, 150	D G C A	5, 5, 3

The following patterns do not refer back to earlier compositions in the set. However, they are related to other patterns in *Viola IV* by pitch content, interval content, contour, and rhythm in various combinations. Again, in the examples below, pitch/interval content is only given for first statement of the pattern in *Viola IV.*

Same interval content

x {1,6}

m. 13, 27–28, 152	G Ab D	1, 6

Same interval and pitch content

y1 {2, 6, 4}

mm. 38–40	D A E G F B Eb G F B Eb	5, 5, 3, 2, 6, 4, 4, 2, 6, 4

y2

mm. 50–51	G F B Eb G F A Eb	2, 6, 4, 4, 2, 4,

Table 5.3c *The Viola in My Life IV*, Viola Patterns, Pitch/Interval Content

Same rhythm and contour.

z

mm. 233–234, 238–239	F C# E B Eb	6, 3, 3, 4

A few other linear events in *Viola IV* part are unique and not obviously connected to the foregoing. Some of these events constitute single notes (bars 19, 35, 126, 128, 130, 241–243). Others are fragments, which, while they may reflect back to previous events, seem too tenuous to be clearly designated as related to any one type of linear event—which may, of course, be the point (bars 9–10, 31–33, 69–70, 72–75, 121, 123, 135–141, 157–158, 263–265, 283).

Oppositional Design

On the local level, the sonic moments that constitute the individual elements of the aforementioned collage-like design of *Viola IV* are often presented as a succession of oppositional pairings of viola patterns versus orchestral sonorities. Musicologist Hermann Sabbe has gleaned the motivation (whether conscious or not) behind such oppositions:

> C5P18 In order to generate genuine processes, i.e. continuities of becoming rather than being—"being" defined as an identity predictively unifying present and future—the composer has to, paradoxically, introduce discontinuity. When he does, i.e. through constantly changing or alternating meter; through the use of grand pauses; through chord or harmonic field change etc. Thus his music proceeds through momentary orientations and reorientations, through temporary conditionings and deconditionings and reconditionings, through continual constructions and deconstructions of sense—not presentation of common, univocally communicable lasting sense.
>
> C5P19 In order to generate this overall continuity, local discontinuities have to be planned and differentiated. In order to constantly reorient the listening process, the composing process must be most carefully oriented.[2]

C5P20 Over the course of the composition, the oppositional pairs become more complex and elongated. They may be generally categorized into four levels of opposition via the degree of both the length of the elements presented in opposition and the intensity of opposition projected in each.

C5S3 Level 1 Oppositions

C5P21 Level 1 oppositions are the least complex. They typically consist of a single chord in the orchestra paired with a single tone or short melodic fragment in the solo part (m. 5). Typically, these follow one another but occasionally they partially overlap. This opposition first appears clearly in bars five and six as the juxtaposition of a single chord in the orchestra followed by a single tone from the unaccompanied viola (Figure 5.9, Figure 5.10). This first statement of the initial Level 1 opposition emerges gradually over the course of the first five bars, during which the soloist and orchestra gradually separate from one another. Level 1 oppositions recur frequently throughout the work. They project the principle of opposition in its most primal state, to which the composition repeatedly returns.

Level 2 Oppositions

A Level 2 opposition consists of a succession of twice repeated chords that alternate with either silent measures (mm. 106–118) or brief unaccompanied melodic events from the viola (mm. 151–154) (Figure 5.11, Figure 5.12). The most significant difference between the Level 1 oppositions and those of Level 2 involves the repetition of each chord in the orchestra paired with the viola playing brief, typically one-measure-long melodic fragments rather than single notes. In this respect, Level 2 oppositions are both more elongated and more complex than those of Level 1.

Level 3 Oppositions

Level 3 oppositions consist of still more extended melodic events from the unaccompanied soloist, typically longer than one bar in duration, alternating with brief quasi-melodic (quasi-neighbor note) events from the orchestra consisting of three chords (mm. 233–251) (Figure 5.13, Figure 5.14).

Figure 5.9 *The Viola in My Life 4*, Initial Opposition (mm. 5–6).

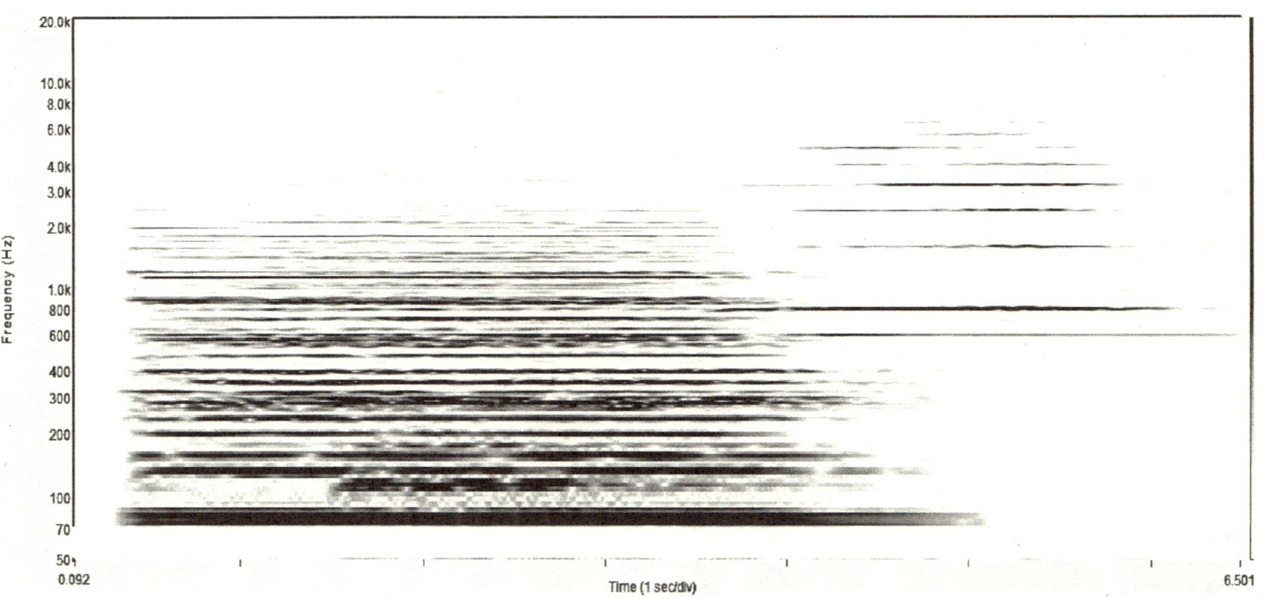

Figure 5.10 *The Viola in My Life 4*, Initial Opposition, Spectrograph (mm. 5–6).

Figure 5.11 *The Viola in My Life 4*, Example of Level 2 Opposition (mm. 151–154).

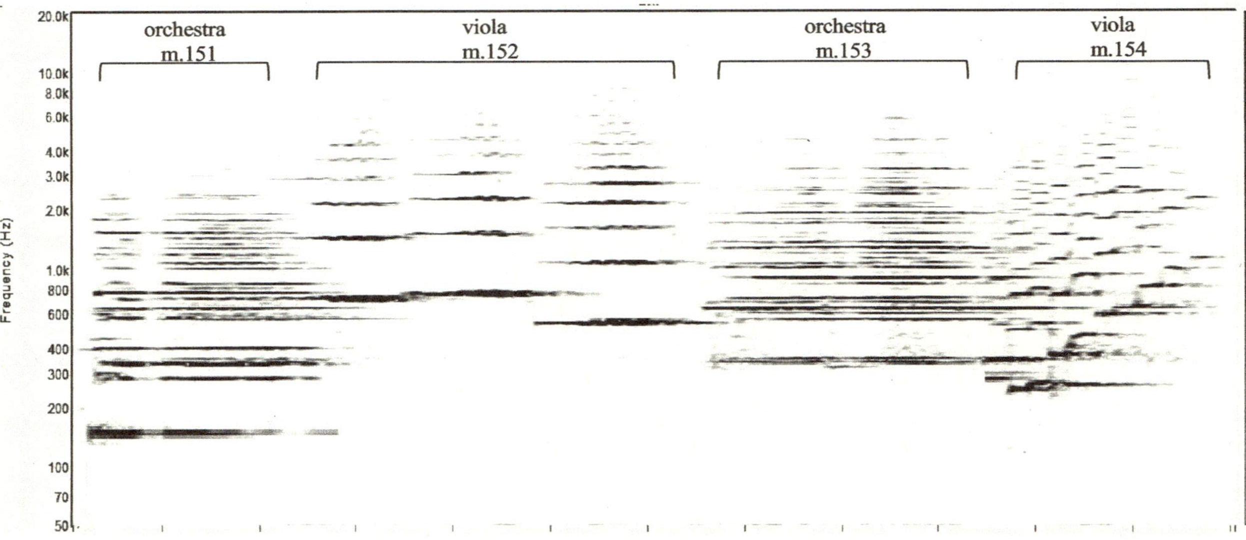

Figure 5.12 *The Viola in My Life 4*, Example of Level 2 Opposition, Spectrograph (mm. 151–154).

Figure 5.13 *The Viola in My Life 4*, Example of Level 3 Opposition (mm. 233–239).

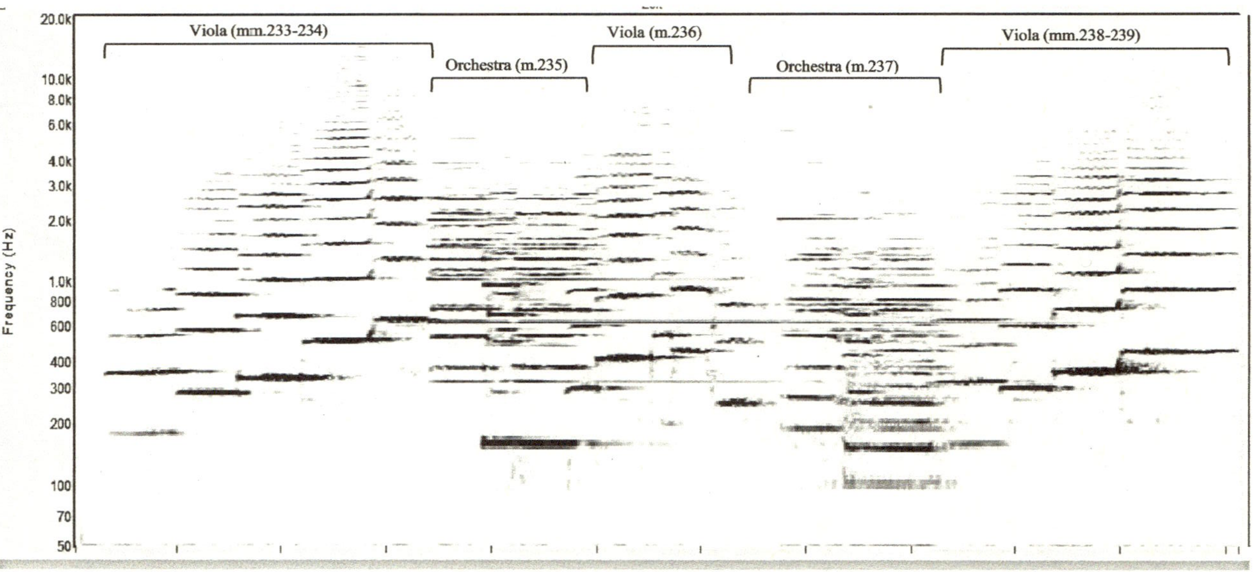

Figure 5.14 *The Viola in My Life 4*, Example of Level 3 Opposition, Spectrograph (mm. 233–239).

Level 4 Opposition

There is only one oppositional pair of events on Level 4, the most complex of the four levels. Here the viola presents its longest and most developed melodic event heard thus far in the work (mm. 169–175), followed by the orchestra which does the same (mm. 176–185) (Figure 5.15, Figure 5.16). Indeed, each of these passages is unique not only to this piece but to the entire set of four compositions. The former is by far the longest melodic line in the solo part in any of the four pieces. It is highly directional, includes internal repetition, and is one of only two melodic events in the viola part in which the dynamic level increases to *forte*. The latter is, similarly, the only event in which the orchestra—without the soloist—plays an extended melodic event, this one also filled with repetition and also the only event in the orchestra that rises in dynamic level, here to *fortissimo*. Interestingly, these two, very special events, immediately follow one another and are of nearly the same duration: the viola line is 39 eighth notes long, and the orchestra passage is 36 eighth notes. These are also the two most dramatic events in the piece—and in this rare occasion "dramatic" seems an appropriate term, though nowhere else is it applicable in these four compositions. It should be noted that this Level 4 oppositional melodic event in the viola part contains not only internal repetition (mm. 171, 172) but an external repetition as well (mm. 174–175, 186–187). The final two bars of the viola line return verbatim at the end of the orchestra melody, and so they frame that significant extended melodic passage from the orchestra (Figure 5.15).

One interesting fact with respect to this viola line in this Level 4 opposition is that it *descends* to its climax, which is marked by the peak of the aforementioned crescendo to *forte*. As the line descends, it becomes progressively louder, causing the upper partials of the viola to sound more prominently. Thus, the descending motion in the fundamental frequencies (the notated pitches) is coupled with an ascending motion of overtones. Of course, this becomes even more apparent as a result of the removal of the mute for this passage,

Figure 5.15 *The Viola in My Life 4*, Viola Solo, Longest Melodic Passage (mm. 169–175, 186–187).

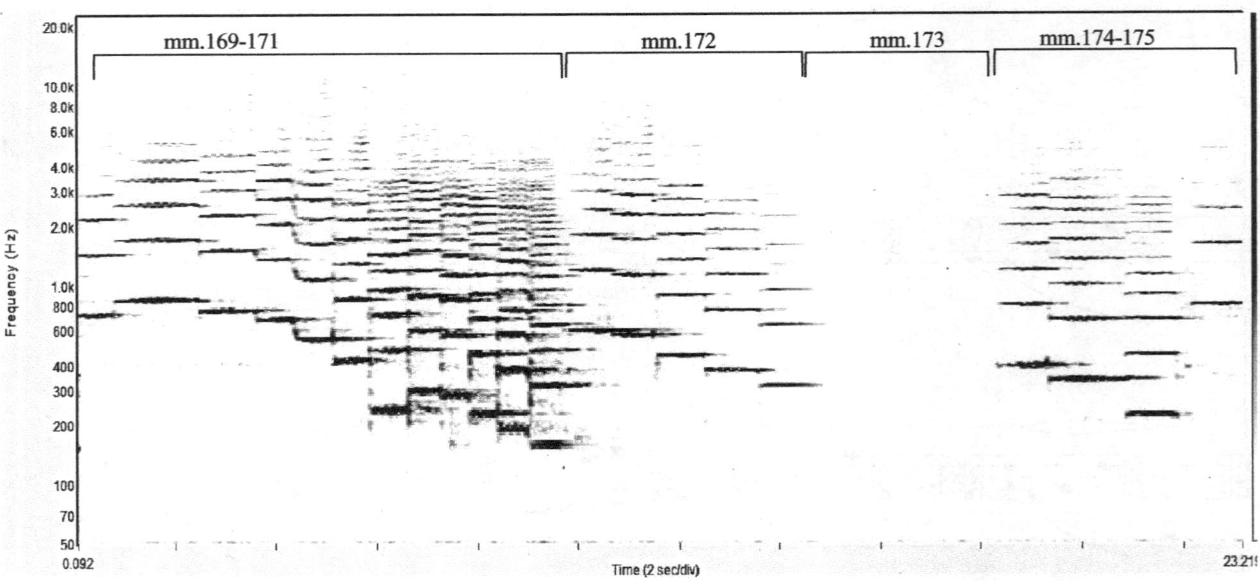

Figure 5.16 *The Viola in My Life 4*, Viola Solo, Longest Melodic Passage, Spectrograph (mm. 169–175).

which intensifies the upper partials of the viola tones. It would appear that at this moment Feldman wants the viola to become not only louder but also brighter, and forcefully break away from both its characteristic sound as projected within all four pieces and the overall texture of this composition.

The melodic event in the orchestra within this Level 4 opposition is quite different from that of the viola in several ways (Figure 5.17). Comparison of the spectrographs of both events reveals not only differences of tessitura between the two but, more importantly, differences of density of spectra (Figure 5.18, Figure 5.19). In the spectrograph of the viola solo, one can clearly see the overtones expand and contract as they rise and fall with changes in dynamics, while in the orchestra passage the density of the chords as well as the orchestration creates bands of clustering (especially in the higher registers of the overtones where the partials are related microtonally) and, therefore, an intensification of beating within the sonority. In this respect, the opposition between these two events reflects an intensification of the transition from tone to noise first encountered in *Viola I* and compounded in *Viola II*, where pure tones of flute and clarinet turned into noise bands of flutter tonguing and then the rolling on the castanets (Figure 3.1, Figure 3.2).

Other significant differences between these two oppositional events on Level 4 arise from differences with respect to pitch content and melodic contour (Figure 5.15). The viola line evolves; it builds to its climax and then recedes from it. As the motion speeds up toward the eighth-note figure in bar 171, it also moves from the line's highest point in the first bar of the passage (Ab^5) to its lowest point at the end of that measure (Eb^3). This climactic moment is, of course, emphasized by the crescendo and accented articulation. The line then moves up toward its original high point and lands only a half-step below that high point in bar 175 (G^5). As it recedes from its climactic low point, the line slows down, creating a momentary sense of cadence. Clearly, this melody is highly directional. It evolves in a classic manner toward a climax and then away from it, and it has a well-defined overall formal design.

In contrast, the melodic event in the orchestra is not directional, nor does it evolve in the same manner. Rather than move toward a climax and recede from that climax, the orchestra's line is constructed from a very short event of two bars in length, which is then repeated several times with no changes with respect to direction, contour, or pitch content. It consists of a compact four-note pattern (E D G F) that simply repeats four and a half times. Compared with the viola line that surrounds it, this melodic event from the orchestra is, by design, quite static. Those few changes that are heard are produced by slight changes in the accompanying orchestration (most notably in the bass instruments: bassoons, horns, trombones) and, of course, dynamics. Unlike the viola line preceding it, this passage seems quite inorganic; nothing in the melodic shape itself projects a motion forward toward a climax, whether in terms of pitch, contour, or register. The orchestra's melodic line seems purposefully artificial, in contrast with that of the viola line—especially with respect to the rather intentionally forced crescendo to its concluding *fortissimo* (Figure 5.17, Figure 5.18).

Clearly, the four aforementioned oppositions become more extended and intense as the composition progresses through the various levels outlined above. Starting with a simple opposition of one chord from orchestra paired with one tone from viola in Level 1, the piece moves toward the rather dramatic opposition of the two extended melodic events of Level 4. The essence of each level of opposition lies in pitting the solo viola timbre against the dense, noise-like cluster sonorities of the orchestra. As the composition unfolds, each of these types of sonic event independently enlarges and intensifies, culminating in the only expansion of the dynamic range heard anywhere in the composition (Figure 5.19). However, these levels of opposition do not seem to develop toward any type of synthesis. The material featured in each opposition is often quite different. This seems deliberate. Feldman's interest seems to be in the existence of the phenomenon of opposition, rather than its particularities at any given moment nor its connection to other oppositions occupying the same sonic space of *Viola IV*. Their oppositional characteristics intensify as the piece unfolds, as if the goal were to draw them apart more and more, intensifying their opposition to one another. The collage design is decidedly nonlinear and nonevolutionary.

The nonlinear nature of this design is compounded by the repeated presence of the extended quote from *Viola II* that occurs numerous times throughout *Viola IV* (mm. 56–65, 84–96, 188–220, 252–259, 274–282). Indeed, this prominent quote seems to exist in

Figure 5.17 *The Viola in My Life 4*, Orchestra, Longest Melodic Passage (mm. 176–185).

Figure 5.17 Continued

a completely different sonic world than the rest of the piece. (As noted earlier, the material of this quote is more diatonic and folklike than any other passage in this composition or its predecessor in which it first appeared, *Viola II*.) Significantly, one of these quoted events, the longest (mm. 188–220), immediately follows the events of the Level 4 opposition, expanding the very process of opposition itself to a new dimension. One senses that all of these events are connected to one another and exist as part of the same composition

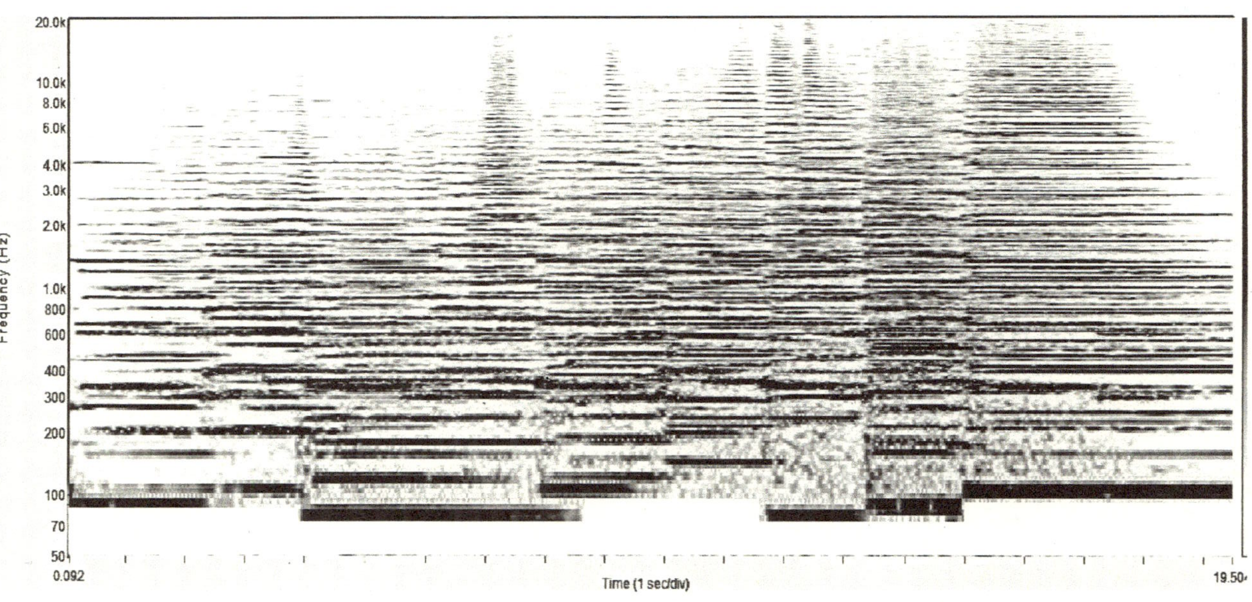

Figure 5.18 *The Viola in My Life 4*, Orchestra, Longest Melodic Passage, Spectrograph (mm. 176–185).

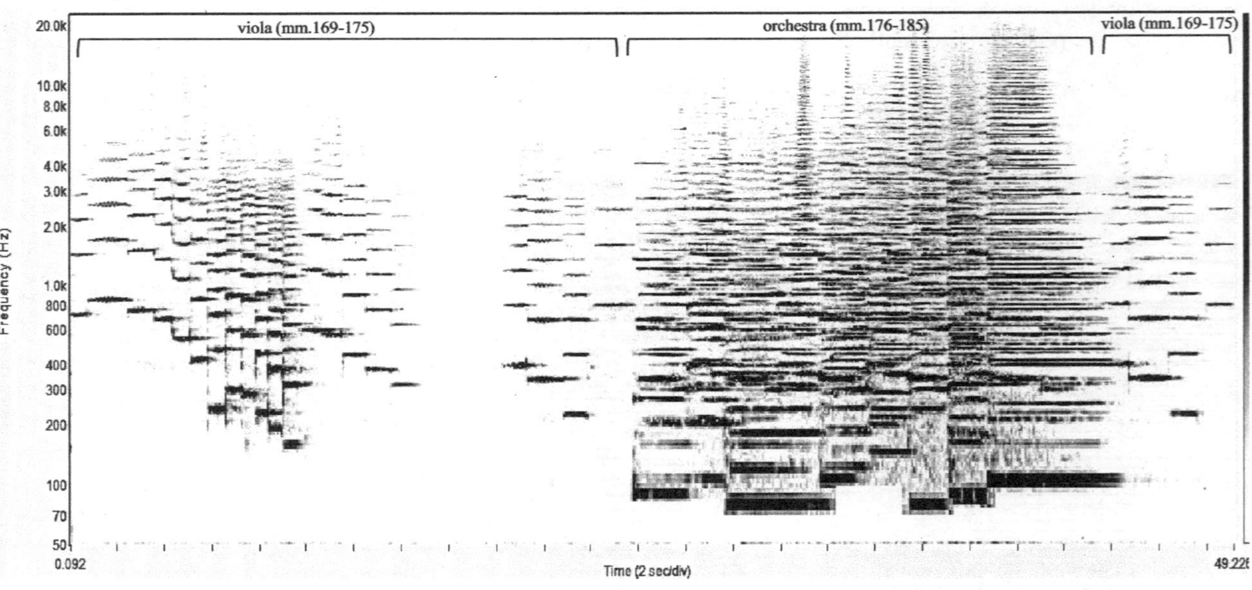

Figure 5.19 *The Viola in My Life 4*, Viola Solo and Orchestra, Longest Melodic Passages, Comparison of Spectrographs (mm. 169–185).

only as a result of their differences. They coexist rather than connect. They are merely different types of elements in the collage that is the form of *The Viola in My Life IV.*

One final note regarding the ending of the composition: the final bars of *Viola IV* are unique and seem to lend further support for this view of coexistence over development. In the third bar from the end of the piece (bar 283), Feldman introduces the piano sounding one chord: DbGACBC. This is the first time the piano has appeared in *Viola IV.* It played a prominent role in both *Viola I* and *Viola III*, but it did not appear in *Viola II* at all. Perhaps it too is intended as a quote of some kind, a reminder of the earlier pieces in the set simply through a return of one prominent tone color. The piano sounds its chord and decays over the final three bars. There is no pedal indication. It is accompanied by the viola sounding a tritone, Ab-D, *forte*, followed by a low Ab in the contrabass. Together these tones constitute two half-step clusters: BCDbD and GAbA. This is only the third moment of the work where the volume rises above its generally soft dynamic level (the other two being the aforementioned melodic events of Level 4).

Synthesis

Once again, the formal design of this piece is quite different from that of the earlier three pieces in the set. The work does not divide into separate parts (previously called panels) but rather forms a collage of seemingly distinct, disconnected moments. As outlined in the foregoing discussion, these moments are related in two ways: as quotations from earlier works and as elements of the four levels of opposition, the first three of which recur throughout the piece. Moreover, they do so within a clear, *though nonlinear*, hierarchy (Table 5.4). When examining the proportions of the various elements as they appear throughout the work, it is clear that the elements of the Level 1 opposition are most abundant, sounding far more often than any other (and, not surprisingly, they are the most diverse in terms of orchestration, rhythm, and pitch content,

Table 5.4 *The Viola in My Life IV*, Formal Design

L1 – Level 1 Opposition
L2 – Level 2 Opposition
L3 – Level 3 Opposition
L4 – Level 4 Opposition
D/d- Quote of Sonority D/pattern d from *Viola 2*

Measures																			
		D/d 53-64		D/d 84-92									D/d 188-220			D/d 252-260		D/d 274-282	
	L1 1-52		L1 65-83		L1 93-105		L1 119-132		L1 145-150		L1 159-168			L1 221-232			L1 261-273		L1 283-285
						L2 106-118		L2 133-144		L2 151-158									
															L3 233-251				
												L4 169-187							
Total Number of Measures	52	11	13	8	12	13	12	11	5	7	11	18	22	11	18	8	12	8	3
Total Number of Beats in Eighth Notes	332	69	79	63	46	53	79	32	30	48	57	90	152 56+46+50	67	112.5	51	110	46	26

which keeps them from becoming redundant and predictable, apt examples of Feldman's concept of variation). They constitute the background against which all other activity emerges as foreground. Interestingly, the next most often heard event is the quotation of event D/d borrowed from *Viola II.* This, in itself, seems to constitute yet another level of opposition in that it is quite different in character and sonority from anything sounding within Level 1. The material on Oppositional Levels 2 through 4 occurs less often but stands out as unique moments that intensify the oppositional development of the relationship between soloist and orchestra.

If one divides the piece around the appearance of its most dramatic event, the single instance of the Level 4 opposition, one notes a clear change in character (Table 5.4, Table 5.5). Prior to the appearance of this event, Level 1 oppositions clearly dominate the texture and establish an overall sonic character for this part of the work. However, from the appearance of the Level 4 opposition onward, there is a distinct change in the nature of the collage in favor of the more diatonic, folk-like tune that constitutes Sonority/Pattern D/d. The numerous repetitions of this quote in this latter part of the work create a new sonic focus within the piece. It seems that the quality of oppositional form is carried to yet another higher level in this latter part of the composition. Prior to the appearance of the Level 4 opposition, the highly fragmented, cluster-like sonorities and patterns of Level 1 dominate, while following the appearance of the Level 4 opposition focus shifts to the more diatonic, linear D/d quotation. One senses that, at least statistically, the balance among the materials that make up the collage has changed. Thus, while there are no clear formal divisions in the work, there are areas of contrast which create a cumulative sense of order, one that is, once again, distinctly nonlinear.

As is typical of much of Feldman's work, *The Viola in My Life IV* is perceptually open ended. Connections among events are made available to the listener, as are potential hierarchies among those events, but they are never made explicit (hence the constant slow, steady, uninflected surface of all his music). Ultimately, Feldman places the

Table 5.5 *The Viola in My Life IV*, Proportions among Levels of Opposition

The chart below shows the proportions among the major events sounding over the course of the *entire piece.*

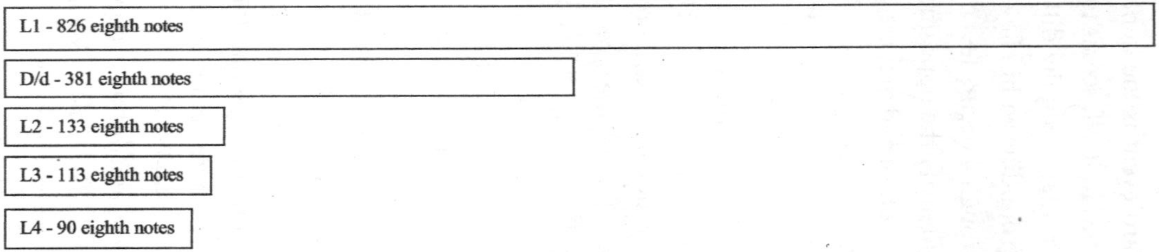

L1 - 826 eighth notes

D/d - 381 eighth notes

L2 - 133 eighth notes

L3 - 113 eighth notes

L4 - 90 eighth notes

The next chart shows the proportions among the major events sounding *up to the entrance of the Level 4 oppositions* (neither L3 nor L4 events sound up to this point):

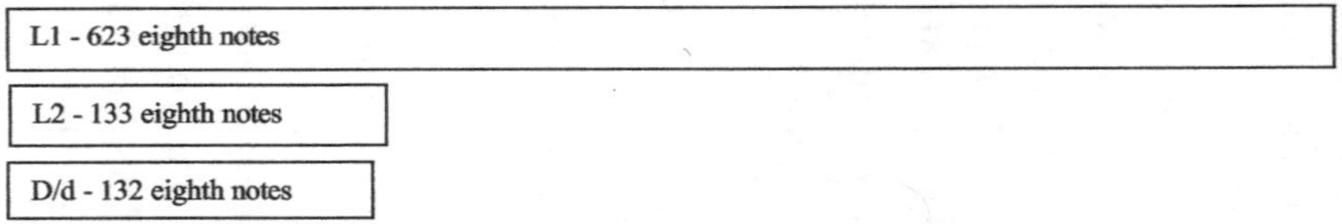

L1 - 623 eighth notes

L2 - 133 eighth notes

D/d - 132 eighth notes

The final chart shows the proportions among the major events sounding *from the entrance of the Level 4 oppositions* (L2 no longer sounds after this point in the piece):

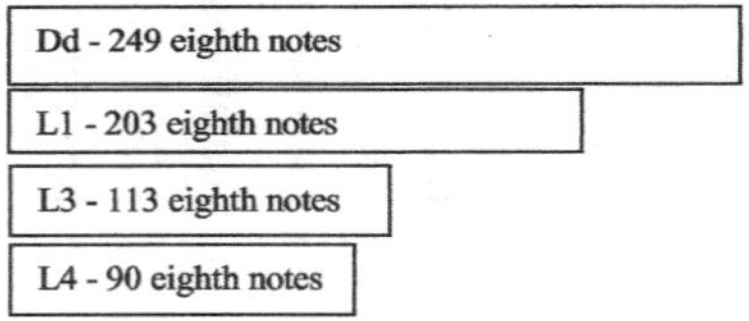

Dd - 249 eighth notes

L1 - 203 eighth notes

L3 - 113 eighth notes

L4 - 90 eighth notes

listener in the position of one who will realize those connections, and such realization, of necessity, will vary among all who experience the work. Toward this end, the open-ended design of such a work as *Viola IV* is essential, for, as I have noted elsewhere, for Feldman, "to expose the process of creating order as one which is imposed from without, is, in the end, to rob the work of its immediacy for the listener."[3]

The collage-like form of The Viola in My Life IV clearly supports this kind of listening experience. In it, each event is, in itself, independent, but when experienced in the context of all other events, they cohere through their differences. They do not evolve, interact, or develop together toward a goal. Instead, contrasting sonic events establish a statistical balance in which they constantly reflect upon one another, leading to a sense of statistical balance. *They cohere only through the fact that they exist in opposition to one another within the same compositional space.* What helps the listener bring the elements of this collage together is their constant referential function with respect to earlier pieces in the set. In a sense, *The Viola in My Life IV* is held together through a collective memory of the entire set of *The Viola in My Life* compositions. Whether or not any listener needs to hear the earlier pieces of the set in order to understand this is an open question. Since the most often repeated quotations can seem so "out of place" in this piece, they feel as if they have been borrowed from some other sonic space and have not been logically derived from surrounding material, even if the listener does not know their origin in *The Viola in My Life* set. Hence, they may seem to have been drawn from elsewhere, outside of any shifting context that may exist within the framework of this piece itself, whether the source of that material is known or not. This is especially true of the quote from *Viola II* first heard in bars 53–64 in *Viola IV* and repeated several times throughout. This is a well-defined, chamber-like, melodic event that is seemingly quite foreign to the rest of the material of *Viola IV* and might well appear to a listener as a quote borrowed from some other source, and, as noted before, given its nature perhaps even from some folk source.

6
Conclusions

In a lecture delivered at Black Mountain College in 1953, Stefan Wolpe, one of Morton Feldman's teachers, stated:

> It is certain that a piece of music is stripped of all rational content. We do not put ideas and theories into music. Theories and ideas may give birth to musical works, but between these works and the psychological, emotional, and intellectual soil from which they spring there is absolutely nothing in common. Language is a system of signs which we decipher to get at their meaning, and the whole value of words rests for us in this meaning. But when, on the other hand, we try to decipher the meaning of a piece of music, when we attempt to treat it as a system of signs, to pass through it to something else, we cease to listen to music. We let the sounds escape and have found nothing in their place.[1]

These words certainly resonate with our developing apperception of the nature of Feldman's music.

As is typical of Morton Feldman's work, the evolution of each composition in *The Viola in My Life* set is, literally, a search for the possibility of order, an order that is immanent in its materials but never stated explicitly. He is careful never to allow the listener to feel that a structure has been imposed from without (hence the overall soft and slow nature of his music); rather, he allows order to emerge as if from within each sound itself. The listener is always left feeling that he or she is organizing the materials of the piece through their own perceptions at the moment when each sound is heard. *This*

The Marvelous Illusion. Thomas DeLio, Oxford University Press. © Oxford University Press 2024.
DOI: 10.1093/9780197759967.003.0006

is Feldman's marvelous illusion. Encountering this music, one feels that the composer has stepped back from the act of composition, that he has let sounds loose into the air and that each listener, individually, is organizing them as they are encountered. Of course, as one perceives, one appropriates, and, finally, one conceptualizes an order in the mind. *Feldman's compositions are literally an enactment of this process.* It is in this respect that his music is organic, for as one experiences it, one becomes aware that order can only arise from that experience itself, never from any abstract, preconceived design. Feldman's work embraces a fundamental premise of the arts as they evolved in the twentieth century. In the words of the distinguished literary critic Joseph Conte:

> The postmodern artist has little confidence in suprahuman orders, and will readily concede that whatever order may be apparent in the world is largely a projection of the human mind. Our sense of the universe as ineffable is stronger now than it was a century ago because we are that much more inclined to disbelieve the fictions of its coherence. Consequently, postmodern artists consider human orders to be arbitrary and occasional, and they are rather skeptical regarding any claims that such orders are endorsed by anything beyond our own immediate political, ethical or utilitarian convenience.[2]

Putting aside for the moment the assumption in this remark that there is a distinction between so-called modern and postmodern art in this regard—which I do not believe exists—one should note how accurately it identifies the very essence of Feldman's creative impulse. For, if his music may be said to have any subject, it is the fact of pluralism, that there is no single, best way to experience the world. This, indeed, is one of the cornerstones of the most progressive art, music, and literature of the twentieth century. Of course, pluralism may appear in different aesthetic manifestations. For instance, often one encounters works that occupy a curious position in which the artist, through the work, speaks *about* pluralism but does not literally *enact* the condition of pluralism. In such work, the experience of fragmentation and multiplicity is described through the lens of one centrally unifying consciousness. In music, this can be seen in the work of someone like Elliott Carter, whose polyvalent compositional approach—brilliantly realized as it is—clearly acknowledges the decentered nature of experience but only as seen from one particular vantage point, that of the composer, through the specificity of his designs. In contrast, composers such as Feldman and his colleagues of the New York School do not just describe the state of pluralism through their work; they literally enact instances of it. This is not to say that Feldman, John Cage, Earle Brown, and Christian Wolff—to name but a few—are all addressing this creative stance in the same way. Each one embraces the condition of multiplicity differently.

Such an approach to making art is not unique to musicians such as Feldman or the other members of the New York School of composers. Indeed, it was crucial to the work of many of the important visual artists of the so-called Abstract Expressionist movement in the United States in the 1950s and 1960s. Referring to the work of the American Abstract Expressionist painters (with whom Feldman was closely associated), art critic Meyer Schapiro noted that a work by any one of these artists "is an ordered world of its own kind in which we are aware, at every point, of its becoming."[3] Feldman's music represents another example of such radically new art. In his music, he never highlights structural connections, nor does he focus on them in any way. Instead, he gives the listener an opportunity to organize events for himself. He, quite literally, builds into the piece the possibility that the listener *may* perceive connections. In a sense, he builds in the *possibility* of order.

The four compositions that comprise Morton Feldman's *The Viola in My Life* series—as, indeed, all of his works—are often described in such terms as:

> Each sound floats in space, is entirely independent of what has gone before and what has yet to come. Sounds do not progress but merely accumulate in the same place.[4]

> Not for him the fabulous interplay of parts in Boulez. Not for him the gnomic succession of sound and silence in Cage. Not for him the architectural cathedrals of Ligeti. Feldman's music is exceedingly straightforward in its procedure. Choose a sound, then another, and follow this example without recourse to events that would imply an opposition. By and large, this was Feldman's technique throughout his life.[5]

> Chords arrive one after another, in seemingly haphazard sequence, interspersed with silences. Harmonies hover in a no man's land between consonance and dissonance, paradise and oblivion. Rhythms are irregular and overlapping, so that the music floats above the beat. Simple figures repeat for a long time, then disappear. There is no exposition or development of themes, no clear formal structure.[6]

While such statements are, to some extent, true with respect to the more superficial aspects of the music—most notably the slow and soft surface presentation of the sonic material—they belie the fact that the music is indeed rigorously organized. Whether its organization comes about through conscious design or subconscious intuition is irrelevant; both offer a path toward the perception of order for the listener to explore. The marvel of Feldman's music for me is the fact that, despite its organization, it projects the impression that it lacks any logical design. On the surface, to the casual listener, it does indeed seem to consist of a random set of sounds floating freely in space and time. Of course, in part, he conveys this impression through his typical performance indications to play slowly and softly at all times. But, I believe, he uses such tools because they afford the means to placing the listener in a position in which he or she feels that the listener, not the composer, is organizing an experience of the composition into some ordered design, a design which, however, the composer himself has indeed created. As I have written in a previous study on Feldman:

> Feldman's is a music in which there is no apparent structuring of sound prior to its actual unfolding in time. It seems natural, then, that the composer would choose to work within a compositional format in which relationships appear to emerge at the very moment sound is first perceived by the listener and never in any sense prior to that moment; a format in which order never seems imposed by the will of the composer but rather evolves within the perceiver's own awakening consciousness. As such, Feldman avoids all procedures that might tend to reveal his own presence consciously shaping the surface of the music for the listener.[7]

Musicologist John McGrath further elaborates on this key point:

> Feldman's desire to stop time, and to "hold the moment" is reminiscent of [Samuel] Beckett's concept of time. . . . In her work on Feldman's concern for the sustainable moment, [musicologist] Catherine Laws posits the composer's intent in terms of an ungraspable narrative:
>
> To create a purely spatial object would, therefore, be no more appropriate than the "measuring out of time" that Feldman finds in most Western musical composition. Feldman's undertaking is more complex; the attempt to hold the moment is the attempt to capture time—an impossible task—but in the attempt Feldman exposes the *experience* of the attempt, taking us close to grasping the ungraspable.[8]

This resonates with my assertion throughout this book that what Feldman is doing is creating an opportunity for the listener to discover what Law describes as the "experience of the attempt" to capture time through his music by situating him in the same vantage point as the composer himself.

In all four compositions of the set *The Viola in My Life*, the solo viola represents the possibility of linearity, hence the possibility of ordering events over time. The emphasis here is on *possibility.* In each of these four compositions, the viola strives to emerge from the ensemble and create linear connections, *temporal connections.* This process comes to a head in *Viola 4* when the soloist literally emerges from the complex texture of the orchestra and constructs a complete melodic idea in the aforementioned Layer 4 opposition in that work. This melodic construct is deliberately paired with its opposite—the orchestral event in that same layer—in order to emphasize the fact that this construct may be only one of many such possibilities. Indeed, any momentary sense of order is of less significance than the *possibilities* from which it emerged. Herein lies the source of the interplay between soloist and ensemble in each of the *Viola in My Life* compositions.

In his commentary on the *Viola in My Life* series, critic Paul Griffiths identifies one of the underlying developments that runs through the entire set and tracks the relationship between soloist and ensemble:

> *The Viola in My Life 1* is unusual, too, in that it is made almost entirely of single notes from the viola with chiming chords from the ensemble . . . but the viola's single notes grow into melodies, which they are just at the point of doing as the first piece draws to its close. In this respect, *The Viola in My Life 1* is not so much a movement within a larger work as a movement towards that work.[9]

The concept of melody (linearity) is central to these four works. In *Viola 1* the soloist primarily sounds isolated tones. Only a few moments in this piece (mm. 54, 60, and 67–70) present vestiges of linearity, breaking into some semblance of brief melodic fragments. In *Viola 2*, more numerous and extended melodic material emerges, and, finally, in *Viola 4*, this process reaches its culmination in bars

169–175, the longest, most directed, and most complete linear event of any of the four compositions. And, as stated in the previous chapter, this moment is highlighted, as it is underscored by the only crescendo to *forte* from the viola soloist in any of the four works, lending it a certain dramatic force not experienced before in any of the compositions. It constitutes a brief, yet distinct, moment of clarity with respect to the relationship between soloist and ensemble. (Curiously, *Viola 3* seems to back away from the trend of moving toward the creation of linear connections, returning to the texture of predominantly single notes. (However, as seen in Chapter 4, it does occasionally repeat one brief, though well-defined, melodic figure borrowed verbatim from *Viola 2*, as if to keep the idea of melody alive, in memory.)

Contributing to this overall tendency to build longer linear connections is the gradual accretion of repeating patterns and sonorities, again spanning the entire set of four pieces. This is intensified as a number of the repeating patterns from each composition are quoted, verbatim, in succeeding pieces in the set, creating a memory bank of melodic ideas. Such quoting is made more and more explicit as four compositions progress. Not only does it increase over the course of the four works, but each composition moves toward more quotation as it unfolds: for example, *Viola 3* ends with a quote from *Viola 2*, and the final pages of *Viola 4* are saturated with repetitions of a lengthy quote from *Viola 2* as well. In relation to such a use of quotations Feldman once said:

> My intention was to think of melody and motivic fragments—somewhat the way Robert Rauschenberg uses photographs in his painting—and superimpose this on a static sound world more characteristic of my music.[10]

This reference to the use of photos in Rauschenberg's collages brings to the fore the presence of quotations among Feldman's four compositions. They may function as echoes or memories, as the listener reacts to them. But most importantly, they do not develop; they do not coalesce into a form larger than themselves. As Marjorie Perloff notes:

> In Rauschenberg's work . . . the objects to be collaged are not transformed by their absorption into the pictorial design or tone; they are simply transferred, "taken out of the space of the world and embedded into the surface of a painting, never at the sacrifice of their density as material. . . . By never transcending the material world the image is unambiguously identified with that material world.". . . The space of the collage thus becomes a kind of memory-space, for only in memory does such levelleing occur. . . .[11]

With respect to the presence of repetition in Feldman's music, Paul Griffiths so aptly notes:

> Repetition, whether exact or gently disturbed, is a way of going nowhere, Often it is in repetition that a piece will end, stranded. Statement is replaced by restatement, echo, memory.[12]

There is indeed no sense of larger development either within each piece in *The Viola in My Life* set or across all four. This resonates with John McGrath's notes with regard to repetition in Feldman's work:

> . . . repetition provided Feldman with a method for undermining clear semantics, The composer strove for the same fluidity in music that [Samuel] Beckett sought in literature: a way in which he could negate function and form, in order to reveal sounds in and of themselves.[13]

As we have seen, this is precisely the way each of these four pieces ends, with near-static repetition.

Morton Feldman once characterized his compositions as "time canvases in which I more or less prime the canvas with an overall hue of music."[14] In the words of art critic Dore Ashton:

> Morton Feldman . . . has often devoted himself to a linear single-dimensional system in which space, as Frank O'Hara has pointed out, is comparable to the space in certain "all-over" Jackson Pollock paintings. . . . His music—hesitant, reticent, disembodied and non-symbolic in the sense that the sounds have not reference to anything but themselves—refuses the architectural tradition of music and aligns itself with the expansive space of contemporary painting. . . . By giving performers great latitude, the composer brings about a diminution of his own choices, just as the painter diminishes his choices when he allows a rill of paint to slide down the canvas's surface unimpeded.[15]

Feldman seems to embed sound within the acoustical space of a composition in a way that makes the space surrounding each sound equal to the sound itself. This enables him to project sound as if in a raw state, before it has taken on the baggage of "structure." Indeed, we need only recall his many statements about engaging sound directly, rather than through systems or musical languages: "I never had an idea when I sat down to work . . . my ideas came out of the piece."[16] He also spoke of developing a "more perceptive temperament that waits and observes the *inherent* [my italics] mystery of its materials."[17] As I have noted in another context:

> Rejecting the most basic tenets of conventional musical discourse, [Feldman] moved toward a creative stance in which sounds appear to move freely in time and space without the interference of any compositional rhetoric or *a priori* procedures. Each of his compositions represents a sensitive transcription of the creative moment. Indeed, one is often tempted to refer to them not so much as pieces of music, but rather as actions in the

> process of becoming musical works; as examples of one impulse toward the experience known as art.[18]

For Feldman, sound is the basis of music; not pitch/interval hierarchies, nor temporal complexes, but sound in its raw state. I believe that his particular approach to composition as outlined above is rooted in this fundamental proposition. Throughout his career Feldman favored the succession of slow and soft presentations of sound. His use of time, in particular, was quite unique. Traditionally, a composition begins with its first sounds (which may be a series of chords, themes, or rhythmic patterns), and a temporal flow of some kind draws this material through many transformations toward a conclusion. Sounds evolve over time toward a goal. But in Feldman's music time is treated quite differently. Time defines the boundary of the listener's engagement with his sonic matter, but it does not push those sounds along. It does not create or support the movement of sounds through some process or evolution. Rather, Feldman treats time as a container in which sounds can be placed. In other words, in his conception of time, movement through some goal-oriented evolution is thwarted. His treatment of dynamics is similarly employed to thwart a sense of movement toward a goal. Typically, a composer uses dynamics to shape a linear evolution of sounds through time. Changes in dynamics create connections (perhaps through a long crescendo toward a climax or a diminuendo toward a conclusion). But his use of the flat uninflected surface—always soft—presents a challenge for the listener who is never drawn toward any specific goal or conclusion.

In this way, Feldman places a great burden on the listener. If there is order in his materials, he does not make that order explicit. The listener is forced into the position of either discovering order or abandoning the musical experience to chaos. Feldman clearly always strives to place listeners in the position of acquiring order for themselves. Of course, such order may, indeed one would expect, should be different for each listener, and in my view this is the most profound sense in which one may say that his music is indeterminate—not merely in terms of whether he composes with graph paper or notates his music fully, but where it places the listener within the creative process.

In this regard, it is interesting to note that there are, in fact, two moments in *The Viola in My Life 4* that seem to violate this principle—the two events within the Level 4 opposition. These are clearly fully composed in such a way that there can be no doubt in the listener's mind that Feldman has stepped in and consciously shaped these events himself in a very specific way. The distinct shape of each melodic line—its pitch content, contour, rhythmic thrust, and dynamic evolution—is both specific and unifying. At these moments the composer emerges as a guiding force, *leading* the listener toward an experience that he has precisely defined in such a way that is quite foreign to the rest of the composition. These moments add yet another level of opposition to the collage that is the design of *Viola 4,* one that actively engages the question of the composer's presence or absence within the listener's experience of the composition. Throughout *Viola 4*, and indeed all four compositions in the set, the composer has stepped back, leaving each of us to discern the composition's inner logic without guidance. However, at the moment in *Viola 4* when the Level 4 opposition emerges, the composer himself comes to the fore and for one brief moment reveals his presence. This is perhaps the final opposition of the work, Feldman's presence versus his absence in the listener's experience of the work.

In light of these observations, one might also consider the music Feldman wrote after the period in which *The Viola in My Life* set was written. About a decade after these compositions appeared, he began to write extremely long compositions that often exhibited even less surface variation, not only in terms of rhythm or pitch but of sound material itself. Compositions such as *Piano and String*

Quartet (1985) and *for Philip Guston* (1984), among others, intensify the sense of separation between composer and listener as they each place the listener in an extremely tenuous position. In his critique of another later work of Feldman (*Crippled Symmetry* [1983]), critic Andrew Clements writes:

> The lack of precise co-ordination creates the sense of every sound constantly being reassessed and placed in a slightly different context. The same idea acquires a whole spectrum of inflections as it's repeated, and even the most commonplace musical shape—a rising major scale for instance—can seem utterly strange and freshly minted.[19]

The compositions are extremely long, and their surfaces are so uninflected that the listener is pushed into a constant state of reorientation, where one must perpetually re-focus one's attention on each succeeding moment as the piece unfolds. Each presents a succession of moments that are often quite similar, and yet are constantly being pushed into isolation through the lack of surface contrast. These works are also, in a very real sense, and despite being fully notated, indeterminate in that the listener comes to the fore and is left to constantly reassess his or her ability to organize the experience in any meaningful way.

Perhaps now we can reconsider Feldman's relationship with other members of the New York School. With respect to his close association with John Cage, it should be clear that the two, while supportive of one another both artistically and philosophically, were in fact quite different composers. Immediately apparent from his early works such as *Amores* (1943), *She is Asleep* (1943), and *Sonatas and Interludes* (1946–1948), Cage was interested in creating temporal designs that were less organic and more abstract. Time existed as a series of containers to be filled (though 'containers' in a different sense that that of Feldman's music). Referring to the period in which these works were created, Cage wrote in his lecture of 1958, "Composition as Process":

> . . . with particular reference to what a decade ago I termed "structure" and "method" . . . [by] "structure" was meant the division of the whole into parts; by "method" the note to note procedure. . . . Composition then I viewed ten years ago as an activity integrating opposites, the rational and irrational, bringing about, ideally, a freely moving continuity within a strict division of parts, their combination and succession being *either logically related or arbitrarily chosen.* The strict division of parts, the structure, was a function of the duration aspect of sound . . . a division of actual time by conventional metical means, *meter taken as simply the measurement of quantity* [my italics].[20]

For Cage time became a container in which sounds could coexist; sounds "were chosen as one chooses shells while walking along a beach. . . ."[21]

This position vis-à-vis the relationship of what Cage calls form to the content within that form was key to his concept of indeterminacy at this time and culminates in a work such as *4'33"* (1952–1953) in which time periods are determined and the sonic content to fill those time periods—the random sounds of the audience—are unknown until the actual performance takes place. Eventually, this led Cage toward a broader concept of indeterminacy as exemplified by works such as *Variations II* (1961) wherein the principle of nonintentionality was fully realized. From this point on Cage's process of composition was intended to avoid the specific predetermination of some or all of the sonic result of each composition.[22] About such works Cage has noted:

> The early works have beginnings, middles, and endings. The later ones do not. They begin anywhere, last any length of time. . . . They are therefore not preconceived objects and to approach them as objects is to utterly miss the pint. They are occasions for experience.[23]

The sentence "They are occasions for experience" encapsulates the essence of the work of Cage and the other composers of the New York School. They created musical works in which they eschewed the desire to create specific personal expressions in favor of creating opportunities for others (the listeners in the case of music) to "create" an utterly personal experience that might lead to an awareness of their own need for personal expression.

Feldman comes closest to Cage's vision of indeterminacy in his early graphic scores such as *Two Instruments* (1958), *Atlantis* (1959), and *The Straits of Magellan* (1961). However, he gradually broke away from such indeterminate notation when he decided that he wanted to specify the sonic quality of each piece with more precision than the graphic notation allowed. Feldman realized that he wanted a sonic result that was very specific and carefully heard. He and Cage continue to intersect but only where the listener is concerned. Throughout their careers neither wanted the listener to feel that the hand of the composer was at work creating the sound events that he or she was experiencing. Eventually, each went about achieving this goal in completely different ways.

Indeed, this is what seems to unify all the diverse compositional styles of the various members of the New York School of composers, as well as many of their epigones. Each found a specific way of removing their personal expression from the creative process while still directing it. For Cage it involved the introduction of chance operations to his compositional process. At various times in his career, these took the form of rolling die, consulting the *I Ching* or Book of Changes (an ancient Chinese divination text), or using the random number generator on a computer to produce a series of randomly chosen values to be used in making compositional decisions.[24] For Christian Wolff, especially in his work from the 1950s through the 1970s, it was the creation of a notational system designed to direct the performer's interactions with one another, without determining the specific sounds produced by their interactions.[25] With this notational system, Wolff was able to externalize the listener's experience of his music. In his work, form became an extension of human behavior. He never sought to project his own personal preferences for certain sound combinations and forms, but he "composed" the actions of the performers leading to totally unpredictable sound events. Action, literally, became form. Perhaps, in this regard, Wolff's music from this period comes closest to the so-called action paintings of Pollock. For Earle Brown, the approach to indeterminacy—for which he coined the term *open form*—involved the development of a notation that allowed performers to create the form of each composition, allowing them to shape both the local details and larger design of each composition. Brown typically chooses the sounds to be played at each moment of the composition but leaves the ordering and expressive shaping of those sounds to the performers' discretion. From one performance to the next, the ordering of those sounds would be different, but the sounds themselves were the same. The title of one of his most successful pieces, *Available Forms I* (1961), clearly speaks to his intentions.[26] Bradley Green's research of Earle Brown's music is especially germane to the present study. Green has employed spectrographs to study different performances of one of Brown's open-form works, *String Quartet* (1965). Through the use of this analytical tool, he has revealed the aural transformations that are produced when string players choose different formal designs available through the score for their performances of this work. Green's spectrographs vividly demonstrate how the performers' decisions can radically affect what is heard from one performance of this composition to another.[27]

In each of these cases (Cage, Wolff, and Brown) the identity of the individual work is lost. Each performance will be different, so much so that a listener—even a discerning one—may not realize that they are hearing the same compositions from one performance of that work to the next. In each case, the result is the removal of each composer's signature from the final result. Each composer gives up his or her ability and desire to make specific choices as to how his or her music is to sound and therefore what it might express. This ability is transferred to the performers and in turn to the listener, whose presence becomes an active force in constructing an experience of the artwork.

Perhaps Feldman's most enduring legacy vis-à-vis his many friends among the New York School of Painters remains his composition *Rothko Chapel* (1971). As is well known, in the 1960s Mark Rothko was commissioned to create a series of paintings to be installed in a Catholic chapel (later converted to an interdenominational chapel) in Houston, Texas. Rothko completed the paintings but died before they could be installed. Feldman, known to have been a good friend to Rothko, was commissioned to compose a work for the chapel. As musicologist Steven Johnson has noted in his excellent study of this work:

> Feldman was a particularly suitable choice for the commission, for he had regularly used visual arts to explain his music and especially stressed the connection between himself and the Abstract Expressionist painters of the 1940s and 1950s. Believing that he and they shared a "powerful, mysterious aesthetic," Feldman credited their paintings with showing him "a sound world more direct, more immediate, more physical than anything that had existed heretofore." At first glance, [Feldman's] *Rothko Chapel* seems just one of many pieces—like *For Franz Kline* or *de Kooning*, for instance—that Feldman titled to underscore this kinship. But in fact it occupies a unique place. According to Feldman, the earlier titles were dedications and weren't intended to signal a correspondence between the music and a painter. *Rothko Chapel*, however, contained abundant extramusical references, and Feldman left no doubt about its special character: it was, he said, "the only score where other factors determined what kind of music it was going to be," the "only piece—and it will never happen again—when all kinds of facts,

> literary facts, reminiscent facts, came into the piece." Indeed, the singular relation between *Rothko Chapel* and Rothko's chapel led Feldman to write one of his most unusual pieces.[28]

Painting such as Rothko's holds a strong kinship to the music of Morton Feldman. Rothko's atmospheric, layered, abstract color fields seem to parallel Feldman's typically soft, slow compositions, (as reflected in his constant admonition to performers to begin a tone with a minimum of attack). Moreover, his focus on the decay of sound, seems to place his music in the same perceptual frame as the hazy edges of Rothko's color fields. Both seem to place their material in a place where the viewer/listener is left to feel that the work had no physical source.

> His stylistic evolution, from a figurative visual repertoire to an abstract style rooted in the active relationship of the observer to the painting, embodied the radical vision of a renaissance in painting. Rothko characterized this relationship as "a consummated experience between picture and onlooker. Nothing should stand between my painting and the viewer." His color formations indeed draw the observer into a space filled with an inner light. Rothko always resisted attempts to interpret his paintings. He was mainly concerned with the viewer's experience, the merging of work and recipient beyond verbal comprehension.[29]

This characterization of Rothko's relationship to the viewer is also noted by Thomas M. Messer in his *Preface* to the catalog for the Mark Rothko retrospective at The Solomon R. Guggenheim Museum in New York City in 1978, the first major retrospective of this artist's work.

> Mark Rothko shares with composers of music an absence of explicit imagery and a correspondingly developed capacity to evoke content by association; an ability to engage the responding

organ (in his case, the eye) in a process that is akin to listening because it involves attention to consecutive passages; an interest in rhythmic structures (in his case spatially articulated); and the use of color to achieve modulations that can be subtly chromatic or dramatically contrasted. . . . Rothko is a creator of melodic surfaces rendered vital and sonorous by means of formal structures *which are, for the most part, hidden* [my italics].[30]

I believe that this is the source of the humanistic side of abstraction. The artwork—whether of sound or paint—never forces its meaning onto the one experiencing it but leads one to discover meaning for oneself, thus, implicitly recognizing that every individual will have a unique experience with the work. One might also note that in his *Rothko Chapel* Feldman features a viola solo. The work was written just after he completed *The Viola in My Life* series. It continues many of the ideas laid out in the *Viola* set: the opposition of viola soloist and ensemble (here including chorus), the development of melodic writing (taken even further than in the *Viola* set). Indeed, some of the soloist's melodic figures in the *Rothko Chapel* (see mm. 25 and 26 in *Rothko Chapel*) are strongly reminiscent of melodic figures in the *Viola* set. Moreover, *Rothko Chapel* features a rather lengthy viola solo near the end that is reminiscent of the folk-like tune that runs through *Viola 2* and *Viola 4.* One might even suggest that *Rothko Chapel* is a culmination of what was accomplished in *The Viola in My Life* set.

In addition to Rothko, among the New York painters Feldman was quite close to Philip Guston. They were friends and shared common aesthetic values. As McGrath perceptively notes: "With reference to the work of Philip Guston, for instance, Feldman once said that the art is not imprisoned in a 'painting space' but instead inhabits 'somewhere in the space *between the canvas and ourselves.*'"[31] The constant push to find and settle in the liminal spaces separating measured time and unmeasured time, pitch and noise, and finally, sound and silence, lies at the very heart of the creative act for Feldman. He seems to have gravitated toward those visual artists who also sought to reside in such spaces.

With respect to the poets of the New York School, we now can see that someone like Frank O'Hara was very close to Feldman with respect to his artistic intentions. As noted literary scholar of the New York School poets Lytle Shaw has observed:

> [O'Hara] is famously attracted to immediacy. But what links all of the writings . . . is a process of denaturalizing the field of attributes one associates with seemingly immediate markers or marks: the meaning of a proper name, painterly gesture, or collage configuration. The phantom immanence of the proper name might thus be considered along a continuum with the seeming immediacy of gestural painting and supposedly autobiographical collage: would-be markers or designators in language behave instead as wild signs; seemingly emphatic and particular marks by painters that would index private psychic states instead escaping into more public fantasies and nightmares of popular culture (especially Hollywood) and the Cold War; or, what appears to be the visual proof of a self and its history in collage keeps turning in on the syntactical codes by which such a self has been educed, mingling with other selves and with culture more broadly. *It is the gradually destabilized rhetoric of immediacy that guides each of these processes—the vanishing of secured immanence* [my italics].[32]

Shaw recognizes that O'Hara and indeed others of the New York School are trying to achieve the same sense of immediacy as Feldman through the "destabilized rhetoric" of their work. They place the reader in the same position vis-à-vis the work as Feldman places his listeners. In O'Hara's own words:

> Abstraction in poetry . . . is intriguing. I think it appears mostly in the 166 minute particulars where decision is necessary. *Abstraction . . . involves personal removal by the poet* [my Italics].[33]

In his poetry we often do not know who is being addressed, and a deliberate confusion ensues as to whether the addressor or addressee is one and the same, or whether one or both are indeterminate. In each poem O'Hara seems to deliberately eschew self-expression in favor of the creation of a field of possibilities in which each reader must discover his own path.

In thinking of Feldman's music, I am often reminded of the work of some of the so-called Black Mountain poets and, even more recent poets, such as Clark Coolidge, Leslie Scalapino, Robert Grenier, Tina Darragh, and P. Inman. It is perhaps with respect to Inman's work that I see the clearest parallel to Feldman. In his texts, words and lines function as forces, always on the verge of accruing meaning, yet never reflecting any single fixed meaning. As noted by literary scholar Craig Dworkin, Inman's poetry is "classically indeterminate. . . .: neither simply meaningless nor capable of meaning anything whatsoever, but *suspended between irresolvable possibilities* [my italics]."[34] An Inman poem is neither a literal statement of an idea nor a series of abstract sound patterns. His poems are filled with clusters of fragmented words that imply multiple trajectories of meaning, none of which are realized, as in this fragment from his poem "*Sam*":[35]

tan
covered
with
size
effect
    throat
        shore by
    neap
    inch

or the following fragment from "*Think of One*":[36]

the page fell out
at St Cloud
the Atlantic of things
minus another look
at some forest

Such work reminds me of the constant push and pull we experience with Feldman's music: the constant interplay between the polarities of individual, seemingly disconnected sonorities, juxtaposed with moments when the music seems on the verge of linking sounds to one another, pushing the music toward completely formed melodic statements, which never quite crystallize. With respect to Inman's poetry, Dworkin continues: ". . . the fundamental irresolvability persists: the various parts cannot be assimilated into a coherent whole, and the tension between abstract 'dissolve' and referential 'meaning'. . . is maintained with an astonishingly steady balance."[37] In Feldman's music as well, we feel the achievement of such a constant balance between oppositional forces—the push toward order and the pull of dissolution. Indeed, such balance constitutes his sense of form. In place of more traditional formal concerns with evolution, development, culmination, and conclusion, Feldman holds his materials forever in suspension, allowing their inherent differences to counteract and counterbalance one another.

It is interesting that one of the leading figures of the New York School of composers, John Cage, is now considered a major figure of new poetry as well as new music. In her influential book *The Poetics of Indeterminacy*, critic Marjorie Perloff devotes chapters to the study of poetry by Arthur Rimbaud, Gertrude Stein, William Carlos Williams, Ezra Pound, Samuel Beckett, and John Ashbery, and concludes with a chapter devoted to the work of David Antin and John Cage![38] Perloff clearly locates Cage's writings—including his poetry—in the lineage of poets of the twentieth century whose work reflects his same concerns with indeterminacy and pluralism. Early on, Cage realized that his chance operations need not be limited to the creation of sounds but could also be applied to words. He created a fascinating body of poetry that leaves the reader in the same position as his musical audiences, searching for connections that are present but embedded within multiple layers of possibilities. In this respect, his writing is closely allied with that of the poets discussed above.

To create poetry such as that of Inman and the other writers mentioned above demands much of the poet. First, the poet must strip words of their accreted meanings, then project them to us through a newly defined context (a poem) disengaged from any impulses toward singular coherence. As Inman has pointed out, such poetry can never be paraphrased, for in such work language is never used as a conduit for images or ideas, but rather is recontextualized as a frame for the engagement of our perceptions. It seems to me that, in Feldman's music, experience is similarly decentralized. Feldman is never after a universal expression; hence he never leaves us with the sense that he has shaped his materials into specific forms, an act that would, of course, collectivize the experience of multiple listeners. This desire seems to be rooted, in some very deep way, in his personal experience of sound.

> One day my mother gave me some money and said to me: Here you are, go and buy yourself a piano." And there I am, a kid, twelve years old, at a merchant of Steinway pianos and there were all kinds! Finally, I chose one and my mother had a hard time paying for it. I still have it, it's "my piano," the others are not pianos. My piano always plays Feldman. If you play Chopin, Schumann, Mozart, on my piano it's always Feldman. You understand through this memory why I hold on to it. The one I have at [Pontpoint, a village where Feldman was staying in France at the time of this conversation] is very good but it's not a piano![39]

I believe that what Feldman is saying here is not that the piano at his house in France is not a piano, but that to him its sound does not represent what his personal experience has come to understand to be the piano, his personal sense of what a piano *is*.

Feldman's music teaches us that musical ideas cannot exist outside the frame of a composition, that is, apart from our first experience of its material substance.

> . . . I don't want to create a finite thing, I don't want to make monuments to things or about things or about myself or combinations of both. I want it almost the way I live within this structure. I am the play within the structure. How to do it without metaphor, you see this is for me the important thing.
>
> And so for me the real is not the object, the real for me is not the compositional system, the real for me is to what degree, almost in Kierkegaardian terms, I can exist, I can plunge, I can leap into this thing which I call life, which I call the environment. . . .
>
> What it really amounts to is whether you want to be in the work, in the medium or outside it, that's what it amounts to.[40]

In each of Morton Feldman's compositions, we, as listeners, are forced to confront the possibility that materials may, in fact, not cohere into some organized whole. At every moment, we must confront the possibility that form may or may not emerge; we must discover ourselves within the piece and through the piece. This, for me, is the essence of his art.

Discography

The Viola in My Life I

Seymour Barab, Paula Robison, Raymond Des Roches, David Tudor, Karen Phillips, Anahid Ajemian (CRI, CD-620; and New World Records, 80657; 1992)

Ensemble Recherche (Montaigne, MO-782126; 1994)

Cikada Ensemble (ECM New Series, ECM-1798; 2008)

The Viola in My Life II

Seymour Barab, Paula Robison, Arthur Bloom, Raymond Des Roches, David Tudor, Karen Phillips, Anahid Ajemian (CRI, CD-620; and New World Records, 80657; 1992)

Ensemble Recherche (Montaigne, MO-782126; 1994)

Das Neue Ensemble (CordAria, CACD-548; 1999)

Collegium Novum (æon, AECD-0425; 2004)

Cikada Ensemble (ECM New Series, ECM-1798; 2008)

The Viola in My Life III

Karen Phillips, David Tudor (CRI, CD-620; and New World Records, 80657; 1992)

Marek Konstantynowicz, Kenneth Karlsson, *Cikada Ensemble* (ECM New Series, ECM-1798; 2008)

Rossella Spinosa, Maurizio Barbetti (STRADIVARIUS, STR-33819; 2009)

John Tilbury, Nick Pendulbury (MATCHLESS, MRDVD-03; 2016)

The Viola in My Life IV

Jesse Levine, June in Buffalo Festival Orchestra (EMF, EMF-CD 033; 2001)

M. Konstantynowicz, *Cikada Ensemble*, Norwegian Radio Orchestra (ECM New Series, ECM-1798; 2008)

Notes

Chapter 1

1. Guy Davenport, *Every Force Evolves a Form* (San Francisco: North Point Press, 1987), ix. Mark Stevens and Annalyn Swan, *de Kooning: An American Master* (New York: Knopf, 2005), 359–360.
2. Mark Stevens and Annalyn Swann, *de Kooning: An American Master* (New York: Knopf, 2005), 359–360.
3. Robert Rauschenberg: *Erased de Kooning Drawing* (1953, traces of ink and crayon on paper, 25¼" x 21¾"); in permanent collection of San Francisco Museum of Modern Art; https://www.sfmoma.org/artwork/98.298. A discussion of the work by the painter is available at: http://www.youtube.com/watch?v=tpCWh3IFtDQ.
4. Claude Lévi-Strauss, *The Way of the Masks*, as quoted in Davenport, *Every Force Evolves a Form* (San Francisco: North Point Press, 1987), 68.
5. Gertrude Stein, *Writings Volume 2:1932–1946* (New York: Library of America, 1998), 356.
6. Hermann Sabbe, "The Feldman Paradoxes" in *The Music of Morton Feldman*, ed. Thomas DeLio (Westport, CT: Greenwood Press, 1996), 11–12.
7. Maurice Merleau-Ponty, "Cézanne's Doubt," in *Sense and Non-Sense*, trans. Hubert L. Dreyfus and Patricia Allen Dreyfus (Evanston, IL: Northwestern University Press, 1964), 13–14.
8. Dore Ashton, "Music and Painting" in *The Unknown Shore: A View of Contemporary Art* (Boston: Atlantic Monthly Press, 1962), 200–201.
9. Philip Guston, "On Survival" in *Philip Guston: Collected Writings, Lectures, and Conversations*, ed. Clark Coolidge (Berkeley: University of California Press, 2011), 252.
10. Morton Feldman, "Give My Regards to Eighth Street," *Art in America* (September 1973). Reprinted in *The Music of Morton Feldman*, ed. Thomas DeLio (Westport, CT: Greenwood Press, 1996), 199–204.
11. Harold Rosenberg, "The American Action Painters," *ARTnews* (December 1952), 22–50.
12. Feldman, "Give My Regards to Eighth Street," 202–203.
13. Sabbe, "The Feldman Paradoxes," 10.

14. Feldman set poetry by two other writers of great significance. He worked with the poetry of e. e. cummings quite early in his career, and Samuel Beckett near the end. Of course, Beckett became the writer with whom Feldman has become most closely associated. Though he obviously was not a member of the New York School, his work shared many traits with the poets of that school and was a significant influence on their thinking. Feldman created his only opera, *Neither* (1977), to a text Beckett wrote specifically for him. In addition, he wrote one of his last pieces in homage to the writer, the magnificent *For Samuel Beckett* (1987). At Beckett's request Feldman also set one of his plays to music:

    In 1961 Samuel Beckett wrote *Words and Music* for BBC radio, a play featuring the two characters "Words" and "Music" (also referred to as Joe and Bob). The work was withdrawn following the première due to Beckett's dissatisfaction. Twenty years later, Beckett suggested that Morton Feldman should compose the music, resulting in the first complete performance in 1987 (the year of Feldman's death), produced for the American Beckett Festival of Radio Plays. In Feldman's words: 'It was a huge amount of fun to do something for Beckett, a sort of tribute to him, i.e. someone who has been part of my life since the '50's . . . it was to some extent a labour of love, which I happily undertook. https://www.universaledition.com/morton-feldman-220/works/samuel-beckett-words-music-4505

15. Will Montgomery, "In Fatal Winds: Frank O'Hara and Morton Feldman," in F*rank O'Hara Now: New Essays on the New York Poet*, eds. Robert Hampson and Will Montgomery (Liverpool: Liverpool University Press: July, 2010), 195–210.
16. Morton Feldman, record liner notes, *Mainstream Records* (MS 5007), 1.
17. Sabbe, "The Feldman Paradoxes," 9–10.
18. Among the few rare exceptions are: Ray Fields, *Morton Feldman's Piano and String Quartet: Analysis, Aesthetics, and Experience of a 20th-Century Masterpiece* (Lanham, MD: Rowman & Littlefield, September 2022), a thorough and revealing examination of one of Feldman's late works; Alistair Noble, *Composing Ambiguity: The Early Music of Morton Feldman* (Ashgate, 2013), , a serious attempt to carry out detailed analysis of several of Feldman's early works in conjunction with discussion of Feldman's notes and sketches; Thomas DeLio, "The Marvelous Illusion: Morton Feldman's *The Viola in My Life (1)*," *Contemporary Music Review* (Vol. 32, No. 6, 2013), 589–638; Steven Johnson, "Organic Construction in the Music of Morton Feldman" in *Essays on the Music and Theoretical Writings*

of Thomas DeLio, Contemporary American Composer, ed. Thomas Licata (New York: Edwin Mellen Press, 2008), 245–272; Wes York, "For John Cage (1982)," in *The Music of Morton Feldman*, ed. Thomas DeLio (New York: Excelsior Music Publishing Co, 1996), 147–195; Thomas DeLio, "Last Pieces #3 (1959)," in *The Music of Morton Feldman*, ed. Thomas DeLio (New York: Excelsior Music Publishing Co., 1996), 39–68,; Thomas DeLio, "Toward an Art of Imminence: Morton Feldman's *Durations III*, No. 3," *Interface* (Vol. 12, No 3, 1983), 465–480, reprinted in *Circumscribing the Open Universe*, ed. Thomas DeLio (Lanham, MD: University Press of America, 1983), pp. 29–47, www.cnvill.net/mfdelio1.pdf.

19. See, for example, Catherine Hirata, "The Sounds of the Sounds Themselves: Analyzing the Early Music of Morton Feldman," *Perspectives of New Music* (Vol. 34, No. 1, 1996), 6–22. In an attempt to understand her own perceptions, Hirata substitutes vaguely subjective observations for real attention to the experience of Feldman's music. Following these observations, she introduces a very suspect concept of voice leading in order to analyze Feldman's work. In my view, talking about one's perceptions is only useful if it leads to synthesis of justifiable observations.
20. Morton Feldman, "XXX Anecdotes and Drawings," in *Feldman Essays*, ed. Walter Zimmermann (Kerpen, Germany: Beginner Press, 1985), 146.
21. Arnold Schoenberg, *Theory of Harmony*, trans. Roy E. Carter (Berkeley: University of California Press, 1983), 421.
22. Paul Griffiths, "Morton Feldman Talks to Paul Griffiths," *Musical Times* (Vol. 113, No. 1554; August 1972), 758–759.
23. All four compositions in the set are published by Universal Editions. *The Viola in My Life I* (New York: Universal Editions, 15394); *The Viola in My Life II* (New York: Universal Editions, 15399): *The Viola in My Life III* (New York: Universal Editions, 15402): *The Viola in My Life IV* (New York: Universal Editions, 15408).
24. Morton Feldman, quoted on Universal Editions website, https://www.universaledition.com/morton-feldman-220/works/the-viola-in-my-life-1-5335.
25. Feldman, "Morton Feldman Talks to Paul Griffiths," 758–759.
26. Robert Cogan, "Varèse: A Sonic Poetics," liner notes, *Neuma* (CD 450-74).
27. Robert Cogan's three books on this subject are essential to understanding the power of this tool for the analysis of music—from all eras and numerous cultures: *New Images of Musical Sound* (Cambridge, MA: Harvard University Press, 1984); *Music Seen, Music Heard*

(Cambridge, MA: Publication Contact International, 1998); *The Sounds of Song* (Cambridge, MA: Publication Contact International, 1999).

28. *Spectra Plus*, Pioneer Hill Software, https://www.spectraplus.com.
29. Cogan, *Music Seen, Music Heard*, 2
30. *The Viola in My Life I* and *II* have been recorded by the Ensemble Recherche on *Morton Feldman* (Montaigne; MO 782018). *The Viola in My Life I, II*, and *III* by an ad hoc ensemble on *Morton Feldman: The Viola in My Life* (New World Records, B000J0ZPDS). All four pieces in the set have been recorded by the Cikada Ensemble and the Norwegian Radio Orchestra on *Morton Feldman: The Viola in My Life* (ECM; 028947657774). For a complete list of recordings of these works, see the Discography at the end of this book.

Chapter 2

1. Paul Griffiths, "Morton Feldman Talks to Paul Griffiths," *Musical Times* (Vol. 113, No. 1554; August 1972), 759.
2. For a very interesting discussion of attack noise in Feldman's music, see Jonathan Bernard, "Feldman's Painters," in *The New York Schools of Music and Visual Arts*, ed. Steven Johnson (New York: Routledge, 2002), 181–182.
3. Walter Zimmerman, "Morton Feldman," an interview in *Desert Plants: Conversations with 23 American Musicians* (Vancouver: Aesthetic Research Center Publications, 1976), 7.
4. Jan Williams, "An Interview with Morton Feldman," *Percussive Notes* (September 1983), reprinted in *Morton Feldman Says: Selected Interviews and Lectures (1964–1987)*, ed. Chris Villars (London: Hyphen Press, 2006), 151.
5. Steven Johnson, "Jasper Johns and Morton Feldman: *Why Patterns*?" in *The New York School of Music and the Visual Arts* (New York: Routledge, 2002), 217–247.
6. Cole Gagne and Tracy Caras, "Morton Feldman," interview in *Soundpieces: Interviews with American Composers* (Metuchen, NJ: Scarecrow Press, 1982), 170.
7. Robert Rauschenberg, *Studio Painting* (1960–1961), combine of mixed media with rope, pulley and canvas bag, consisting of two adjacent, contrasting panels; Robert Rauschenberg Foundation, New York. https://www.rauschenbergfoundation.org/art/artwork/studio-painting
8. Jasper Johns, *Untitled* (1972), oil, encaustic, and collage on canvas with objects, consisting of four equal-sized panels placed side-by-side; Reynolda

House Museum of American Art, Winston-Salem, NC. https://reynoldahouse.emuseum.com/objects/90/four-panels-from-untitled-1972

9. For a detailed look at these "crosshatch" paintings and their connection to Feldman's music, see Steven Johnson, "Jasper Johns and Morton Feldman: *Why Patterns*?" in *The New York School of Music and the Visual Arts* (New York: Routledge, 2002), 218–219.
10. Fred Orton and Gavin Byars, "Morton Feldman Interview," *Studio International* (November 1976), 247.
11. Williams, "An Interview with Morton Feldman," 158.
12. Morton Feldman, "*Crippled Symmetry*" in *Morton Feldman Essays*, ed. Walter Zimmerman (Kerpen, Germany: Beginner Press, 1985), 127.
13. Maurice Merleau-Ponty, "Cézanne's Doubt," in *Sense and Non-Sense*, trans. Hubert L. Dreyfus and Patricia Allen Dreyfus (Evanston, IL: Northwestern University Press, 1964), 14–15.

Chapter 3

1. Regarding the indication to play *coperta*, scholar and percussion specialist Christopher Shultis has noted: "If I were playing this I would probably use mallets and roll on machine castanets covered with cloth." From email correspondence with the author on April 21, 2022.
2. Again, percussion specialist Christopher Shultis notes: "this is a kind of terminology typically used for marching percussion, outdated though and not used anymore. A tenor drum would be a deep tom-tom size drum but with heads on top and bottom. It was originally a marching drum with no snares. Field drum would be another term for side drum . . . it's like a marching snare drum. So if Feldman really wanted these instruments I would use two deep two-headed drums, one with snares on and the other without. I can't help but wonder though how much specificity Feldman was after with his use of these terms. It could simply be two drums, one with snares and the other without snares." From email correspondence with the author on 4/20/2022.
3. See discussion and overtone structures of wind instruments at various dynamic levels in Robert Cogan and Pozzi Escot, *Sonic Design* (Prentice-Hall, 1976), 350–365.
4. There is one misprint in the full score. In bar 24 the violin should have Ab/Db as in bars before, not A/D natural. This has been confirmed in correspondence with Universal Editions. Julia Pekovics, from the Division of Rights and Customer Relations, has checked the parts and confirmed

that in the parts the violin does play Ab/Db in this bar. From email correspondence with the author on May 19, 2022.

5. Morton Feldman, "XXX Anecdotes and Drawings," in *Morton Feldman Essays*, ed. Walter Zimmermann (Kerpen, Germany: Beginner Press, 1985), 178.

Chapter 4

1. Jasper Johns, *0–9* (2013), a series of ten lithographs, Museum of Modern Art, New York. https://www.moma.org/collection/works/171335?association=series&page=1&parent_id=169050&sov_referrer=association
2. Morton Feldman, "Morton Feldman Talks to Paul Griffiths," *Musical Times* (August 1972), 758–759.
3. Wesley York, "For John Cage," in *The Music of Morton Feldman* (Westport, CT: Greenwood Press, Contributions to the Study of Music and Dance, No. 46, 1996), 147–195.

Chapter 5

1. Robert Cogan, "Reconceiving Theory: The Analysis of Tone Color," *The College Music Symposium*, published online, October 1, 1975), n.p.; https://symposium.music.org/index.php/15/item/1734-reconceiving-theory-the-analysis-of-tone-color
2. Hermann Sabbe, "The Feldman Paradoxes" in *The Music of Morton Feldman*, ed. Thomas DeLio (Westport, CT: Greenwood Press, 1996), 10.
3. Thomas DeLio, "Toward an Art of Imminence: Morton Feldman's Durations III, #3," *Interface* (Vol. 12, No. 3, 1981), 465–480; reprinted in *Analytical Studies of the Music of Ashley, Cage, Carter . . .: Essays in Contemporary Music, Collected Essays Volume I*, ed. Patricia Burt (1980–2000), 117–138.

Chapter 6

1. Stefan Wolpe, "To Understand Music," lecture delivered at Black Mountain College (February 1953); reprinted in *Sonus* (Vol. 3, No. 1, Fall 1982), 7–8.

2. Joseph M. Conte, *Unending Design: The Forms of Postmodern Poetry* (Ithaca, NY: Cornell University Press, 1991), 17.
3. Meyer Schapiro, "The Liberating Quality of Avant-Garde Art," *Art News* (Vol. 56, No. 4, Summer, 1957), 38–39.
4. Universal Editions, https://www.universaledition.com/morton-feldman-220/works/the-viola-in-my-life-1-5335.
5. Nils Vigeland, program notes for *Morton Feldman: The Viola in My Life* (New World Records, No. 80657).
6. Alex Ross, "American Sublime," *The New Yorker* (June 19, 2006), n.p.; https://www.newyorker.com/magazine/2006/06/19/american-sublime.
7. Thomas DeLio, "Morton Feldman's Last Pieces #3," in *Analytical Studies about Music*, ed. Patricia Burt (Lewiston, NY: Edwin Mellen Press, 2017), 330.
8. John McGrath, "Beckett and Feldman: Time, Repetition and the Liminal Space," in *Samuel Beckett, Repetition and Modern Music* (New York: Routledge, 2017), 89.
9. Paul Griffiths, program notes for the CD *Morton Feldman: The Viola in My Life* (ECM New Series 1798, 2008), 8–9.
10. Morton Feldman, quoted by Paul Griffiths in program notes for the CD *Morton Feldman*, 10.
11. Marjorie Perloff, "The Portrait of the Artist as a Collage-Text: Pound's *Gaudier-Brzeska* and the "Italic" Texts of John Cage" in *The Dance of the Intellect* (Cambridge: Cambridge University Press, 1985), 63.
12. Griffiths, *Morton Feldman: The Viola in My Life*, 10.
13. McGrath, "Beckett and Feldman: Time, Repetition and the Liminal Space," 92.
14. Morton Feldman, "Between Categories," *Contemporary Music Review* (Vol. 2, No. 2, 1988), 4.
15. Dore Ashton, "Music and Painting," in *The Unknown Shore: A View of Contemporary Art* (Boston: Atlantic Monthly Press, 1962), 205–206.
16. Fred Orton and Gavin Byars, "Morton Feldman Interview," *Studio International* (November 1976), 247.
17. Morton Feldman, "The Anxiety of Art," *Art in America* (September 1973); reprinted in *The Music of Morton Feldman*, ed. Thomas DeLio (Westport, CT: Greenwood Press, 1996), 208.
18. DeLio, "Morton Feldman's Last Pieces #3," 295.
19. Andrew Clements, https://www.theguardian.com/music/2012/aug/15/feldman-crippled-symmetry-review.
20. John Cage, *Silence* (Middletown, CT: Wesleyan University Press, 1973), 18–19.

21. Cage, *Silence*, 19.
22. Thomas DeLio, "The Morphology of a Global Structure: John Cage, *Variations II*," in *Circumscribing the Open Universe* (Lanham, MD: University Press of America, 1984), 9–28; reprinted in *Analytical Studies of the Music of Ashley, Cage, Carter, Dallapicccola, Feldman, Lucier, Reich, Satie, Schoenberg, Wolff and Xenakis: Essays in Contemporary Music*, ed. Thomas Licata (Lewiston, NY: Edwin Mellen Press, 2017), 1–22.
23. DeLio, "The Morphology of a Global Structure: John Cage, *Variations II*," 31.
24. DeLio, "The Morphology of a Global Structure: John Cage, *Variations II*," 1–22.
25. See Thomas DeLio, "Structure as Behavior: Christian Wolff's *For 1,2 or 3 People*" in *Circumscribing the Open Universe* (Lanham, MD: University Press of America, 1984), 49–68; reprinted in *Analytical Studies of the Music of Ashley, Cage, Carter, Dallapicccola, Feldman, Lucier, Reich, satie, Schoenberg, Wolff and Xenakis: Essays in Contemporary Music*, ed. Thomas Licata (Lewiston, NY: Edwin Mellen Press, 2017), 155–174.
26. Earle Brown, *Available Forms I* (Associated Music Publishers, 1961).
27. See Bradley Green, "Performer Choice and Earle Brown's *String Quartet* (1965): The Formal and Aural Implications of Open Form," *Indiana Theory Review* (Vol. 35, No. 1–2, Spring and Fall, 2018), 58–92.
28. Steven Johnson, "Rothko Chapel and Rothko's Chapel," *Perspectives of New Music* (Vol. 32, No. 2, Summer, 1994), 7.
29. Unattributed, *Mark Rothko and His Paintings*, https://www.mark-rothko.org.
30. Thomas M. Messer, "Preface" to the catalog for *Mark Rothko: A Retrospective* (New York: Harry N. Abrams, in collaboration with The Solomon R. Guggenheim Museum: 1978), 12.
31. McGrath, "Beckett and Feldman: Time, Repetition and the Liminal Space," 97.
32. Lytle Shaw, *Frank O'Hara: The Poetics of Coterie* (Iowa City: University of Iowa Press, 2006), 233.
33. Frank O'Hara, "Personism" Manifesto (1959), n.p.; https://blogs.baruch.cuny.edu/studiesinamericanpoetrys17/files/2017/01/Frank-OHara-Personism-A-Manifesto-1.pdf.
34. Craig Dworkin, "The Logic of the Work," in *Radium of the Word: A Poetics of Materiality* (Chicago: University of Chicago Press, 2020), 82.
35. P. Inman, "*Sam*," from *Vel* (Berkeley, CA: O Books, 1995), 15.
36. P. Inman, "*Think of One*," from *Think of One* (Elmwood, CT: Potes and Poets Press, 1986), 67.

37. Dworkin, "The Logic of the Work," 83.
38. Marjorie Perloff, *The Poetics of Indeterminacy: Rimbaud to Cage* (Evanston, IL: Northwestern University Press, 1981.
39. Martine Cadieu, "Morton Feldman—Waiting," a conversation originally published as "Morton Feldman: l'attente" in *A l'écoute des compositeurs* (Paris: Minerve, 1992), 202–205; reprinted in *Morton Feldman Says: Selected Interviews and Lectures (1964–1987)*, ed. and trans. Chris Villars (London: Hyphen Press, 2006), 38–40. It is unclear if this is a quote or a paraphrase.
40. Alan Beckett, "Interview" with Morton Feldman," *International Times* (November 1966); reprinted in *Morton Feldman Says: Selected Interviews and Lectures (1964–1987)*, 32.

Bibliography

The following is a list of writings pertinent to this study.

Ames, Paula Kopstick. "Piano (1977)." In *The Music of Morton Feldman*, edited by Thomas DeLio. New York: Excelsior Music Publishing Co, 1996, 99–143.

Ashton, Dore. "Music and Painting." In *The Unknown Shore: A View of Contemporary Art*. Boston: Atlantic Monthly Press, 1962, 200–206.

Asplund, Christian, and Michael Hicks. *Christian Wolff*. Evanston: University of Illinois Press, 2012.

Baldridge, Wilson. "Morton Feldman: One Whose Reality Is Acoustic." *Perspectives of New Music*, 21 (1982/1983): 112–113.

Barlow, John D. "Witkiewicz's Theory of Pure Form and the Music of Morton Feldman." *The Polish Journal of Aesthetics*, 31, no. 4 (2013): 109–120.

Benson, Stephen. "Beckett, Feldman, Joe and Bob: Speaking of Music in 'Words and Music.'" In *Essays on Music and the Spoken Word and on Surveying the Field*, edited by Suzanne M. Lodato and David Francis Urrows. Amsterdam: Rodolpi, 2005, 165–180.

Bernard, Jonathan W. "Feldman's Painters." In *The New York Schools of Music and Visual Arts*, edited by Steven Johnson. New York: Routledge, 2002, 173–215.

Blum, Eberhard. *Choice & Chance: Bilder und Berichte aus meinem Leben als Musiker*. Berlin: Berlinische Galerie, Landesmuseum für Moderne Kunst, Fotografie und Architektur, 2008. Includes many recollections of the author's years as a close friend of Feldman and member of the performing group, "Morton Feldman and Soloists."

Blum, Eberhard. "Morton Feldman and Soloists." In *Choice & Chance: Bilder und Berichte aus meinem Leben als Musiker*. Berlin: Berlinische Galerie, Landesmuseum für Moderne Kunst, Fotografie und Architektur, 2008.

Bonet, Juan Manuel. "I Learned More from Painters Than I Learned from Composers." In *Vertical Thoughts: Morton Feldman and the Visual Arts*. Dublin: Irish Museum of Modern Art, 2010, 6–23.

Böttinger, Peter. "Das exakte Ungefähre: Ein analytischer Versuch über *Instruments I* (1974) von Morton Feldman." *Morton Feldman. Musik-Konzepte*, 48/49 (1986): 105–114.

Boutwell, Brett. "'The Breathing of Sound Itself': Notation and Temporality in Feldman's Music to 1970." *Contemporary Music Review*, 32, no. 6 (2013): 531–570.

Cage, John. *Silence.* Middletown, CT: Wesleyan University Press, 1973.

Cage, John. *For the Birds.* London: Marion Boyars, 1981.

Chase, Stephen, and Philip Thomas. *Changing the System: The Music of Christian Wolff.* Aldershot, UK: Ashgate, 2010.

Claren, Sebastian. "Woran man sich erinnert: Morton Feldmans Konzeption des instrumentalen Bildes." In *Bilder - Verbot und Verlangen in Kunst und Musik*, edited by Sabine Sanio and Christian Scheib. Friedberg, Germany: Pfau Verlag, 2000, pp. 123–141.

Claren, Sebastian. *Neither: Die Musik Morton Feldmans.* Hofheim, Germany: Wolke Verlag, 2000.

Cline, David. *The Graph Music of Morton Feldman.* Cambridge: Cambridge University Press, 2018.

Cogan, Robert. *New Images of Musical Sound.* Cambridge, MA: Harvard University Press, 1984.

Cogan, Robert. *Music Seen, Music Heard.* Cambridge, MA: Publication Contact International, 1998.

Cogan, Robert. *The Sounds of Song.* Cambridge, MA: Publication Contact International, 1999.

Cogan, Robert. "Varèse: A Sonic Poetics," liner notes. Acton. MA: *Neuma Records*, (1990): 450–474.

Coolidge, Clark. "Regarding Morton Feldman's Music and Wherever It All Now Goes." *Sulfur* 22 (Spring 1988): 123–129.

Davenport, Guy. *Every Force Evolves a Form.* San Francisco: North Point Press, 1987.

DeLio, Thomas. "Toward an Art of Imminence: Morton Feldman's *Durations III*, no. 3." *Interface* 12, no. 3 (1983): 465–480. Reprinted in Thomas DeLio, *Circumscribing the Open Universe.* Lanham, MD: University Press of America, 1983, 29–47.

DeLio, Thomas. "Structure as Behavior: Christian Wolff, *For 1, 2 or 3 People.*" In *Circumscribing the Open Universe.* Lanham, MD: University Press of America, 1984: 49–68; reprinted in *Analytical Studies of the Music of Ashley, Cage, Carter, Dallapicccola, Feldman, Lucier, Reich, satie, Schoenberg, Wolff and Xenakis: Essays in Contemporary Music*, edited by Thomas Licata. Lewiston, NY: The Edwin Mellen Press, 2017, 155–174.

DeLio, Thomas. "The Morphology of a Global Structure: John Cage, *Variations II.*" In *Circumscribing the Open Universe.* Lanham, MD: University Press of America, 1984, 9–28; reprinted in *Analytical Studies of the Music of Ashley, Cage, Carter, Dallapicccola, Feldman, Lucier, Reich, satie, Schoenberg, Wolff and Xenakis: Essays in Contemporary Music*, edited by Thomas Licata. Lewiston. New York: Edwin Mellen Press, 2017, 1–22.

DeLio, Thomas. "Last Pieces #3 (1959)." In *The Music of Morton Feldman*, edited by Thomas DeLio. Westport, CT: Greenwood Press, 1996: 39–68; reprinted in *Analytical Studies of the Music of Ashley, Cage, Carter, Dallapicccola, Feldman, Lucier, Reich, satie, Schoenberg, Wolff and Xenakis: Essays in Contemporary Music*, edited by Thomas Licata. Lewiston. New York: Edwin Mellen Press, 2017, 295–334.

DeLio, Thomas. *The Music of Morton Feldman*. Westport, CT: Greenwood Press, 1996.

DeLio, Thomas. *The* Amores *of John Cage*. Hillsdale, NY: Pendragon Press, 2009.

DeLio, Thomas. "The Marvelous Illusion: Morton Feldman's *The Viola in My Life (1)*." *Contemporary Music Review* 32, no. 6 (2013): 589–638; reprinted in *Analytical Studies about Music: Essays on the Music of Beethoven, Carter, Chopin*, et al., edited by Thomas Licata. Lewiston, NY: Edwin Mellen Press, 2021, 177–240.

De Visscher, Éric. "Surfaces de temps. À propos de Morton Feldman." In *Les écritures du temps (musique, rythme, etc.)*, edited by Fabien Lévy. Paris: L'Harmattan (Les cahiers de l'Ircam), 2001, 141–153.

Dohoney, Ryan. "Mourning Coterie: Morton Feldman's Posthumous Collaborations with Frank O'Hara." In *New York School Collaborations: The Color of Vowels*, edited by Mark Silverberg. New York: Palgrave Macmillan, 2013, 183–197.

Dohoney, Ryan. *Saving Abstraction: Morton Feldman, the de Menils and the Rothko Chapel.* Oxford: Oxford University Press, 2019.

Dohoney, Ryan. *Morton Feldman: Friendship and Mourning in the New York Avant Garde*. London: Bloomsbury Academic Publishing, 2022.

Dworkin, Craig. *Radium of the Word: A Poetics of Materiality*. Chicago: University of Chicago Press, 2020.

Feldman, Morton. *The Viola in My Life I*. New York: Universal Editions, No. 15394, 1970.

Feldman, Morton. *The Viola in My Life II*. New York: Universal Editions, No. 15399, 1970.

Feldman, Morton. *The Viola in My Life III*. New York: Universal Editions, No. 15402, 1971.

Feldman, Morton. *The Viola in My Life IV*. New York: Universal Editions, No. 15408, 1971.

Feldman, Morton. *Essays*, edited by Walter Zimmerman. Kerpen, Germany: Beginner Press, 1985.

Feldman, Morton. *Morton Feldman: Ecrits et Paroles* edited by Jean-Yves Bosseur and Danielle Cohen-Levinas. Brussels: Les presses du reel, 2008.

Feldman, Morton. *Morton Feldman Says: Selected Interviews and Lectures 1964–1987*, edited by Chris Villars. London: Hyphen Press, 2006.

Fields, Ray. *Morton Feldman's Piano and String Quartet: Analysis, Aesthetics, and Experience of a 20th-Century Masterpiece.* Lanham, MD: Rowman & Littlefield, 2022.

Figal, Günter. "Intangible Matters: On Color and Sound in Art (James Turrell, Morton Feldman)." *Research in Phenomenology* 48, no. 3 (2018): 307–317.

Friedman, B. H. "Morton Feldman: Painting Sounds." In *Give My Regards to Eighth Street: Collected Writings of Morton Feldman.* Boston: Exact Change, 2000, xi–xxx.

Goldstein, Louis. "Morton Feldman and the Shape of Time." In *Perspectives on American Music Since 1950 (Essays in American Music, Vol. 4)*, edited by James R. Heintze and Michael Saffle. New York: Garland Publishing, 1999, 67–80.

Goulish, Matthew. "The Next Ten Minutes: Morton Feldman and Samuel Beckett." In *Beckett and Musicality*, edited by Sara Jane Bailes and Nicholas Till. Farnham, UK: Ashgate Publishing, 2014, 171–186.

Green, Bradley. "Performer Choice and Earle Brown's *String Quartet* (1965): The Formal and Aural Implications of Open Form." *Indiana Theory Review* 35, nos. 1–2 (2018): 58–92.

Griffiths, Paul. "Morton Feldman: Shimmering Orchestral Tapestries." *New York Times* (January 31, 1999).

Guston, Philip. *Philip Guston: Collected Writings, Lectures, and Conversations*, edited by Clark Coolidge. Berkeley: University of California Press, 2010.

Hall, Tom. "Notational Image, Transformation and the Grid in the Late Music of Morton Feldman." *Current Issues in Music* 1 (2007): 7–24.

Hutton-Williams, Francis. "Samuel Beckett and Morton Feldman's 'Text-Music Tandem' in *Words and Music*." *Modernist Cultures* 8, no. 1 (2013): 100–119.

Johnson, Steven. "*Rothko Chapel* and Rothko's Chapel." *Perspectives of New Music* 32, no 2 (1994): 6–53.

Johnson, Steven. "Jasper Johns and Morton Feldman: What Patterns?" In *The New York Schools of Music and Visual Arts*, edited by Steven Johnson. New York: Routledge, 2002, 217–247.

Johnson, Steven. "Organic Construction in Music of Morton Feldman." In *Essays on the Music and Theoretical Writings of Thomas DeLio, Contemporary American Composer*, edited by Thomas Licata. Lewiston, NY: Edwin Mellen Press, 2008, 245–272.

Johnson, Steven. "It Must Mean Something: Narrative in Beckett's *Molloy* and Feldman's *Triadic Memories*." *Contemporary Music Review* 32, no. 6 (2013): 639–668.

Josek, Suzanne. *The New York School. Earle Brown, John Cage, Morton Feldman, Christian Wolff.* Saarbrücken: Pfau Verlag, 1998.

Kane, Brian. "On Repetition, Habit and Involuntary Memory: An Analysis and Speculation upon Morton Feldman's Final Composition." www.cnvill.net/mfkane.pdf

Knockaert, Yves. "Systemlessness in Music: Composing Without a System: A Comparative Study of Systemlessness in the Works of John Cage, Morton Feldman and Wolfgang Rihm." In *Order and Disorder: Music-Theoretical Strategies in 20th Century Music.* Leuven, Belgium: Leuven University Press, 2004, 53–104.

Laws, Catherine. "Feldman—Beckett—Johns: Patterning, Memory and Subjectivity." In *The Modernist Legacy: Essays on New Music,* edited by Björn Heile. Farnham, UK: Ashgate, 2009, 135–158.

Lunberry, Clark. "In Living Memory: Morton Feldman's Departing Landscapes." In *Sites of Performance: Of Time and Memory.* London: Anthem Press, 2014, 133–166.

McGrath, John. "Beckett and Feldman: Time, Repetition and the Liminal Space." In *Samuel Beckett, Repetition and Modern Music.* New York: Routledge, 2017, 86–123.

Moelants, Dirk. "Feldman, Memory and the Perception of Slowness." *Tijdschrift voor Muziektheorie* (a Dutch Journal of Music Theory) 8, no. 3 (2003): 215–226.

Nadrigny, Pauline. "Music/Painting, the Temptation of Analogy: The Case of Morton Feldman." *Archives de Philosophie* 80, no. 2 (2017): 269–293.

Nicholls, David. "Getting Rid of the Glue: The Music of the New York School." In *The New York Schools of Music and Visual Arts,* edited by Steven Johnson. New York: Routledge, 2002, 17–56.

Nimczik, Ortwin. "'Each Sound with a Minimum of Attack': Morton Feldman: 'De Kooning' und 'Intermission 6.'" *Musik & Bildung: Praxis Musikunterricht* 32, no. 4 (August-September 2000): 44–47.

Noble, Alistair. *Composing Ambiguity: The Early Music of Morton Feldman.* Farnham, UK: Ashgate, 2013.

Perloff, Marjorie. *The Poetics of Indeterminacy: Rimbaud to Cage.* Evanston, IL: Northwestern University Press, 1981.

Perloff, Marjorie. *The Dance of the Intellect.* Cambridge: Cambridge University Press, 1985.

Perloff, Marjorie. "The Beckett/Feldman Radio Collaborations." In *The Beckett Circle* 26, no 2 (2003): 207–211.

Philippi, Daniela. "Klänge-Farben-Flächen. Bewegung jenseits von Prozeßhaftigkeit in Orgelkompositionen von John Cage und Morton Feldman (Sounds, colors, surfaces: Moving beyond process in the organ compositions of John Cage and Morton Feldman)." In *Orgel International* 3, no. 2 (1999): 148–151.

Sabbe, Hermann. "The Feldman Paradoxes: A Deconstructionist View of Musical Aestherics." In *The Music of Morton Feldman,* edited by Thomas DeLio. Westport, CT: Greenwood Press, 1996, 9–20.

Shaw, Lytle. *Frank O'Hara: The Poetics of Coterie.* Iowa City: University of Iowa Press, 2006, 233.

Shultis, Christopher. *Silencing the Sounded Self: John Cage and the American Experimental Tradition.* Boston: Northeastern University Press, 1998.

Stollberg, Arne. "Klangfarben auf der Zeitleinwand: Morton Feldmans Konzeption des musikalischen 'all over.'" In *Musik-Wahrnehmung-Sprache.* Edited by Claudia Emmenegger, Elisabeth Schwind, and Olivier Senn. Zurich: Chronos Verlag, 2008, 39–49.

Thomas, Margaret. "The 'Departing Landscape': Temporal and Timbral Elasticity in Morton Feldman's I Met Heine on the Rue Fürstenberg." *Ex tempore: A Journal of Compositional and Theoretical Research in Music* 11, no. 1 (2002): 73–86.

Villars, Chris. "Karen Ann Phillips: Composer, Violist, Pianist and Music Educator—A Chronology." www.cnvill.net/mf-karen-phillips.pdf

Wiener, Oliver. *Morton Feldman: "The Viola in My Life."* Saarbrücken: Pfau Verlag, 1996.

Williams, Jan. "An Interview with Morton Feldman, 22nd, April, 1983." In *Percussive Notes* 21, no. 6 (September 1983): 4–14.

Wolpe, Stefan. "To Understand Music." Lecture delivered at Black Mountain College (February, 1953); reprinted in *Sonus* 3, no. 1 (Fall 1982): 4–17.

Wolpe, Stefan. "On New (and Not-So-New) Music in America," translated by Austin Clarkson. *The Journal of Music Theory* 28, no. 1 (1984): 1–45.

York, Wes. "For John Cage (1982)." In *The Music of Morton Feldman*, edited by Thomas DeLio. Westport CT: Greenwood Press, 1996, 147–195.

Index

For the benefit of digital users, indexed terms that span two pages (e.g., 52–53) may, on occasion, appear on only one of those pages.

Tables and figures are indicated by an italic *t* and *f* following the page number.